A ROUGH RIDE

by

C. P. MAN

C000108843

ISBN 978178

www.chimerabooks.co.uk

New authors are always welcome, or if you're already a published author and have existing work, the rights of which remain with or have reverted to you, we would love to hear from you at **info@chimerabooks.co.uk**.

A Rough Ride published in 2014 by Chimera Books.

This novel is fiction - in real life practice safe sex.

Contents

Lead me not into temptation; I can find the way myself. Rita Mae Brown

Fight It Out

Mark had already begun to saunter towards his prize. She had directed her delicious gaze into his eyes long enough for him to be called out the winner, and he was in a hurry to claim her. Thoughts of her body under his ignited a whole array of brain cells and made his mouth water. At last he could work on getting the little minx out of his system; over a period of several months, of course, or perhaps years if his luck held. The main thing was that he would be getting his hands on the goodies. He had a very potent itch that required immediate scratching.

Holding his stare in place as he moved forward, he noticed her lips twitch. What was the damn fool trying to do now? Was she trying to speak? He hoped not, for she'd pay dearly for that folly in front of all these people. Another twitch, a shake of her head and then she dropped a bombshell:

'I want the blond one with the boots.'

Mark had to work to make sure his jaw stayed firmly closed. If he'd heard correctly, and he prayed he hadn't, the chit had just chosen a complete bastard to complete her training with. She'd already had a taste of pain with the guy; what on earth was she thinking? The woman was nuts. What she'd endured in the training room was small fry for Levison. It would be a matter of hours before he'd decide to try bigger and better things with her body, and he would put money on the fact that she wouldn't like it. So why choose him? Had he got her all wrong? Was she a diehard masochist through and through? He didn't think so. Perhaps she was blinded by pretty-boy's good looks? There must be another reason. Surely she could not be that shallow. No matter. Thinking fast he decided to call the auctioneer's bluff. The rules stated 'no talking', so in his mind her secondary choice was null and void.

'If you'd be so kind as to hand over her reins,' he politely asked one of the thickset men behind her, whose eyes were still goggling from the outburst. His comment fell on deaf ears because the giant had just managed to gather his wits about him and grab the vicious looking bamboo cane, propped up against the corner of the magnolia wall behind him. His meaty wrist swung in a wide arc before Mark's tensioned fist caught it sharply in mid-air.

'Her reins, gentlemen. I'll see to her chastisement in just a minute.' He released the hand of the monster and eyeballed the guy, who was at least a foot taller than himself, to make sure his message was correctly received. The cane wavered in big-boy's hand before he grimaced and reluctantly backed down.

'Not so fast, Matthews,' drawled a voice from behind him. 'I don't think the little pony likes you. No, I don't think she likes you *at all*. This must be a first, Matthews. Maybe you're getting a little too old for this business? A few too many grey hairs?' Kyle laid on his Deep South accent, thick and syrupy. He didn't want Petal to connect him in any way with the events of yesterday.

Mark turned slowly on his heel and stared at the smug face a couple of metres away from him. He noted that the nose he had smashed his fist through a couple of days ago looked none the worse for wear, unfortunately. If he got the opportunity to break it again he'd make sure he did the job properly.

'Kyle. Pleasure is all mine. Shouldn't you be out somewhere herding cattle? Oh yes, that's right. You're the only cowboy in the history of the US who doesn't know how to use a bullwhip.' Ignoring Kyle's slack jaw, Mark approached the auctioneer and asked for the matter at hand to be clarified.

Matthius was clearly perplexed as to the outcome of the proceedings but not completely stupid. He had money riding on Mark as the victor, but so as not to appear as though he was backing the obvious favourite he made a show of considering the matter, before bending down over his stand to murmur softly in Mark's ear.

'Can I just announce you the winner?' The whisper was a conspiratorial one.

'No, you can't,' said Mark, gritting his teeth, whilst wondering where on earth Albrecht managed to get these people from. 'You need to consult the rule book.'

Matthius pursed his lips. He then chewed upon a knuckle and fiddled with his red silk tie before finally asking, 'We have a rule book?'

'Of course we have a rule book. How can you not know that?' Mark resisted the urge to slap his hand across his forehead.

'Well, I've been here five years and I've never had to use a rule book!'

'Good for you,' said Mark, his dark stare indicating that he was not amused by this knowledge. 'Now you do.' He propped both of his elbows upon the ledge of the auctioneer's podium and tapped his fingers together impatiently.

Matthius scanned the immediate area for any sign of a book. There were a couple of silver ballpoint pens, several sheets of paper with the details of the ponies to be auctioned and his rather crumpled copy of the Daily Mail, from which he had managed to complete approximately half of the 'quick' crossword. There was little else underneath the podium bar his feet and he was at a complete loss as to where a book might be stashed. 'Assuming there really is a rule book, where might it be hidden?'

'It's in the drawer directly under your newspaper. Incidentally, two across is dive, ten across is halcyon, twelve down is renegade and eighteen across is ether.'

Matthius, who had been working the whole morning to try and discover those words with the aid of an internet connection, was not impressed to have his fun curtailed so abruptly. His eyebrows furling in irritation, he fumbled for the drawer in front of him. Pulling out the slim red vellum tome, he perused its contents in a brisk fashion. He was beginning to wonder if he should have backed Levison. What on earth was he supposed to be looking for anyway? Noticing the stares of many of the room's occupants were now upon him and his ultimate decision, he began flipping through the pages with increased vigour.

'Page thirty-two, "if there is a dispute with the outcome of the auction..."' added Mark, after Matthius had been through the book from cover to cover three times.

'Ah, yes, here we are,' said Matthius, and clearing his throat delicately with the air of one who knew what he was speaking about, even though he didn't, he began:

'Rule two point three states that there will be no speech allowed by any of the auctions "equine" participants and,' Matthius ran his finger down the page until he came to the next item he was looking for, 'rule three point four states that the novice shall pick his/her trainer of choice by eye contact alone.' Leaving a delicate pause, he cleared his throat and smiled before announcing, 'So I declare that Mark Matthews is indeed the winner.' There was a small smattering of applause.

'I object.' Kyle had his hands on his hips and his voice rang out loudly around the room. His aggressive stance did not go unnoticed by the auctioneer, who gave a worried look in Mark's direction.

'Can he do that?' Matthius' eyes looked askance at Matthews and all of his previous bluster quickly left him as he scanned the rule book yet again.

'No, he can't,' said Mark loudly, and moved to take Jenny's reins for the second time. His pony was quivering with rage at having being overruled so abruptly, but it was nothing compared to the anger he felt at her for having nearly jeopardized the outcome of the auction. She was shortly going to feel his displeasure via the bite of his crop and learn the meaning of obedience, so help him God. But then all his feelings of malice towards his new pet evaporated when her big blue eyes turned upwards to meet his and he caught sight of the malevolence there, displayed for the world to see. It made him want to get down on his knees and kiss her. So much for having been serviced by the two blondes this morning, he thought. His hormones were once again swimming to the parts that vanilla sex couldn't reach.

'Yes, he can.' Kyle watched as Mark's grip descended on the thin leather reins. He winked at Petal and turned to face his opponent.

Mark raised his eyebrow in a bored fashion and waited for whatever rot Kyle was about to spew forth. His annoyance at the delay was more due to the fact that his time with Miss Redcliff would be cut short, rather than any lingering grudge towards Kyle's previous behaviour. He just wanted to get out of here and... into something tight, wet and juicy.

'Rule five point six states that a pony will exercise her own choice with regards to her trainer. She does not want Matthews. She wants me. She chose me and I object to Matthews obtaining her against her will in this one particular decision she is allowed to make.' Kyle looked very pleased with himself.

Mark's head tilted to the side in contemplation, and by the narrow look he gave his combatant it was clear he suspected something was amiss. 'Since when did you read the Albrecht Auction Handbook from cover to cover?'

Kyle ignored him and directed his next words at Matthius. 'Call the Stable owner. There's a number at the back of the rule book to be used in the case of disputes.' A single finger pushed the rim of his Stetson a little higher up his forehead, so he could lavish a glower upon the auctioneer. It was abundantly clear that he was going nowhere until the matter was resolved.

'This is utter nonsense. Untie the pony now!' Mark grabbed Jenny's reins and demanded that she be released instantly.

'I am not going anywhere with you! I have chosen my trainer.'

Jennifer Redcliff still had an impressive set of lungs, especially when you took into consideration that her lung capacity had been reduced by half due the tight corset she was currently sporting. It took a moment for Mark's eardrums to clear before he could fully witness the carnage she had wreaked with her last outburst.

The two giants behind her, now infuriated beyond reason, had both reached for their canes and began thrashing the backside before them with a great deal of enthusiasm. Only after a good ten strokes had befallen their victim did one of them pause briefly in his administrations, in order to reattach her bridle and bit to ensure no further outbursts were forthcoming. The remaining occupants of the room then became rather boisterous and animated, having been given a grand show of entertainment that not even they had bargained for. It was simply unheard of for a pony in Albrecht Stables to break the rules in this manner. Excited jeers and clapping began in earnest from the few remaining bystanders. Spirited ponies were a rare beast in Albrecht and when one did make an appearance the occupants of the stables almost held their breath in glee. Jennifer Redcliff would be the talk of the stables before the day was over.

Mark watched the proceedings with acute disbelief. It was official: the girl was certifiable. He could not help but watch, along with everyone else, as she was given a sound thrashing with the canes. The giants were not particularly gentle with their instruments of torture. They were not used to being thwarted in any shape or form. Biceps rippled, fingers flexed and loud grunts of exertion could be heard as their rods flew everywhere, reflected a thousand times over in the array of ornate mirrors that decorated the room. It was a wonder the Murano chandeliers hadn't started to sway. Mark felt an urgent need to halt the pair, although he couldn't exactly put his finger on why.

'Call the owner now, Matthius. Let's put an end to this dispute.' Mark had to raise his voice to be heard above the din of the zealous spanking, and it was something he did very rarely. Things were not going quite as planned and it didn't happen too often in his world. He was not at all pleased. Watching Miss Redcliff get a good dressing down from the burly black-coverall crew should have had him aroused, but all he wanted to do was stop them in their tracks. He had no problem with her ass getting a sound flogging, but he wanted to be the one to administer it. Watching her face as she tried to slice her teeth through the rubber of her bit, he could only be impressed at the way she held herself taught against her bonds and refused to utter a single sound. How did she have such a high tolerance for pain? Had her earlier words in the barn been more than a mere flippant remark? *I've had worse.* She hadn't answered his question at the time and now he was more than curious about the answer. Had she experienced pain before? She was tightly in control of herself under the pounding canes and while they weren't hard enough to induce tears, she should have been venting some rather nasty noises about now. She would remain an enigma for the time being, but he intended to get to the bottom of it.

'Enough, gentlemen; either myself or Mr Levison might want to admire her ass later and I, for one, don't want it to be a bruised mess.' Mark regretted his outburst as soon as it had left his lips. Watching Kyle's smile widen he hoped to hell that whoever the owner of this stable was, he was prepared to be reasonable.

'Getting squeamish in your old age, Matthews?'

Mark didn't grace Kyle's question with a reply. Instead he watched intently as Matthius picked up his cell and began dialling. There was an anxious look upon the man's face as his thickset fingers punched in the numbers and awaited an answer. As he began to apprise the owner of the situation his brow creased in concentration, before finally the cell was removed from his ear and placed gently upon the podium in front of him. The room had become silent once more as the spanking stopped. Miss Redcliff could be heard panting for breath in the corner, but all eyes were now on Matthius and the outcome of the telephone call. There was an awkward pause as he cleared his throat.

'We are shortly to receive an answer via the intercom so that all present may hear the verdict. Meanwhile, the owner has suggested that the remaining participants amuse themselves by accompanying the pony to the veterinary surgery where she will be given a physical examination and, due to her recent disobedient behaviour, she will be fitted with the "device". I have it on good authority it is a spectacle well worth witnessing,' and with that Matthius led the way out of the glittering mirror mass, causing dozens of prisms to refract themselves around the pristine white walls as the crystal face of his watch caught a dazzling ray of sunlight.

Jenny watched the proceedings in miserable silence. Her breathing had now slowed and her head cleared from the fury of having been expected to fall at Mark Matthews' feet. Whoever the owner of this godforsaken place was, they had better not give her to him. A fountain pen would be the least of his worries. As one of the incredible hulks behind her began unfastening the ropes and spreader bar which held her legs taught, she could only think of the humiliation that would follow being awarded as Mark's prize pet, to be trotted around and made to do tricks. Although her backside stung and a fierce wave of heat emanated from the tender flesh, the sensation did little but fuel her ardour and it was all down to that one infernal man. The sooner he was out of the equation the better. At least she'd be able to think clearly and form a sensible escape plan.

The ogres were rough but worked with a speed and agility that belied their size. In no time at all she was free of the rope that had been coiled around her wrists, knees, calves and ankles, but the effects of the rope burn she had managed to achieve during her orgasm dance would stay with her for a few days to come. Her arm-binder, which had been roughly ripped off just before the auction began, was beyond repair and as there didn't appear to be another in sight, Jenny supposed she could be thankful for small mercies. At this precise moment in time there wasn't a lot she felt thankful for. Her limbs ached and her jaw felt like someone had driven a transit truck through it. Both mouth and pussy were filled with an unpleasant heat that simmered uncomfortably and the heavy saddle she wore buckled on her back made breathing through her corset even more difficult, if that were possible. When a heavy hand landed on her backside with a smack, she mewled pitifully through her gag.

'Move!' It was apparent that the beefy twins were men of little words. The command was grunted loudly and accompanied by a boot in her sex, so Jenny had little choice but to obey. Stumbling forward, a stout hand slapped her rump again and squealing loudly Jenny raced across the room.

Fighting her way through a jungle of meandering legs she had plenty of time to admire the opulent dress and footwear of her audience. These were people from her world; the world of the rich and famous which housed the powerful, compelling forces of the upper echelons of society. A Gucci stiletto whizzed past her nose, followed by a Dolce and Gabbana shoe which took a more leisurely path. From her vantage point of only a few inches above the floor she watched glossy gold buckles fly past her nose and highly polished leather brogues flirt with leopard-skin Jimmy Choo's. Was this to be her life from now on? Examining the footwear of the high and mighty? The swish of a long silk skirt brushed over the highly sensitised skin of her back and she shuddered with longing.

'Oh, what a delightful wiggle those ass cheeks have, and just look at that tiny tail. Lots of room for improvement, don't you think? I wonder if she'll be worth buying after she's finished her training?' The voice was female and her English was tinged with an Italian accent. Her comment was met with a mumbled reply from her male companion. Walking slowly behind the errant pony, the woman was now examining her attempt to tackle the concrete corridor.

Jenny could feel the eyes of the pair boring into her back. Having forgotten how brutal crawling was on her hands and knees, she was now going as slowly as possible in order to lessen the abrasive impact against her skin. Falling behind the main group quickly, she struggled to keep her hands and knees moving against the cold and unforgiving floor.

'I think Petal needs some encouragement, darling,' said Miss Italy, and there was another mumbled reply. The next thing Jenny knew, a pointed heel was being firmly pressed into her left buttock and Miss Italy was putting some considerable weight behind it. Jenny shrieked loudly and darted off up the corridor, uncaring of the rubble underneath her. A few minor scratches were nothing when compared with a five inch heel trying to stab for entrance into an already very tender backside.

'Hmm, pity,' said Miss Italy, her lips forming a delicate moue as Petal raced off ahead. 'I was just thinking that the little horsie would make an amazing footstool installed permanently in the centre of our lounge, darling.'

Jenny raced on ahead, not wanting to hear the rest of that particular conversation, and bemoaned the new throbbing pain in her ass cheek. It was obvious who wore the trousers in their relationship, she thought sourly. Darting in between legs once more as she caught up with the main group, she gave no thought to anything bar escaping the pair behind her. Her lungs burned for air but she paid them little attention. She was too intent on trying to listen to Matthius, who was giving his captive audience a taste of what was to come.

'The device is quite possibly one of the 'worst punishments that can be awarded to a novice pony,' said the auctioneer, turning around to give his spectators a wide smile. 'It is a suit of perfectly tailored, form-fitting latex which will hug every curve and contour of the pony-girl's body. It provides sensory deprivation in many different ways. Her ears can be filled with wax, to ensure she cannot hear a thing. While two small slits will be provided for her eyes to enable walking, an additional blackout blindfold is provided if her trainer wishes to deny her the pleasure of sight. Her mouth will be plugged with a small ball-gag, but this can be removed should there be any additional requirements for her mouth.

'And there will be,' drawled a now familiar voice. Laughter bounced off the narrow walls and Jenny felt her throat go dry. Would the cowboy be as demanding as Mark? Would he treat her gently? She cursed herself a thousand times over for thinking such thoughts. She would be rescued. She would! If it took her rescue team a few more days to find her, she'd cope. These people only had her body to amuse themselves with. She still had firm control of her mind; except when she was anywhere near Mark, that was. *Please, anyone but him*, she begged silently, and could only hope that someone somewhere was listening.

'Tiny wires are situated all over the insides of her new bodysuit and will pulse electrical current through her body in order to keep her aroused and stimulated. The suit features a special "chastity belt" which will be locked in place automatically and a timer will be set for the duration of forty-eight hours, whereupon the locking mechanism will be released automatically. The chastity belt itself features two dildos which, although initially quite small and comfortable in size, can be inflated, elongated and pulsed within her body. There is a clitoral stimulator which will be fitted with precision around either side of her clitoris and a tiny pincer-like contraption will reside above it. If the internal computer contained within her suit decides she is becoming too aroused, she will received a sharp nip for her troubles and all titillating sensations will cease abruptly. The suit will then decide when to restart its devious ministrations. There might be as much as thirty minutes between near orgasms, or there could be less than five. As you can imagine, little sleep will be achieved in a suit that turns its victim's body into an orgasmic ticking time-bomb. More laughter echoed around the corridor.

'Can such a suit be purchased from Albrecht? For the use of our own slaves, perhaps?' The gentleman who asked the question was tall, obviously French judging by his accent, and his face was screwed up in fierce concentration.

'I'm not sure,' replied Matthius, who had little to do with the inner dealings of Albrecht, 'but for a price, pretty much everything is for sale around here.' He turned his head back over his shoulder and gave an exaggerated, cheeky wink to the spellbound participants.

'Could the suit be worn for extended periods of time? Perhaps five, six or even seven days, Monsieur?'

'That I cannot tell you. But hold on to your questions, ladies and gentlemen, because the vet will probably be able to answer them very shortly.'

Jenny veered well away from Mr France and his unsettling inquiries. She did note that the rather disturbing gentleman wore a pair of Berluti loafers, easily costing over four hundred pounds for the pair and that if he could afford shoes such as those, along with the suspected Valentino suit he wore; a latex cat-suit wouldn't prove too big a problem for his budget. All this talk of restrictive clothing and denied orgasms was making her hungry again, and it wasn't for food. The menu at Albrecht had already put her off fruit and vegetables for life...

'Our little pony is lagging behind again, Giles. I think she's heard a little too much. Perhaps we should give her an added incentive to get her ass moving?'

Jenny's head swung around awkwardly to discover the whereabouts of the new voice, this time of thoroughbred English descent. A gentleman in his late fifties smiled lecherously back at her.

'I think you're right, Crawford,' said his purring companion, also male, but of much younger years, 'or we may have to wait until Christmas to see this "device".' After a few seconds of high-pitched laughter Jenny discovered something slim, smooth and made of leather being run up her inner thigh. It didn't take a brain surgeon to guess what the man was waving around and she surged forward to avoid its exploratory path.

Unfortunately the crop appeared to move with her and it quickly reached higher, probing for entry at her slippery sex. Jenny swung left to avoid its path and was rewarded with more laughter. She did not manage to avoid its path a second time. A loud smacking sound could be heard as the tip of the crop caught her left buttock. Jenny wailed as best she was able through her thick rubber bit. Although it had been little more than a light tap, the pain was maddening after her buttocks had been cruelly ravaged by the canes. Thinking it wise not to allow the crop another attempt to rest upon her poor ass cheeks, she fled through the ranks and was somewhat surprised when Matthius left the confines of the building and continued walking out into the open. Where on earth were they going?

When her knees hit grass Jenny contemplated the thought of getting up on all fours and making a run for it. The idea soon manifested itself as ridiculous in her brain. She knew without a doubt that Mark, Kyle and possibly Matthius would be fast enough to catch her and the electrified fence was still in place. All she would be doing would be inviting further punishments upon her body and it looked like she already had enough to cope with in that department. Erasing the thought of escape from her mind for now, she appreciated the cool dirt beneath her hands and knees. Never in her life had she thought she might enjoy the rigors of crawling through mud and muck, but oh how times had changed. Right now she would love to immerse her steaming backside in a pile of gooey mud and wiggle about in it to the best of her ability. She burned and she hungered; next she'd be begging to stay. Trying to oust the annoying thought from her head, she became increasingly annoyed when it refused to budge.

'And here we are, ladies and gentlemen,' said Matthius, stopping outside a rather unremarkable outbuilding built of red brick with corresponding red slate tiles. As per nearly all the buildings in Albrecht, its entrance was through a double set of brightly painted, white timber doors. When they opened they revealed a man in a white coat and various surgical contraptions that did not look welcoming. She would have immediately retreated backwards, but the spectators had formed a semicircle around her, effectively blocking any departure.

'If you'd like to file around either side of the "breeding station", which we will use for her preliminary examination, I think all of you will manage to achieve quite a good view from that perspective.' Those were Matthius' ominous last words as she was driven forward by a dozen or so pairs of moving feet.

The Veterinarian

The first thing Jenny noticed upon entering the new building was that the floors were made of sparkling white marble, a thin vein of grey running through each impressively sized slab. It was amazing what you noticed when your head was only inches from the floor. The smell of antiseptic and bleach was fresh upon the tiles and it was obvious they had been recently cleaned. Her face was reluctant to stretch itself to examine higher objects, but in the end she decided it was better to have some idea of what might be about to happen to her.

Finally, lifting her eyes off the floor and straining to look upwards in her tight leather collar she immediately wished she had kept her nose down. Directly in front of her was the young man she had spied earlier. Dressed in a lab coat, which revealed a neatly ironed blue shirt beneath, she placed him somewhere in his thirties. He sported a stethoscope around his neck and a pair of stainless steel forceps hung over the single pocket upon his breast. Of slim build, he wore rimless glasses delicately balanced upon his roman nose and generated a somewhat bookish and geeky look. Glancing down at her in a detached manner, he beckoned her forward.

Jenny did not move an inch. She had spotted a T-shaped wooden contraption in the middle of the room, and if that wasn't frightening enough, there were an array of microscopes and buzzing machines stowed in the far corner, along with a table filled with scalpels, syringes and all other manner of paraphernalia she was unable to put a name to. Spying clamps, pins, needles, thermometers and electric trimmers, her heart rate pounded into emergency mode. She wanted to run out of the door as fast as her legs would carry her but Mark, as usual, was one step ahead of her.

'You can't run when someone is holding your bridle.' He spoke gently but firmly, and his fist gripped the thin leather of her reins tightly.

The scrabble of her back legs against the marble stopped, but her whole body rebelled at the thought of being forced to play their naughty games in such a way. This was too much. They had crossed the line. Hell, no, they had crossed the line about three seconds after she'd entered the tack room two days ago, but it wasn't as if she could voice her complaints.

Mark lowered his head to whisper in her ear. 'You'll give them exactly what they want if you kick and scream now. Two days with the device and a trip to the dungeon would probably be more than most trained submissives could manage. If I were you I'd go up to the vet and offer your body for his inspection. Do the exact opposite of what they're expecting, Princess, and keep them on their toes.' Winking at her, he used the rough ends of her leather bridle to caress her cheek before stepping back to the outer circle of gathered guests, but his penetrating eyes remained trained on her face.

The vet, who had been moving some instruments about on his table and preparing for his examination while Mark had given his brief pep-talk, appeared satisfied with his work. Turning around to face his new patient once more, he repeated the action of beckoning her forward with the crook of his finger. 'Just wait on your knees beside the breeding station. I'll be with you in a moment.'

His words did not decrease Jenny's anxiety in the least, but knowing there was little hope of escape with so many people watching her, she decided Mark's advice was the only sensible course of action. Crawling slowly up to the 'breeding station', the words alone causing a shudder to ripple through her body, she meekly awaited the attentions of the vet, her heart banging inside her ribcage.

Quickly unbuckling the heavy leather saddle from her midriff, the vet patted her head and muttered, 'Good girl.' Then he produced a pair of thick black leather cuffs for her wrists and elbows, and folded her arms up her back towards her neck, fastening the cuffs as he did so. There was a metal chain that linked each cuff together and this was attached to the rear D-ring in her white collar by means of a large karabiner. It was even more uncomfortable than the arm-binder had been, and Jenny noted ruefully that she was once again an object to be toyed and played with.

'Stand up,' said the vet, hoisting her up by the waist so she had little choice in the matter. He led her over to the wooden frame and began to feed her head and upper body through a small rectangular opening in the top. Her stomach now rested on a square plate and her upper body was tipped forward over the fame whilst her backside was pushed up and outward. Her knees were forced down towards the floor and a spreader bar was once again fastened around her ankles, leaving her sex wide open and on display for the amusement of the many bystanders. Then a long rectangular panel positioned directly above was drawn down upon her back and she felt the pressure of the wood graze the tips of her elbows. The clamp held her body tightly in place. It appeared that he didn't want much patient participation, Jenny thought, growling around her bit. The sound drew amused laughter from the crowd.

'They said she was feisty,' sneered Miss Italy, 'but I wonder how feisty she'll remain in this "device".' Her comment drew a few sniggers from the people around her, who were avidly looking around the room to discern the methods of torture and torment that might soon be doled out to the hapless pony-girl. Jenny noticed, with some trepidation, that there was not a kind or sympathetic glance amongst them, with the exception of Matthews perhaps, and she did not want to look in his direction to find out.

The vet simply raised his eyebrows in reply, before clapping his hands together to gather the attention of the group. 'OK, ladies and gentlemen. I'm going to talk you through what you are about to witness in our surgery. The frame Petal is currently restrained upon is called a breeding frame because that is how our mares are restrained before we have one of the stallions cover them. It's an effective piece of equipment, because the mare cannot collapse her body against it or stand up. She can stay in this position, reasonably comfortably, until such time as you are confident that your stallion has performed his duty.' He looked around to ascertain there were a few nods being directed his way before he continued. 'Today the frame is just a convenient way to secure her body while we do a dental exam and brief physical. She will also be fitted with a RFID tag, to enable us to accurately track her whereabouts at all times within a position of several hundred metres. We will end our session by securing her in a very special latex bodysuit that will test her endurance, over the next few days, to the absolute limit. Are there any questions before we start?'

The audience, glancing coyly at one another, shook their heads and waited in breathless anticipation for what was to come next. After a brief pause the vet continued with his narration. 'First, I need to check that everything is in working order. So we will start with the ears.' Reaching into one of the larger pockets positioned at his hips he pulled out an otoscope. Pulling Jenny's ear to open the canal he inserted the instrument's tip inside it and flicked on the light. Stooping down to carefully examine her right ear, moving the instrument this way and that as he worked, he quickly moved across to repeat the procedure on the other side. 'Good news, ladies and gentlemen. Everything seems in perfect working order, which means there will be no problem plugging her ears with the wax earplugs that are commonly worn with the device, inside its hood. As this suit is worn in punishment we often try to remove as many of the senses as possible when the occupant is inside it. Her trainer will be able to engineer her suit so she won't be able to see, hear, talk or use her hands and feet to touch or feel. Her movement may also be restricted, although she will be given regular daily exercise. All of that will help to focus her concentration on what the "device" will be doing to her body. Now I will examine Petal's body for any signs of abnormalities, enlargement or tenderness.'

Jenny listened with trepidation. If she'd thought she was helpless before, that was nothing compared to what they were planning to put her through in a few minutes' time. She would be encased in a world of silent darkness and completely reliant on her captors for food, shelter and a guiding hand to help her move from one place to the next, if the vet was to be believed. They were going to lock her tight inside her head and watch her suffer the torments of sensory deprivation. It was solitary confinement, but worse. Her body would be constantly primed for orgasm only to have it denied at the last instant. This was intolerable. It was just beginning to dawn on her that the position she would soon be in was worse than that of even the lowliest of animals. They could not expect her to endure this, surely? Were they messing with her head? But even as the thought crossed her mind she knew these people were deadly serious in their intent. They meant to break her. After two days of this, if she made it, there was a very real possibility she would be exactly like the girls in the stable; meek, mild-mannered and ready to obey every little command at the earliest opportunity. Thrashing about in her bonds as the thought took hold, she screamed through her bit and made her displeasure at their treatment be known. A few errant tears leaked from eyes, but her fury kept most of them at bay.

'See the beauty of the breeding frame? Try as she might there is very little movement Petal can achieve within it. She cannot hurt herself, she cannot hurt others and I can continue the examination in confidence.' The vet was as good as his word and his hands stroked and kneaded all available flesh, from the tops of her thighs to the tips of her fingers. Her upper back, neck and shoulders were manipulated under his efficient hands, and struggle as she might it made no difference to his thorough inspection. When his fingers approached her mouth, however, Jenny ground her teeth over the bit before snapping at him. 'Ahh, I wondered if you might prove difficult,' he said. Reaching inside his deep pocket once more he pulled out what appeared to be a thick rubber ring, with two studded leather straps attached to it. Jenny hadn't a clue what he was showing her, but apparently the audience did as there were a few nods of appreciation.

'I can see you're going to need calming down before we dress you up in your shiny latex suit, but that can be arranged, I think, with a bit of audience participation. Are there any volunteers?' He looked pointedly at the crowd gathered around him, and most could be seen nodding their heads or raising their hands. Indicating the two men closest to him and beckoning them forward, he issued his instructions. 'Handling a human pony can be a difficult business which will often require speed and agility, so I have a challenge for you. If you are successful in your task, I will allow you the reward of soothing Petal in her hour of need, gentlemen. What say you?' Both men nodded heartily and smiled. 'One of you will need to remove her bit and bridle, while the other will need to squeeze her jaw open and insert this ring gag firmly inside her mouth, just behind her teeth. I need to examine her mouth and I am wary of doing so while she is in such a spirited mood.' Having said that he dangled the gag in front of Jenny's eyes and waited for someone to grab it. He didn't have to wait long.

There was barely time to blink before fingers were hastily undoing the silver buckles of her bridle and trying to squeeze the bit from her mouth. She did not make it easy for them. Clamping her teeth firmly into the rubber she shook her head madly, as best as she was able, and made all manner of unladylike sounds. It didn't make the least amount of difference as with a hard wrench one of the men before her pried it from her mouth, watching as she showered spittle over the spotless white floor in front of her. Wanting to scream bloody murder, but knowing that would give them exactly the leverage they needed, Jenny clamped her jaws firmly shut and continued thrashing her head around. The crowd were in fits of hysterics by now, but the only thought in Jenny's head was the need to deny them access to her mouth. Realising what they shortly had planned for her she was all for biting and chewing any piece of flesh that came her way, but there was little she could do when a strong hand cupped her jaw and fingers roughly levered her teeth apart. Even though the opening was only a few millimetres the man used the space to the best of its advantage by threading the red rubber ring inside her jaw horizontally, before tightening the leather straps behind her head which caused the ring to pop up vertically and force her mouth open wide. Yet again she hadn't stood a chance.

After the men received an appreciative round of applause the vet continued his examination. Having donned a pair of clear latex gloves, a long mouth swab was already in his hand as he approached his patient's face. 'There, there, filly.' He patted her head. 'I'm just going to take a look around and get a sample of your DNA. It's nothing to worry about.' Lifting her face in one hand and pulling up her top lip with the other he began to carefully inspect the area. His fingers pressed down upon her upper gums for a few seconds before they moved inside the 'O' of her gag and began to palpate her tongue gently.

'I'm checking her mouth for pallor and moistness and her tongue for any signs of ulceration. You'll be pleased to know she's got some excellent colour and no abnormalities that I can see.' He dragged the swab through her mouth and replaced it in a test tube for safekeeping.

Jenny was being driven insane. She was wearing herself out with futile struggling and her body was already limp and lethargic from the rigours of the auction. She could hardly believe what these people were doing to her. What did they want with her DNA and how dare they take it without her permission?

'We take samples of all our ponies' DNA and blood. It can be useful to treat or diagnose illness and these particulars are often scrutinised by buyers before purchase, especially if they want to breed them.'

Especially if they want to what? Jenny did not hear the mumbled comments and general chatter of the people gathered around her after that little titbit of information. She was absolutely shell-shocked. If her jaw hadn't been wired open it would have hung so, and quite unattractively. Breeding? They could not be serious. Goddamn! Alas, she could not even stamp her feet, spread apart as they were with the metal pole. Who were these people? What did they want with her? And where, for the umpteenth time, was her ticket out of here?

If the vet saw the multitude of questions bouncing off Jenny's temples like a slew of grand slam ace tennis balls, he chose not to pay them too much attention. His fingertip was over her eyelid and stretching the delicate membrane upwards. 'I'm just checking her sclera for signs of discoloration or reddening.' He moved to the other eye and repeated the same invasive treatment. 'Once more it appears that she is in tip-top shape.' Inserting the stethoscope into each of his ears, with some struggle he managed to place it just below Jenny's corset, directly above her heart. 'I have not been instructed to do a thorough examination today, so I'm going to note her heart rate and blood pressure before and after the relaxant.' The smile he gave Jenny was not comforting in the slightest. She had a mouthful of saliva caught behind her ring gag that could not be moved, which was unfortunate, because if she could have moved it the vet would be wearing it right now. Whilst pooling saliva might have been the least of her discomforts at this moment in time, it was the one she was focusing on to keep herself sane.

Placing the stethoscope back around his neck he commented, 'Her heart rate is a little elevated at this moment in time, but that's to be expected and I suspect her blood pressure will also reflect her anxiety.'

Easy for you to say, thought Jenny, whose anxiety levels had already rocketed to the Milky Way and beyond. She was only just coping with this new onslaught of information. The blood pressure cuff was placed around her upper arm and inflated. She concentrated on breathing. In and out, she guided her misshaped lungs, in and out.

There was a lengthy pause while the vet appeared to study his apparatus, and finally he concluded, 'Just as I thought. A bit elevated but nothing to be too concerned about.' A long breath whooshed out of her as she prayed that was the end of the check-up. 'Now, I'll just examine her tail, take her temperature and then you're good to go, gentlemen.' He patted Jenny's rump and she shrieked and bucked in protest. It did her little good; the breeding frame held her fast and did not budge an inch.

'I am going to lift her tail,' and good as his word, he did exactly that, pulling the plaited tail gently but firmly upwards, 'and assess her anal reflexes.' Drawing his gloved finger slowly around her sphincter he watched as Jenny contracted her muscles reflexively. Then he slowly pulled her tail from within its tight resting place and, with a good slow tug, waited for it to pop free. Walking over to his table in the corner of the room, he placed it into a jar of sterile liquid. With the vet out of the way for a moment the two gentlemen volunteers were openly examining Jenny's backside with obvious delight, admiring its beautiful pink tone and deep red stripes. Fingers had begun to explore the raised marks and appreciated each little quiver of torment the bound pony-girl was forced to exhibit, along with each precious little mewl of protest.

'Not so fast, gentlemen,' said the vet on his return, gesturing for the two overzealous males to move back and allow him room to complete his last assessment. They did so reluctantly. Taking a pale white tube of lubricant from his pocket he liberally applied the gel over his index finger before inserting it into her rectum. The patient was none too happy about the fact, but all of her squirming served to spread the lubricant around in a much quicker time than he would have normally accomplished the task. Pulling his finger from her ass he continued with his examination. 'See how the plug has already begun to soften this incredibly tight muscle? Already we can see it will take some time for her to recover complete closure, which will allow me to insert this thermometer with relative ease.'

A long, freezing cold thermometer made its way deep into her bowels and Jenny had little effort left to fight it. She watched the crowd's eyes as they stared at her and then at her backside, most of them smiling and thoroughly enjoying the show. The room suddenly felt very small and Jenny wanted, more than anything, to teleport her body away from these people, because she was now becoming horribly aroused at the humiliation of being publicly displayed and used so basely. She could feel intense heat penetrate her cheeks but there was no way she could hide either her embarrassment or her awakening libido. The vet must have been able to discern the flood of arousal to her clitoris because he took the opportunity to thrust a single digit into her pussy, before finding room for another to join it.

'Just as I suspected. Our little pony-girl is going to enjoy being used anally, but that's by the by for you two gentlemen, as that area is off limits for now.' There was a chorus of groans around the room as he slowly withdrew his thermometer and read the temperature. 'Excellent. She's in fine form and probably ready for some fun. The stage is yours, gentlemen, after one last little thing.' Without warning the vet pulled out a transponder syringe, much like a normal vet would use to tag a cat or dog, and it dived towards her upper arm. There wasn't a thing she could do about it, bar howl in protest. This was not a small injection. This was a needle containing a microchip, and when it went in she let everyone know about her displeasure, screaming and shaking her head madly in displeasure.

'There, there, all done,' said the vet, who was completely unconcerned by Jenny's tantrum and made no show of noticing her ill humour or bad behaviour.

'No point in trying to escape now, young filly. You can easily be tracked by that little chip, and from quite a distance. We correlate all your medical data on that chip too, and you just need to be scanned before each check-up in order for us to have a computer full of relevant information to look at. Which makes life for me considerably easier, considering you ponies are unable to talk.' He took a sterilised tissue from his pocket and ripped the package open, swabbing at the indentation of the needle and wiping away a tiny spot of blood. 'We try to decrease the risk of infection where we can.' Carefully placing the tissue and his latex gloves in a medical waste bag that he pulled from his pocket, he said, 'If you will now excuse me, ladies and gentlemen, I had better go and tidy up.' He patted Jenny's head and his footsteps could be heard receding into the distance. 'Have fun, gentlemen,' were the last words he aimed at his audience.

Uh oh. All eyes were on Jenny, but the two pairs in front of her were the ones she was most concerned about. The pain of the needle had vanished and she was already concentrating on her next challenge. Not having paid much attention to either of them while the vet had been in attendance, she finally took the time to size up her adversaries. Both men had the look of fanatical zealots clearly inscribed upon their faces, and it was clear that the religion they worshipped was sex. The man to the left of her was probably of Middle Eastern origin and featured beautiful coffee-coloured skin, complemented by dark caramel eyes. He had bow-shaped lips, which were currently posed in a rather sensuous pout, and his thick dark hair was cut in a fashionably modern style, with flicks and edges. Jenny was going to call him *Good-Looking*. The first thing she noticed about the guy to the right of her was that he was massive. Easily six foot four inches in height, he was thickset, black, and the whites of his eyes were almost gleaming with vitality and health. His biceps rippled under the soft, cream chambray shirt he wore and his black eyes were enormous in their hunger for her. Fine, she'd call him *Big Guy*. Jenny could not help but notice the rather impressive bulge in his slacks because her face was lowered at just the right height upon the breeding frame for his waist to be directly in front of her eye line. His cock twitched. Jenny's heart pounded and her pussy clenched. It appeared he was big *there*, too. She had all but forgotten her humiliating treatment under the hands of the vet. Finally it looked like she might just get some of the good stuff. Her mouth watered, quite literally, out of the corners of her gag.

'Would the little pony like to be fed?' The accent was beautifully rough, raspy Spanish and it made her insides clench.

Oh, yes. Yes please. Jenny was aware, somewhere in the back of her head, that she should not be responding to this type of treatment; this sexual madness that had taken over her body. She was almost aware, somewhere through the lustful haze of thoughts that now flooded her brain, that Albrecht was priming her to crave sex and the release it would bring. It appeared they'd brainwashed her well. She needed this. Her whole body was squirming and imploring the men to take her in any way they saw fit. It had been three long days without sex and amazing orgasms aside, being filled by these two gorgeous men had her dribbling in excitement - even more than she was already. When Big Guy continued to look at her in a questioning manner Jenny realised he expected a reply. She nodded her head enthusiastically, her mouth biting down upon the rubber ring as she tried to reply with an affirmative. Big Guy bit his wonderfully full bottom lip and gave her a searing look of longing. *Yes, yes, yes. Feed me those juicy big cocks gentleman and rock this body of mine into the next century.*

The two guys must have heard her thoughts for Big Guy was already fondling his impressive piece through the fabric of his slacks and Good-Looking was unbuttoning his fly. Jenny's struggling had completely ceased. A voracious appetite for pleasure was spiralling through her body and she wanted someone to act upon it. Good-Looking now had his cock within his delicately boned hands. It was obvious he had enjoyed the appetiser Jenny had presented and would require little in the way of foreplay.

'Shall we see if she's wet?'

Jenny almost rolled her eyes in frustration and would have stomped her hooves had she been able. Hadn't the vet just demonstrated that only two minutes ago?

Good-Looking smiled and inserted his two longest fingers inside the hole of her gag. He slowly stroked her tongue, which was still very sensitive and slightly swollen from the ginger spice salve and dildos that had been used at the auction. That quickly captured her attention and she couldn't help a moan of delight. His fingers continued to dip and dive within the confines of her jaw, his fingernails gently skimming the inner walls of her mouth before he used a generous dollop of her own saliva and began to use it to paint her lips. She couldn't help but watch in fascination as the two clever fingers scooped up all of the available spittle which had pooled behind the gag and applied it around the entrance to her mouth in a similar fashion to that of a tube of lip gloss.

'I am preparing you for my cock. Would you like to suck it?' Good-Looking, for all his Middle-Eastern good-looks, spoke with a guttural, German accent. Jenny knew enough about languages to know the accent was slightly forced, as if he was trying to disguise his original country of origin. He obviously didn't want the spectators to trace his whereabouts back home. Daddy might not approve of his 'recreational' pursuits. Jenny raised her big blue eyes to his and watched them devour the sight of her mouth, spread wide open, lips glistening invitingly as he had readied her to receive him. He awaited her response with his hands in the pockets of his open jeans. A tuft of dark hair appeared enticingly at the V of his zipper. In response she thrust her tongue out from behind the metal ring and licked her top lip provocatively. She wanted to be filled and she wanted to suck. It was hardly a secret that she was aroused and there was little point in playing hard to get, displayed as she was. His eyes danced at her response.

'You'll have to beg me for the privilege, Pretty Pink Petals.'

His leering glance over her body could have been an incendiary device, for she exploded in flame everywhere. She could not think straight. Her mind was a muddled mess and she was being controlled by nothing more than hormones. Beg? What did he mean beg? She couldn't talk, dammit. She groaned in frustration, watching longingly as he palmed his erection and stroked himself.

Although Big Guy was behind her, Jenny was aware he was not playing the same game. That was because he was currently sliding his big hands under her ribcage, dwarfing her breasts as he cupped them. The heat of his hands felt heavenly upon her cool skin and as his fingers began to pull at her nipple clamps she groaned in torment.

'Would you like me to cover you, Petal, as Amand fucks your face?' Big Guy pressed his body firmly against hers and she could feel the bulge in his pants press up against her ass.

'Unnnnghh.' It was as close to a yes as she was going to get. He leaned into her neck and his lips grazed her earlobe. 'Unngghhhh.' *Yes, yes, yes, fill me, fuck me. Don't make me wait. I don't want to wait.* Jenny jiggled her hands around in her cuffs but they would not move and her body had no leverage to speak of. How did she beg? She wanted, no, she *needed* to be used by these men. Oh God, what was happening to her?

'I'm waiting, Petal.' Good-Looking raised an eyebrow at her and the action instantly reminded her of Mark. Mark! Goddamn, he was in the audience watching her. Where? Her eyes scanned the small crowd of people nervously as she fixated on the men, taking in their leering glances and lascivious winks as her eyes met theirs. Big Guy had now got down on his knees behind her and was running his hands up her widely splayed legs. He worshipped her calves through the thick leather of her boots and when he reached her upper thighs he moaned in pleasure, his fingers stretching out to caress the silken flesh before him. Jenny's whole body shuddered in need. Her clit pulsed with a fury that was unholy and no one had gone anywhere near it, yet.

'I'm still waiting.' The voice had taken on a sing-song quality, as if the man behind it was slightly annoyed. Well, he could join the group. She was annoyed too; annoyed and needy. Beg how? 'Unnnghhh,' she moaned, her voice louder, almost pitiful in its attempts to cajole him to place his cock in front of her lips. And still her eyes scanned the crowd who had dispersed around the surgery, some in order to get a better view whilst others sought comfort either in a chair or upon a countertop. Miss Italy had her silk skirt around her waist and her back to the wall as her enthusiastic partner began to lap at her sex. Her large brown eyes centred on Jenny and she winked her approval at the proceedings before her, of which she was watching with avaricious glee. Turning her eyes away hurriedly, shame coursing through her body at the thought of so many faces staring at her, she concentrated on Good-Looking. It wasn't a hard task; he was beginning to undo the shiny black buttons on his crisp black shirt and his beautifully tanned body was mesmerising. Shrugging the shirt away roughly he let it slip to the floor. Taking her face in his two hands, he raised her head so she could admire his straining cock, now just inches from her nose.

'I don't think she knows how to beg, Domingo,' said Good-Looking, running his shaft teasingly along her upper lip. A drop of pre-cum oozed from the tip and the salty tang had her mouth watering.

Domingo was using his rather impressive tongue to trail a wet path down her ass cheeks, before he used his meaty hands to spread them wide and admire the tiny, gaping hole before him. 'Amand, I'm hungry, you're hungry. Tell the pony how to beg.' His lips gently circled the tight, puckered rosebud and Jenny squirmed madly. 'Uuuunngggh!' Her hips tried to buck away from him, but she was held tightly in place. It was incredibly pleasurable. When he thrust his tongue slowly inside her she nearly dissolved into a puddle on the floor.

'You're an animal. You need to beg like one. As you can't use your hooves you need to use your tongue. I want you to thrust that tongue out as far as it can go and when I'm satisfied you've got the look just right, I'll let you draw me inside you.' He dragged his cock along her lower lip and watched her body twitch in delight.

Jenny was quick to obey; thrusting her tongue outside the metal ring as far as it would go. She didn't care about the humiliation, nor did she care about her audience. Her thoughts centred solely on Amand and Domingo.

'Wouldn't she look great with her hooves begging upwards in supplication, Domingo?' Pleading for the chance to suck and service us? Do you think she would make a nice addition to our stable in a few months' time?'

Domingo just laughed. 'A few months? Try a few years. This one will wear black.'

'Mmmm. That makes me even harder.' He pumped his cock in his hands, slowly at first but the speed increased with each passing stroke. 'OK, lovely tongue, pony-girl. That's it, thrust it forward and back. You'll get the hang of it. Now I want to see some pleading with those pretty blue eyes.' He grabbed a handful of hair from the top of her head and pulled her face back he could watch every tiny nuance of her expression.

Jenny wanted to scream in frustration. Domingo had resumed his little thrusts into one of the more tender parts of her anatomy and his tongue was wonderfully skilled. He performed little pumps, longer lunges and then more circling, around and around. She was yelling, snuffling and squirming madly and could only hope that the expression in her eyes was enough to please Amand.

'Yes, that's it Petal, you've captured the look perfectly,' and with those words he laid his cock down carefully upon her supplicating tongue.

Jenny sighed. It was warm, soft and silky. There was a pleasant salty taste to it and she couldn't wait to devour the beast.

'Wait. Do not suck until I tell you to. Just hold it right there and let your tongue curl around me.' Jenny did not need to be told twice. Amand sighed and closed his eyes as she did exactly as told.

Domingo had unzipped himself and was rubbing his cock up and down Jenny's backside. Just little strokes to let her know he was there, but the size of the beast behind her both frightened and excited her. This was almost going to be a replay of the auction room, but with the real deal in the form of two warm bodies and two throbbing cocks.

'Should I let her taste me, Domingo?'

Jenny greeted that comment with another pleading look and Amand smiled at her.

'Let her, Amand. She's been a good girl and good girls get to suck. Meanwhile

I'm going to fuck her and bang against these beautifully red-raw ass cheeks. It's going to sting a little but I have a feeling Petal might enjoy the sensation.'

Amand needed no further encouragement as he thrust his cock to the back of her throat. Domingo, meanwhile, rubbed himself up and down the entrance to Jenny's sex. Her lips had already parted prettily, eagerly awaiting his entry but he wanted Amand to get a good rhythm going before he joined in the party.

'Suck, Petal, suck!' Amand had begun thrusting greedily into her mouth and Jenny struggled to keep up. Although she was well lubricated it wasn't the easiest task in the world to suck when the front of her mouth was prised open with a metal ring. She had to concentrate on using her jaw rather than her lips to provide the tight sensation Good-Looking was after. Judging by the look on his face he was reasonably pleased with her efforts. That was when things started to get a little difficult...

Domingo began to plunge his cock inside her pussy, with sharp and powerful thrusts. Her backside, still smarting nastily after its previous treatment with the cane, howled in protest. She, however, did not. Armand was plugging her mouth far too quickly and far too thoroughly for even the slightest whisper to escape her lips. The pain of Domingo's body slamming into her backside was like a fourth of July firecracker to her body. She came alive and it was as if someone had plugged in all the electrical circuits in her brain at once. Domingo grabbed a handful of hair from the top of her head and grazed her cheek with the stubble of his jaw as he banged into her once again.

'Boy is this one tight, Amand. You've got the wrong end,' and with that he used her head as a leverage point to pound into her backside harder.

'I don't think so,' said Amand, struggling to breathe as he continued to bury himself in the depths of Petal's throat. The soft ring of her gag grazed the tender flesh of his cock beautifully and the cool rubber coupled with the warm of her mouth was his undoing.

Domingo's fingers worked the nipple clamps and chain on Petal, tugging and dragging until her poor little buds were straining and swollen. His body worked hers over like a freight train, so big and powerful that each thrust was as much maximum damage as it was pleasure. When his fingers finally dipped and reached for the pulsing nub of her clit, Jenny needed only the lightest of touches before she took the plunge over the edge of consciousness. Her body suffered paroxysms of the grandest order. Each further thrust from Domingo's loins sent another wave of sensation flowing through her, and when Armand erupted in her mouth she vocally gurgled her pleasure. Her body was a riptide of turbulent emotions and for several seconds afterward she could barely breathe.

Domingo cared not. He was concentrating on burying his massive member deep inside her. Lifting Petal up by her inner thighs he angled her backside up towards him to get a better angle on his lunges. Having only managed to bury half of his cock inside her up to now, the improved position allowed him to go deeper, and thankfully this was aided by the fact that his pony was fairly gushing with her very own brand of enthusiasm. His fingers found her clit and forced the poor abused little root to stand to attention once more.

As Amand withdrew from her lips a thick gob of semen and saliva dribbled over the red ring and flowed down her chin. She barely noticed the wet line of goo as it trailed downwards towards the floor. She was too intent on relishing the 'Domingo effect' and savouring the delicious sting as he slapped into her ass. When the gag was removed and in its place appeared Amand's face, she automatically opened her mouth. She had no idea why, the reaction was automatic and fuelled by lust. When his beautifully dark, caramel eyes bored into hers she knew she was lost. Letting him drink his fill, she watched as Amand's soft lips vied with hers in order to drink his own essence. Her legs went weak and would have buckled had they not been held tight in restraints.

Domingo worked her over with his confident stroke and more than competent fingers. They tugged, cajoled, rolled and flicked. Jenny loved it all. Mewling and crying into Amand's mouth she could not believe it when her body was on the verge of yet another orgasm merely seconds after the first. Each little bell attached to her webbing and corset tinkled sweet music as her body quivered. 'Oooh,' she moaned, but the sound was whipped away by the gentle pressure of lips and when his tongue began to war with hers, she was again roaring with need.

Amand finally pulled his lips away to murmur, 'Beg for that orgasm, Petal. Let me see that sweet tongue, pretty Pet. Show me how much you want this.'

Jenny tried to fight the instinct to do exactly as he asked. Her eyes were swimming with arousal and floating around the room, watching the crowd as they got down to business themselves. But Domingo's fingers were relentless in their pursuit. Already she was on the brink of release and she could feel her pussy stretched as never before, the massive cock filling her and banging into her with a frenzied rhythm she could not control.

Armand traced his finger around her swollen lips and tilted his head to the side. 'Show me that tongue, Pretty Pink Petals. Domingo won't let you have the goodies until you do. He's very particular about such things.' There was a knowing nod as he looked over Jenny to watch the powerful black man let loose an almighty roar of satisfaction.

As his cock plied for admission at the entrance to her cervix Jenny gurgled upon the last vestiges of pooled semen in her mouth while her tongue snaked out of its own accord. Please, please, please, she begged silently. She felt Domingo's cock twitch and jerk spasmodically inside her as his fingernails bit into the flesh of her shoulders. Her eyes, still roaming the room, finally caught a glimpse of Mark who had buried himself in the shadows. Back against the wall, with his hands casually at his sides, he gave off a relaxed air until she ventured up to his dark, almost black, unfathomable eyes. His look of fury would be forever imprinted upon her brain as she screamed out the pleasure Domingo's fingers had finally released.

The Device

'I do love a screamer, don't you?' Kyle had sidled up to the wall against which Mark rested and was grinning lewdly at the sight of the ménage before him.

Mark ignored him. Jealousy coursed through his bloodstream, bile forced its way up into his throat and he wanted to rip the heads off both of the bi-brothers who were currently mopping up their own bodily fluids and sweat. He'd never felt anything close to it and he didn't like the emotion one little bit. Jennifer Redcliff looked resplendent wearing her tight white corset. Her new hour-glass figure, swollen lips, glazed eyes and splayed legs were a sight to behold and it was all he could do to control himself. With her head thrown back in the throes of intense pleasure and her short hair plastered to her head, she looked almost divine. The trouble was he wanted to be the one who put a look like that on her face and woe betides anyone else who wanted a go. It was all he could do, at this moment in time, to prevent himself committing mass murder. Breathe, just breathe, he told himself. She would be his soon enough. He scraped his short fingernails upon the plasterboard behind him and tried to divert his concentration from the sublime picture of wanton submissiveness Miss Redcliff had created. He might as well have tried to stop the space and time continuum. As a bucket of tepid water was brought in by a stable hand he found his eyes glued to the poor boy's hands as they began to soap up her body. If he had his crop handy right now, the stable hand would be getting more than just his knuckles rapped. At the ridiculous thought, Mark felt sick.

'I'm going to be getting me a piece of that ass,' said Kyle.

It took a while for the words to register, so intent was he on watching each and every little place the stable hand's fingers were going. He now wanted to rip the poor boy's digits off, one by one and feed them to him. His first foray with the green monster was not going well. Finally, Kyle's words hit home.

'How's the nose, Levison? The concealer you're using to cover up the bruise is dripping down your face, sweetheart.' It had been an educated guess but when Kyle quickly put his hand up to his nose to test Mark's statement and it came away smudged with an orangey paint, Mark couldn't help a snort. 'Now do me a favour and get out of my sight before I rearrange the rest of your face.'

In response Kyle gave him the finger. He'd already begun to walk away, so the threat hadn't really been necessary. Mark would put money on the fact that pretty boy was off to the gents to make sure his face was still reasonably attractive to the opposite sex. What did Jennifer Redcliff see in him? He was distracted from his train of thought by the vet, who had once again taken centre stage and having dismissed the stable hand, thank God, cleared his throat to attract everyone's attention.

'Ladies and gentlemen, I hope you enjoyed our little appetizer and are now ready to move on to the main event?' The vet took a sweeping glance over the room and was rewarded with the rapt attention of his audience. 'Good. Then I shall begin by releasing Petal from the frame and her spreader bar. Now where are the would-be trainers?'

Mark stepped forward smartly. The vet frowned when Kyle was nowhere to be found. 'He's gone to powder his nose,' Mark informed him. 'He has a very delicate constitution and sometimes these types of scenes upset him.' There were a few amused smiles amongst the crowd.

'Ah, OK,' said the vet, having not caught the sarcasm imbued in Mark's statement. He looked rather perplexed at the idea that any of the trainers in Albrecht might be squeamish, but recovering his composure he moved the conversation along. 'Right sir, if you'd like to pick up a crop or paddle I think that will be enough encouragement to ensure our trainee remains still for the fitting.'

Mark chose a black leather crop with a vicious looking tip. Jenny barely noticed. She wasn't used to the kind of exertions Albrecht was placing upon her and all she wanted to do right now was curl up on the floor and go to sleep. When the two of them finally untangled her from the frame she would have fallen into a heap, physically unable to support herself, had they not managed to catch her body and lower her dead weight gently to the floor.

It was obvious to Mark where the problem lay. Jenny was close to exhaustion by the looks of her heavily lidded eyes and trembling limbs. As a result of the auction she wouldn't have had any food or fluids since breakfast, and with all the excitement it appeared everyone else had forgotten. He strode towards the fridge in the corner, near the vet's table, and pulled the door open wide. Scanning the contents quickly, most of which were medical in nature, he found what he was looking for. Positioned along the door compartment of the refrigerator was an array of different flavoured energy gels. He pulled two orange packets out, figuring that was the least she was going to need if she was shortly to be cocooned in stiflingly hot latex. When he walked back to her she had not moved from her coiled position on the floor and her eyes were staring vacantly at the ceiling. It was probably less distressing than focusing on the sea of faces around her, he guessed, or indeed the rubber suit the vet was earnestly preparing behind her.

Ripping the tops off both packets simultaneously with his teeth, he stooped to her inert form and slowly let the fluid pool on her tongue. It seemed to snap her out of her stupor, for she began lapping at the contents of the two packets in earnest. He carefully drip fed her and didn't stop until he had drained the packets dry. Kneeling beside her on the floor he caressed the side of her cheek. As mad as he was at her earlier behaviour, it would wait until later. Right now she would need lots of encouragement to get her through the next ordeal.

'Chin up, Petal. It'll be over before you know it. Besides, I have it on good authority you girls like wearing tight-fitting clothes and fiddling about with vibrators.' He had no idea if she was listening to him. Her eyes were still glazed and, bar the soft swallows of her throat, the girl was as still as a statue. 'Don't give up on me just yet, Pretty Pink. Show these people what you're made of.' He did not want to use the whip to get her to assume the required position for the fitting, which would be on all fours. He figured she'd had enough corporal punishment today, judging by the blazing red stripes which decorated her backside. When the vet cleared his throat, indicating he was ready to begin, Mark knew he had only a few precious seconds to play with.

'I can't wait to finally fuck that delightfully pretty mouth of yours, Petal.' It was no word of a lie. His cock strained against Armani's finest tailoring in its eagerness to complete the task. 'You have no idea how much I look forward to training that body of yours to please mine to my eminent satisfaction. It will be quite a job, but I suspect you'll be dribbling at my feet and awaiting the chance to complete my every command to the best of your ability within a reasonably short period of time. I'm the best there is, sweetheart.'

His pep talk had the required effect. With a concentrated effort Jenny pushed herself up to an all fours position before unleashing the fury contained within her eyes and venting it upon her antagonist. Her inner demon was awake and roaring. Immediately trying to get to her feet she was thwarted, both by her body and her boots. Her body was too weak to stand and her stiff leather boots were not supple enough for her to accomplish the act without help. Mark watched her uncoordinated movements and knew exactly what she was trying to do. The problem was easily solved. Placing the sole of his shoe in the small of her back, he applied enough pressure to make sure she kept her current stance. Although the chit grunted in protest, at least she didn't try to speak. Miss Redcliff appeared to have learnt something from her short stay at Albrecht.

'We'll need to remove the cuffs, corset and boots first; they can be refastened over the suit when we're finished,' said the vet.

Mark nodded in understanding and got to work unthreading the laces of her boots. Before long he had managed to open them up enough that it only took one strong pull on each leg to remove them. He then pulled a Swiss army knife from his pocket and began to saw through the white cords that held her corset secure. When the last of the two ropes had been severed the corset almost sprang off Jenny's back, which indicated that the strain it had been under was great. The fact that his pony was now taking deep, gulping breaths also confirmed this. The cuffs were the easiest thing to tackle and with a couple of twists from the key he was helpfully provided with, her hands were free.

Picking up the rubber suit he had been carefully adjusting, the vet came to stand behind Jenny. 'I'm going to need help getting her into this,' he said, and laying the item of clothing on the floor behind her, he grappled with the left leg while Mark had some fun with the right. Stretching the black material as wide as it would go in their strong fingers, they slowly slid the elastic fabric along her calves and up to her knees. He continued with his explanation. 'The suit encompasses two generous plugs, both of which will pulse, vibrate and elongate at random intervals. It also features a clitoral stimulator and massager, which will tease our little pony to the brink of orgasm again and again over her forty-eight hour period of confinement, tormenting her to exacting standards. She will not be allowed to orgasm. The tiny wires that run around the latex suit will measure her heart rate, breathing rate, temperature, the contractions of both her vagina and anus, and the engorgement level of her labia. When combined these indicators give a very accurate idea of impending orgasm and the suit will shut off all stimulation for at least two minutes, allowing the subject to adequately calm down before its insidious torment may begin again.'

Jenny watched as the vet lubricated the plugs which rested on the seat of the latex, currently beneath her legs, and tested the mechanisms. A faint whirring sound could be heard as they began to hum and shudder, and before long they began to grow in size, both in length and width. They were constructed in flexible black plastic and looked like they could do internal damage. She trembled and tried not to watch as he tweaked the dildos this way and that, watching them inflate and deflate on cue. They would be inside her soon, but strangely enough, the thought was not abhorrent. Her pussy was already clenching in its eagerness to receive them. As the two men pulled the suit up around her thighs one of the plugs gave the merest tickle upon her sex and she moaned with fervent need. Directing her hips downward in order to try and rub herself against one of the dildos, she was immediately thwarted in her attempts by a swift slap from the vet who quickly aligned both of the sculpted black shafts with the correct penetrable holes. She purred. Embarrassingly, when he pushed them forward they began to slide smoothly into place, both of her entrances having been already lubricated by the previous skilled antics of Domingo and Armand.

Mark stroked the strands of Jenny's fine ebony hair and watched the vet's progress with interest. He wasn't going to have a battle on his hands with the fitting, surprisingly enough. He had expected Miss Redcliff to claw, kick and scream the place down, but no, here she was mewling like a kitten. He watched her eyes flutter closed as her neck tried to arch back in pleasure, though the movement was hampered by the thick white collar she wore. He gave her backside a small tap with the crop. It was enough to have her eyes springing open and they quickly darted up to his to display their venom. 'You know better. Keep those eyes open. Everyone wants to see how much you're enjoying the Albrecht experience.' Scowling at him she could do nothing to curtail her immediate reaction, and as her eyes widened searing heat flooded her cheeks. 'That's exactly it,' Mark winked at her, and smiled when her lips compressed in anger.

The vet, meanwhile, had finally encountered resistance with the last inch of both insertables. In order to combat the pony-girl's tight anal walls he began to pump them inside her with a slow and gentle rhythm. Taking a small tube out of his pocket he applied a little more lubrication on the anal plug for good measure.

Jenny was torn between a desire to suck the dildos inside her or try to fight her base instincts and rebel. As her eyes flickered upward to look dubiously in those of Mark's, she already knew what a futile endeavour resistance would be. The man in front of her was a cold-blooded as a snake and his eyes were already drifting away from her. She meant nothing to him. She was a number, one face in a stable full of beautiful female forms or an object that needed to be honed to perfection. That was all. She couldn't, wouldn't endure life like that with him, even if it was only a few more hours until her rescuers would finally manage to locate her. It would be intolerable. Pretty Boy she could handle. With Mark, she would be lost and she had a feeling that she might never find herself again. Snapping back to the present she grunted as the plugs finally slotted home inside her. Her clit was then manipulated carefully between the vet's fingers and inserted between two soft rubber 'ears' that held it firmly in place. Then the tugging began in earnest...

The latex rippled across her body. It devoured inch by slow inch of pale, smooth flesh into its hungry jaws until there was only a sea of black rubber to seen. The material felt tight and suffocating but Jenny was so exhausted by the day's activities that she didn't have an ounce of fight left in her to halt its progress. As her limbs were worked this way and that to accommodate the slick fabric her head reeled. Where was her escape ticket? Had she really been abandoned to this life of sexual servitude? It was certainly starting to feel like it. It was entirely possible that unless she managed to engineer a way out herself, she would remain a pony-girl at Albrecht until such time as someone chose to purchase her. But what if there were no buyers? Would she remain here forever? Mark's previous offer now seemed a whole lot more palatable than life as a dumb animal, trussed up tight and paraded daily around a paddock. She'd rather be a personal sex-slave than endure life with the mud, slop and straw.

The suit began to take hold of her body and its tight confinement was both frightening and exciting. Her thoughts were mush inside her head. One moment she was certain rescue would come, in the next she was convinced it wouldn't. She knew her relationship with her father wasn't good, but she didn't think he hated her enough to arrange to have her kidnapped! Was this all a mistake? It seemed to have been engineered very shrewdly, right from the beginning when she first entered the Pony Rides hotel. That in itself didn't mean her father was responsible; it could have been any one of a number of people - but did anyone really hate her enough to do this to her? It was a crazy thought and no definite answer was forthcoming. Yes, she had been a tease to men but she had also given them what they wanted. She wasn't aware of any of her previous boyfriends holding a grudge of this kind of magnitude against her.

The rubber crept up towards her clamped breasts. Mark lightly tugged on the chain which still connected them and smiled when he heard her gasp.

'You had better remove those,' said the vet. 'Her suit has specially formulated plastic cups which will knead and manipulate her breasts. It also features its own pair of nipple clamps, angled within the cups, which will tighten and release at regular intervals to torment its victim. Some of our ponies find nipple torment one of the easiest ways to achieve orgasm. We'll be watching Petal closely to see if she is one of them.'

Mark did as he was bid and slowly released each of the pretty, filigree clamps that she wore. He admired her face as a delicious look of anguish began to take form. The blood would slowly flow back into those tortured teats and they would throb rather nastily for the next few minutes, he suspected. She wouldn't suffer for too long. They would be replaced by her new ones very shortly.

Jenny felt her boobs being almost sucked into her brand new outfit and when the rubberised plastic moulded to her cleavage in a horribly stiff and unyielding matter, she cried out. It was more from shock than real pain, though. Her whole body was being condensed into this skin-tight bodysuit and her heart rate and breathing were already erratic in panic.

'Now for a little nip. Brace yourself.' The vet simply pinched the tips of two rubber domes in front of him, causing Jenny's compacted breasts to move forward, before he released the twin clamps. The pony in front of him hissed and her eyes watered as two wide pincers bore down upon her tender teats, but the threat of the crop being dangled in front of her eyes made sure she remained motionless.

'Since when do you get to have all the fun?' Kyle had re-entered the room and was looking none too pleased upon having discovered he had missed half of the action. He glared darkly at Mark, who blithely ignored him and continued with his efforts of squeezing the trainee's arms into the corresponding holes of her suit.

Jenny gave a few token squirms and wriggles under the hands of her tormentors, but with a good push and a few hard pulls she was immersed up to her neck. Mark drew the long zipper upwards, from just above the small of her back until it was fastened snugly at her neck. Taking pains not to catch the delicate skin of her throat, he tucked the ends into her thick white collar. Jenny decided then and there that she would never understand the inner workings of his mind. One minute he'd lash at her with a crop and in the next he was as gentle as a new-born lamb. What was with the man?

'How does that feel? Not too tight?'

It was horribly tight, but the vet wasn't really interested in an answer. He pulled her legs and arms this way and that, to make sure she had just about enough room to move, and then squeezed two fingers upon her wrist to feel for her pulse. 'Not too agitated. That's good.'

How wrong could he be? She was disturbed all right. Her suit already felt tacky and sticky. She had no idea how she would be able to spend two days in the thing. It would be hotter than hell. She could feel the minute metal threads that ran up and down the length of it and wondered what they were for. Whatever it was, she suspected she wouldn't like it. What with the new longer style plugs trapped inside her and the tubes and wires, she was beginning to feel like a robot who just needed a power source. An orgasmic power source, as her body already pulsed and contracted around them, seeking fulfilment. Tired as she was, her body was ridiculously greedy for release and it would have to wait two long days before the privilege might be granted. Still, it wasn't that long in the grand scheme of things, was it? It would be over before she knew it.

'You may gag her now.' Jenny looked up as the vet indicated a ball-gag on his table which looked very familiar. Kyle was the nearest and practically ran to the table, fingers clamping swiftly around his prize, even though Mark had made no move for it.

When he returned he grabbed her face in one hand and yanked her chin up. 'Do you find me attractive, Petal?' When the girl foolishly tried to shake her head he nodded it for her with a heavy hand. 'Everyone finds me attractive. That's why you picked me, isn't it?' Jenny didn't bother trying to shake her head this time, as she had no desire to feel her teeth rattle inside her head. 'I'm good at what I do, Petal. We'll make an awesome team. We might even get you that black collar in under a year, if we put our minds to it.' He flashed his brilliant white smile, which had been enhanced with a considerable amount of dentistry, and turned his face around to wink at Mark. 'Bet you wished the girls loved you, huh?'

Mark blinked slowly and decided he might grace Kyle with a modicum of his attention. 'No,' he sighed, 'I go to a considerable amount of trouble to make sure they do not love me. It saves whining and whinging later, I find.' There was a snicker of amusement from the gathered spectators.

'You're missing out, man. If the ladies love you, they worship you. You don't have to love 'em back.'

'Thank you for your psychological perceptions on love, Kyle. Are you going to gag the pony, or can I gag you instead?'

In response Kyle screwed his face up in annoyance and snorted. Mark's words did have the desired effect, however. He moved the gag to Petal's lips and pressed softly for entrance. He could be gentle when there was an audience to please.

He couldn't resist bending down to whisper in the trainee's ear, 'Do you remember meeting me last night at the stables, Petal? I had a lovely gag for you, just like this one.' Watching her eyes widen in confusion as she began to piece the jigsaw together he raised his voice and continued, 'This is how you'll remain in my presence.' He had stopped speaking with his heavy southern drawl and waited to see if any recognition would dawn. It did. She foolishly gasped and while that gave Kyle all the answer he needed, it also gave him a great opportunity to shove the ball-gag to the back of her throat. 'Whether by bit, ball or my cock, you'll never get the chance to use your vocal chords for anything other than neighing and whinnying under my command. To be honest, you'll barely need to use your brain cells. All you need to do is follow my direction and be a good girl.' He patted her rump and grinned when she tried to paw and scream at him. 'Aren't you glad you picked me? We're going to have lots of fun together.'

Jenny recoiled in horror from her assailant and a whopping great mistake that no amount of white-out would ever get rid of. She wondered if she could change her mind. Hell no. She'd take crazy over cold any day of the week. Jenny would have picked Kyle, who was clearly nuttier than a fruit cake, over Mark had he been the only other option. Yes, he was a fruit loop, but at least she wouldn't have to deal with a daily chemical imbalance in her hormone levels.

The vet held up a circular black object and asked, 'Any volunteers?'

Kyle whisked the thin black rubber disc out of the vet's hands and stretched the fabric in his hands, letting it snap back to its original shape in front of Petal's eyes. He laughed out loud when her head whipped back in shock. Wasting no time in getting to grips with the hood of her outfit, which was then dragged roughly over her head with a few hard yanks and tugs, he stood back to admire his handiwork. Tucking the ends of the latex hood smartly into place behind the thick white collar, her temporary disguise was complete. He ran his thumb over her rubberised cheek and took a theatrical bow for his audience before wheeling a free-standing mirror, which had been carefully concealed behind the trainee, in front of her humbled figure. He wondered how she would react. His bet was badly. All eyes in the room turned to stare at Petal's black, oily-looking body and waited expectantly for something to happen. They were not to be disappointed.

It took Jenny a couple of seconds to comprehend exactly what was reflected in front of her. Firstly, because she had a very limited field of vision through her tiny eyehole slits, and secondly because everything swam in a black haze before her. When her eyes finally adjusted and she was able to make out a reasonably clear picture of herself, she just managed to hold back on what would have been an ear-splitting scream. She was no longer human. Albrecht stables had successfully managed to strip every ounce of humanity from her and turn her into the animal they desired.

No one would be able to recognise her in the figure-hugging elastic prison she now wore, unless they had somehow managed to catalogue the size and shape of her breasts or ass, she thought with some measure of incredulity. The only apertures within her hood were the two small slits for her eyes and two round holes beneath her nostrils through which to breathe. Haltingly, she angled her eyes towards the mirror to witness the damage that been had been inflicted upon her.

Immediately shrinking back in horror, Jenny simply stared at herself for what must have been a minute, perhaps more. She simply could not believe her eyes. Reflected in the mirror before her was a human horse, complete with perky rubberised ears. There was also a long, black, horse-hair tail dangling between her legs. She wanted to bawl her eyes out. The suit was now being sprayed and polished to a gleaming shine by both Domingo and Amand, who were having lots of fun with some aerosol canisters and a pair of dusters. At least someone was enjoying themselves, she thought acidly.

There was little time to dwell on her predicament. Two long latex gloves were headed her way, the ends of which were adorned with a pretty accurate, if somewhat small, horse's hoof. Her hands were picked up by both Kyle and Mark and the fingers were bundled into fists. Her vision was beginning to tunnel at this point and only some of the goings-on around her registered within the dark recesses of her brain. This could not be happening. Slowly but surely the pair of lubricated hoof-mitts were worked up her hands. Even though her vision was sketchy she knew which side Kyle and Mark had taken by the way they accomplished their task. Mark was gentle and careful with each of her fingers as he squeezed them into the tight glove. Kyle was impatient. When the latex snagged and wouldn't move on his first attempt, he yanked upon her elbow with a fierce, hash tug. Hang on, that couldn't be right, could it? Mark was the sadist. He was the one who'd nearly crippled her with exhaustion and pain in the training room. Shaking her head to try and clear her clouded vision she eventually managed to confirm what she had already known. Mark was being kind, Kyle was being rough. Ah yes, but Kyle had been her tormenter yesterday evening. He'd fed her a sleeping tablet and gagged her for a whole evening. Nothing made sense any more. Was everybody twisted around here? Maybe she was going mad.

When the hoof-mitts snapped into place they fell at an angle from her wrists, similar to how a real horse's hoof might appear. Once again her hands were useless. She knew it wouldn't be long before her boots and corset followed. Not content with having taken her speech, liberty and free will away, now they wanted to make her look like an animal too. A hysterical fit of spluttering and tears threatened to explode from the back of her throat. She just managed to hold it back, but the effort involved was nearly her undoing. The next thing she knew Kyle was coming at her with a knife, and for some reason the thought terrified her far more than it would have had Mark been the one wielding it. Instinct had her diving her head towards the floor, where she coiled up in the tightest ball she could manage. It was a protective manoeuvre and completely automatic, but when the whole room exploded with laughter she felt the first of what could potentially be a monsoon of tears threaten to spill.

Kyle dragged her up by a handful of her hair, and with his free hand he cut a slit in the front of her hood, aligned with the hole in the black ball which filled her mouth. The knife was quickly pocketed but Jenny did not feel in the least bit comforted.

'You will be fed and watered through the hole in your gag. At meal times you will be presented with a tube which will give you a nutritious balance of all your daily vitamins and nourishment in liquid form. You are now at the mercy of the device and with its many sensors and careful response measurement it will not be a pleasant experience. Oh, the first hour will be entertaining enough, I'm sure, but after that you'll be, a little bit on edge, shall we say?' The veterinarian reeled off his information in a perfunctory manner and looked relieved that his job was nearly over. To finish, he held a narrow black rectangle in the air and all eyes bar Jenny's immediately focused upon the item. 'This is the remote control for Petal's suit. While the suit has an "auto pilot", if you will, it can also be directed by any individual who has charge of this little box. Speed, thrust, inflation, pain and electric shocks can all be delivered by the specific whim of her trainer. So, all that's left to be decided, is who would like to be the first to test her suit?' He waved the black box in the air for effect.

Kyle made a grab for the remote, but this time Mark had anticipated the move and his lightning reflexes slid it out of the vet's hand before Kyle even came close to it. 'Congratulations, Mr Matthews, and have fun with the demonstration.' The vet appeared satisfied with his creation and sidled back to his desk, content to watch the proceedings from a respectable distance.

'You might as well have your fun now, Matthews. I'll be having the last laugh when she's awarded my trainee for the next few years.' Kyle's glare was hostile, but it had little effect on his adversary who was once again training his gaze on the pony before him.

Domingo and Armand had just managed to get her back in her hoof-boots and they were now tackling her corset with a considerable amount of gusto. Unfortunately for them Jenny was now back in the land of the living and she was not going to take being strapped back into the air-sucker-outer lying down.

She wanted to scream. To be exact, she wanted to scream the words, 'Get off me you sonofabitch bastards!' What she actually managed to spurt out through her tightly gagged mouth was 'ggggmmmffhhhh,' and it didn't sound half as promising. The fact that she couldn't articulate a single syllable poured petrol among the already very fiery flames. Now she was *really* mad. Somehow managing to propel her body upwards and get to her feet in a manoeuvre a Chinese gymnast would be proud of, Jennifer Redcliff would have looked tall and imposing on her four inch hooves had she not had a serious wobble on landing, but by some miraculous feat she managed to remain upright. Now what?

Looking around frantically and unable to detect any clear exits within her very limited field of vision, she had few options available to her and they were as follows: a) run as fast as you can and hope for the best or b) lie down and play dead. Obviously, she ran. Unfortunately running was no mean feat when you had four inch hooves, but determination served her where pony hoof-boot design failed. Somehow she made it to the white timber doors with nobody's hands upon her. This was mainly due to the fact that she'd managed what must have been at least a five metre skid upon the smooth marble tiles with her plastic hooves. Sliding precariously, with her balance all over the place, her hooved hands finally managed to bang into the sturdy timber door and she frantically cast her eye slits downwards in an attempt to spy a door handle. Her heart was banging out the good bits of Tchaikovsky's 1812 overture and now that there was a chance of escape in sight her body had infused itself with blood and felt ready to do battle. There was the door handle. It was a simple latch mechanism. She just had to flick the lever upwards and the doors would open outwards. Reaching out and already exulting in her victory, she moved her fingers forward and made to open the metal ratchet. *Bang.*

Her gloved hoof bounced back off the wall and pain splintered through her wrist on impact. The other hoof followed suit, but this time it was a gentler thud because she knew she had already lost. That was why no one had chased her. In her suit she had been rendered as helpless as a baby. There would be no escape for her while she was trussed up like this. Hooves flailing at the door, banging at the lever as if it might magically open, Jenny felt invisible tears leak down her face. Thank God no one could see her now, brought to a new all-time low. Sinking to her knees, still banging at the wood with her mittened hands, she was almost glad of the hood that would hide her tearstained face. The humiliation of crying was enough. She did not need them to witness the act and watch the enjoyment on their faces, which she knew without a doubt would be there. Trying to stifle her sobs, she let them watch her furled back and tried to drown out their laughter, which rang sharply in her ears.

Mark had watched the display of spirit and felt nothing but pride for his soon-to-be apprentice. Jennifer Redcliff had now spent three days of intensive training within Albrecht's walls and she should be feeling the effects. The girl should be hungry, exhausted, emotionally unstable and utterly cowed into submission. Whilst she might be hungry, she was not yet any of the other three on his list. Time would probably see that all of them had a tick beside their respective box, but as of yet, the chit was still fighting and all guns were blazing. She needed to think through her attack plan a little more carefully before acting upon her impulses, but Miss Redcliff deserved some credit for her determination.

He knew what she was doing now. The curve of her body and the slight tremors of her back spoke volumes to him. Knowing he could save her at least some of her embarrassment at having been brought so low, he turned his attention to the remote control he held in his hand. She wouldn't have much time to think when the device came to life within her body. Studying the plastic rectangle carefully, he tried to fathom what was what. He nearly went cross-eyed. The tiny little symbols all looked Greek to him. He grimaced. This looked like it might be a trial and error affair. There were two main control points, all featuring arrows pointing this way and that. He could assume that the up arrows would increase the size of a dildo; down arrows would decrease and perhaps the sideways arrow would inflate? That left several other symbols to decipher, such as thrust, thrust speed, vibration, pain and electrical shocks. Hmm. Deciding to test the arrow theory first, he pressed an upwards arrow.

Miss Redcliff immediately shot off the floor and pawed at her ass, so he quickly took his finger off the button. He watched her breathe a sigh of relief. That probably meant the top portion of controls were for anal use, if a logical pattern were followed. Taking a sideways glance at the vet, who was already nestled on a wooden stool in the corner, inspecting his instruments one by one, Mark took an educated guess. He decided the next set of buttons should do the trick. Pressing the up arrow, he watched his pony closely.

This time her body did not go into a rigid posture as before, but instead she stretched out in a supine, catlike manner. She wasn't purring yet, but she would be. He'd got the right hole and it was high time to play eighteen rounds with it. Letting his finger trail off the pulsating button he allowed her time to get used to the growing intruder. It took all of two minutes before the dildo was fully inflated and the button ceased to pulse beneath his fingertips. He wished he could see her face. If it were up to him there would be no hood and no gag. He liked to witness his submissives' expression and he liked the sounds of their moans and whimpers. He still couldn't quite believe that she had managed to earn herself a punishment this severe in only three days. If she continued on the dangerous path she was forging for herself she'd be doing dungeon time in less than a week. She wouldn't like it. The girl might have a pair of balls that could certainly rival Kyle's and she had a good tolerance for pain, but she had absolutely no idea of the torments down there. Laying your eyes upon the equipment and thinking you could take it, were somewhat different to actually being there and made to take it.

Studying his remote once more he decided that two arrows on top of each other probably meant thrust. Pressing the button down with his thumb his keen eyes took in Jenny's hips and the way she suddenly pushed them forwards and back, gently rocking to and fro. It was official; he was a whizz with technology. The black latex creaked and groaned as she got to all fours to find a more comfortable position. The girl hadn't seen anything yet. Pushing the sideways arrow he once again studied his prey. No squawks or shrieks were forthcoming, so he guessed it couldn't be all that bad. A soft 'unnnghh' left her lips and her body trembled. He was hoping he'd found *inflate*. When she began to whimper the longer he held his finger on the button, he decided it had been a pretty good assumption.

Opting to be kind he pulled his fingers back and didn't let it expand to its full potential. Her hips waggled a little and then she dipped her head to her knees. There was a pause as she gathered her breath and then she looked up and after a quick perusal of the inhabitants of the surgery, her head centred on his and he knew what she was thinking. Revenge.

Miraculously she once again got to her hooved feet and rushed forward, but this time it was not the exit she was after. He suspected she wanted to sink her knee into one of the more delicate parts of his anatomy, and in quite a brutal fashion. Rapidly scanning the rest of the controls he sought either pain or electric shock treatment. His handicap was growing with the vast array of symbols swimming before his eyes. There was a triangle, a fork, a spiral and a circle and he was just getting started. Watching Miss Clomping Hooves tear down the marble floor in what could only be described as a stampede, or slide-eze as she seemed to have mastered the art of skating, he didn't have a lot of time with the decision making process. Triangle, spiral, interconnecting lines or fork? He didn't have a working knowledge of the suit and none of his previous trainees had been required to wear it, so he had no idea which punishment was the kindest to dole out. Not that it really mattered as he still hadn't managed to figure out the symbols. Miss Redcliff hadn't slowed down and if anything she might have managed to speed herself up. The sleek black silhouette flying through the room towards him looked rather disconcerting; a cross between Batwoman and an angry Terrier. Taking a calculated guess he pressed the triangle and hoped it would be somewhat painful and slow her down, but that it wouldn't do any permanent damage.

The Terrier came to an abrupt halt in mid-stride with a loud gurgling sound, before Batwoman took over and flew through the air. The landing needed practise. Spinning around in a one hundred and eighty degree arc, Jenny's head came to rest mere inches from his feet, which was quite worrying as his finger was still firmly depressing what was obviously the electric shock option. She was pawing repeatedly at areas all over her body and had gone into rigid spasms, leaving her face down and twitching upon the cold, unforgiving floor. Taking pity on the captive he released the triangle before pressing the heel of his loafer into the small of her back to make sure she stayed relatively harmless to all and sundry. He didn't have a pen in his jacket pocket, but someone might have a toothpick somewhere and now that he'd directed her to go for the eyes, the results wouldn't be pretty. Actually, come to think of it, in the getup she currently wore she wouldn't be much of a threat to anybody unless she clipped someone with one of her hooves.

He wondered whether he should let up the gentle pressure of his foot. The two glistening metal horseshoes on the underside of her feet discouraged him against the notion. He already had a stab wound to contend with; he could do without half a ton of bruises to accompany it. Now, where was the vibrate button? He assumed fork was for pain but that still left a number of options available to him. Eeny meeny miny... bugger it, he'd go with the interconnecting lines. They looked like they could have something to do with vibration. He took a moment to wonder whether he should keep his foot in place whilst trying the new button or not. There was a risk he might electrocute himself if he kept it there, but there was also a risk she'd do him some personal irreparable damage if he didn't. What was a little electricity between friends? He pressed the button.

No electricity. That was good. There wasn't much of anything else, either. Jenny hadn't made a sound. She'd better not be unconscious under that suit or he was going to get good and mad. He wanted a blowjob as soon as the mysterious owner of Albrecht came on and gave up the results of this ridiculous farce. Which reminded him, it must be getting late by now. It was about time someone got this show on the road.

There it was - the merest whisper of noise. Thank God she hadn't passed out. Mark didn't really do the guilt thing, but there were occasions when he almost managed a semblance of a conscience. All eyes in the room were trained on Miss Redcliff. They wanted pain. One way or another, they'd get it eventually. Poor girl couldn't make much more than a whisper with the ball-gag filling her throat, but she was definitely making some kind of sound. The latex slowly came to life beneath his foot.

There were a few gentle twitches at first. He began to wonder whether she was still feeling the after effects of the shock treatment, but the twitches soon progressed to longer, squirming motions. A grumble of disappointment circled the room. They wanted action. They wanted reaction and the stronger the better. Too bad, because Mark didn't give a damn what anyone else wanted.

She tossed her head from side to side and there was the sharp squeak of plastic as her hooves searched for a hold on the smooth ice-rink her body rested upon. It was clear that the girl was tired. She looked like Bambi experiencing his first winter as she tried to scrabble to her arms and feet, gangly limbs going everywhere and coordination nowhere in sight. He'd nailed the right button by the looks of it. He watched her buttocks clenching, her face twisting around the gag and almost cracked a smile as her hips tried to thrust their way through the floor. Good luck with that move, he thought. He had no idea how to increase the intensity of the clitoral stimulator, but guessed that given enough time the suit would do its own thing anyway. He shoved the remote in his pocket, out of harm's way.

A few minutes later there was an audible moan and some intense fidgeting. He immediately worried that she'd do herself an injury on the unforgiving floor. He got down on his haunches and hauled her up by her underarms. She squeaked and creaked in her rubber captivity and smelt rather pungent, but she didn't resist his attentions when he sat her on his lap. She already had enough to worry about. He suspected she was trying rather hard to rein in her body's reaction to the suit and that the audience gathered around her was another, added incentive to remain impervious to its charms. She didn't stand a chance. The crowd was practically salivating for her downfall. Their greedy, lust-filled, sex-crazed eyes said it all. They wanted pain, humiliation and tears. They would not be satisfied with less. When she buried her head into the crook of his neck, he knew she had seen it too.

Ignoring Kyle's look of rage as Jenny took refuge within his arms, he took a moment to wonder if there was the slightest chance he could get her out of here. Miss Redcliff might be a brat of the tallest order, but no one should be held in a facility of this type against their will. Whilst he knew her body was compliant to the workings of Albrecht, her mind was not and that, in his humble opinion, was reason enough to aid her in any way he could. He decided he'd look into it and see what he and his minions could do. There was always a way.

His train of thought was disturbed as a hum began to sound in the room. It was the loudspeaker coming to life. The gentle whispering of voices in the background suddenly stopped and a throat could be heard clearing itself. He was male, as Mark had expected, and as soon as the voice starting talking he placed the age of its owner somewhere in his late forties or early fifties. The pronunciation was elegant and the accent, other than being clearly English, was untraceable - at least to him. The volume of the voice, unfortunately, was much louder than it needed to be by some margin.

'Ladies and gentlemen, I would like to wish a good afternoon to you all. I hope you are enjoying the hospitality of Albrecht stables and that our training regimes will meet your needs for your future submissive slaves in the coming year.'

Jennifer Redcliff suddenly went rigid in his arms. Had the suit done its duty and stopped just before the moment of truth? There was a long pause, which made him worried enough to place a hand on her chest to make sure it was still rising and falling. Thankfully it was.

'You will be pleased to know I have made my decision with regards to the spirited pony you see before you. It was a hard decision, given the circumstances, but I have tried my best to make sure that the spirit of Albrecht is upheld.'

Mark began to tap his foot. He was nervous and impatient. The impatience he could handle, the nerves made him curse. Of course she would be his. He was the best there was and everyone at Albrecht knew it. The squirms of his pony began afresh and increased rapidly in strength. She had devoted a lot of effort in order to quell them because her body started to shudder, toss and turn with an almost violent force. He shook his head. It was almost as if she was having an orgasm, but that couldn't be possible, could it? The suit she was wearing was designed specifically with the purpose of stopping pleasure, not giving it out. Then he heard the choked sobs and snorts. He realised she was crying. Wrapping his arms tight around her he tried to comfort her, but there was no stopping the sudden torrent of tears that had begun. She had obviously finally realised the predicament she was in and reality was beginning to take a hold. The girl had done well to last out this long. Stroking her back, he made soothing gestures with his hand.

'I am awarding custody of the horse to none other than Mr Kyle Levison, who has a rather impressive reputation with the ladies. The reason for this is because I feel it is very important for a trainer and trainee to start out on a good footing in order to ensure that training will go as quickly and smoothly as possible. I have every confidence that they will work very well together and

make each other proud. I am sure you will join me in congratulating Mr Levison and now, if you will excuse me...'

The hum disappeared abruptly and there was a smattering round of applause, but Mark barely heard it. Kyle had the smuggest smile on his face and began to approach them with a knowing look in his eye. He'd been set up. Who the hell was the owner of Albrecht and what had just happened here? Standing up abruptly he slowly released Jenny into Kyle's arms, and putting on his best face, congratulated him. Unless he wanted to appear a complete jerk, he had little other choice. Though his fist itched to perform a meat-tenderiser type action upon Levison's face, he kept himself firmly in check. He needed to get out of here, quickly. His anger exploded into painful fragments that burrowed deep inside his head at the thought of what Levison might do to Jenny, and that was nothing compared to what was happening in his stomach. There it had gathered itself into a tight knot of adrenaline and was threatening to eviscerate him.

'Make sure you feed her, Levison. She's had a long day on nothing but breakfast, I suspect.'

'Oh I'll be feeding her all right, Matthews,' Kyle called after his retreating form. 'Liquid feed, force-fed and on an hourly basis.' Several sniggers of amusement followed his statement.

Mark made no notion of having heard the comment. Stepping out of the room with all the other spectators he took long, purposeful strides and to all outward appearances he was a man in control. In reality, he was anything but.

Flashbacks and Exercise

Jenny was flailing about madly on the floor. On some level she was aware that everyone had left the room bar Kyle, but he was the least of her worries at the moment. Her breaths were huge, great big choking sobs and her face felt flushed and fevered. Her mind was in meltdown and the explosion was of Hiroshima and Nagasaki style proportions. Had a giant mushroom cloud lined with highly toxic chemicals such as Iridium and Strontium 90 floated down to greet her, she didn't think she would have felt any worse. At least she would have known death was coming for her. There was no such guarantee at Albrecht; quite the opposite, in fact. They wanted her alive - she wouldn't be much use to them in any other state.

She was in shock. Her body was cold, despite the stifling heat of the latex and she felt numb all over. The voice upon the loud speaker continued to echo in her head, even though he had finished speaking over five minutes ago and she still could not believe it was him. There was no mistaking the commanding tone of Michael Redcliff, her father, however. She'd known it was him from the very first word. How could he do this to her? How could he do this to his daughter? Oh God. Oh God. Oh God. The man was a monster. Everything Mark had said before was true. It was her father who was responsible for this mess. He had sent her here knowing there would be no chance of escape. Her mind staggered in disbelief.

The suit managed to take her almost to the point of orgasm before it abruptly stopped its teasing vibrations, but that was the least of her concerns and she barely noted the absence of stimulation as her wardrobe geared up for another attempt sometime in the not too distant future.

Kyle must have picked up her corset, for she felt something being slid under her stomach and wrapped around her rubberised body. He could do his worst. She didn't give a damn. She just wanted to roll up into a little ball and continue to bawl as loudly as the fat gag inside her mouth would let her. She'd kill him. If she managed to get out of this place alive, she'd hunt the man down and murder him in cold blood for doing this to her.

Her father had ruled his household with an iron fist from the very beginning and made it clear that he was a man 'who must be obeyed' from an early age. Oh, her father had never hit her. He had employed others in order to see to her 'correction', and they had been many and varied. More often than not men, but occasionally women had been given her as their 'charge' to teach, mentor and discipline into the ways of the Redcliff household. The teachings had been long and onerous, but the discipline had been loathsome and actively encouraged by Mr Redcliff. 'Spare the rod, spoil the child,' had been his favourite motto, and no one around her had been in the least bit sparing with the rod or any other implement, that was for sure. The switch, cane, paddle, slipper and ruler, or any other item that could be found suitable for chastisement had been used at every opportunity, and in her early years she had tiptoed around everyone and everything.

Whilst some of the episodes had been blurred by her memory over time, there were several that still stood out clearly nearly a decade after they'd been administered. The 'walk of shame' had been a favourite public disgrace favoured by her father. She would be made to traipse down a long stone hallway, adorned by glowering, gilt-framed family portraits, to be greeted by a small walnut end table at the far wall which featured a single drawer. The horror had been in walking the walk and knowing what awaited at the end of it. Her misery would be nearly uncontainable after the first step, and by the last she would be shaking in her patent black shoes. Upon reaching the table she had been expected to open the drawer and pull out whatever resided inside its velour-lined confines. More often than not it would be a paddle or a hairbrush, but the worst occasions were when she was greeted by an empty drawer. That would mean there was probably a switch waiting for her, propped up in the corner. Whatever it was, she was to grip the item between her teeth, pull up her skirt and bend over the table with her arms behind her head.

She was always made to wait for her punishment. Sometimes it might be a mere ten minutes, other times it could be as much as a couple of hours bent in torment with her ears straining for the tiniest of sounds to indicate that her disciplinarian was on the way. Then she would be spanked. The severity of the spanking varied from person to person, but no one that lived in the Redcliff household could have been accused of leniency when it came to doling out her chastisements. By the end of the session her bottom would be bright red and there would be tears, lots of tears. The worst humiliation had been when she was instructed to stand on the table following her ordeal. Her skirt and panties would be removed and then she would be helped atop the sturdy wooden table, where she would be expected to press her nose into the wall and bare her reddened assets for the world to see. Her father always made sure there were a plentiful abundance of people in his household to witness her various humiliations.

The awful memories brought back fleeting images of her mother, and instinctively she reached for the gold tiffany locket that always rested around her throat. A plastic hoof pawed helplessly at her chest before she remembered she had lost it on her very first day at Albrecht, when she was pilloried in front of the villagers. It was one of the only things she had left that connected her to a mother she barely even remembered; a mother who had run out on her child when she was just six years of age. Jenny vaguely remembered painted pink lips, the smell of Chanel and glossy, ebony hair always worn in fashionable up-do. She remembered cuddles, smiles, bedtime stories and a life far removed from the lonely one she was forced to live through growing up in the Redcliff household.

Although she had tried to trace her mum when she reached eighteen, she had been stonewalled at each and every attempt she made. Even a private detective hadn't been able to unearth anything of a concrete nature. She was left with rumours, probabilities and maybes. For all intents and purposes her mother had vanished off the face of the earth and had never been heard of again. Jenny had no idea if the woman was dead or alive, but she had finally put the past to rest. Her mother obviously wanted no part of her, so she gave up the search. If she were honest, though, she would admit that she hadn't given up hope. The locket was her last link to a time long since departed, when laughter and joy had been present in her life, and she needed it back. Tears poured down her face as the last three days finally caught up with her. She was not going to be rescued and escape was virtually impossible. It was time she faced up to the facts.

Back in the land of the living, her corset was being tightened around her body once more and Kyle was no less lenient in his vicious tugging than Hetty had been, two days ago in the tack room. It was easier to bear this time around, though. She simply did not care. Self-pity had consumed her and she intended to wallow in her deep pool of quicksand. Soon enough the corset was tightened fast around her waist, allowing the twin mounds of her latex covered breasts to rest over it. She could be grateful for the fact that Kyle wasn't quite as experienced as Henrietta, because if he had been she wouldn't have been able to draw in a single breath through her hiccupping sobs.

'Sensible choice you made there, darlin'. Can't wait to begin training that delightful little mouth of yours again. So fucking tight, mmm.' Kyle patted her backside and gave the long black tail on the rear of her suit an impressive yank for good measure. He laughed when she jumped.

Again? Where had that come from? Bar last night, she'd never met the man before. Had they drugged her sometime during her stay? Not to her knowledge. Besides, she could hardly suck someone off whilst asleep. She was good, but she wasn't that good. Great, it appeared she'd met another crazy. This one might be from way across the large pond of the Atlantic Ocean but he was ocean-going all right. Her sobs increased in their intensity, if that were possible.

'Will you shut the fuck up, you snivelling wretch?' said Kyle, and he gave her backside a sound slap to drive his point home. He laughed as she yelped pitifully. 'There'll be plenty of time for moaning and groaning with your pony friends in the stable later, Pretty Pink. We've got a schedule here. We need to get you fit enough to haul your ridiculous ass and numerous suitcases along the racecourse for the required two laps. I want to see you in your yellow collar. As all the other trainees bar you managed to get theirs yesterday, we're already behind schedule and you're making me look bad. Believe me when I say you don't want to make me look bad. You make me cranky and I'll take out my frustrations on you, babe, not that I won't be anyway.' He gave her a lascivious grin and looked every inch and curve of her body up and down to indicate exactly what he meant. 'I'm already bent out of shape that you've managed to deny me two outa three holes on our very first two days together. What kinda gal does that to her Dom on their first date?'

Jenny barely listened to Kyle's little speech. Her sobs were drying up, but that was only because they were being replaced by cold hard anger and it was directed exactly where it should be - at her father. She just needed a way to channel that anger into something useful, something that would bring about her emancipation and departure from his life, period. She never wanted to lay eyes on the man again. At the moment she was a girl in freefall, but she would get it together. And when she did Michael Redcliff would need more than one person watching his back. He'd need a whole bloody army if she had anything to do with it.

A mere half hour later Jenny found her anger had dissipated quite rapidly. Kyle had led her out of the surgery by her bridle and she had been allowed to walk, which was a bonus, as her knees still hurt like hell from the scrapes she had managed to acquire from the concrete. Finding movement in the latex suit difficult and restrictive, she managed to overcome it with a little more aggression in her step. The gag made her pant and snort through her nose when any exertion was forced upon her, and it wasn't a pretty sound. It didn't seem to bother Kyle in the slightest, however. Although her vision was severely limited by the two tiny slits in her rubber hood, Jenny clearly saw a smug smile of satisfaction grace his face on more than one occasion. It appeared there was something between Mark and himself and he was feeling rather pleased to have come out the victor. He wouldn't be smiling for long. She was going to make it her mission to make everyone's life hell in Albrecht, be they pony-girls, boys, trainers or owners - especially owners. It was brave talk. The thought of doing dungeon time still made her quail.

'Right, nearly there. I hope you're feeling frisky, Petal.' Kyle yanked on her bridal and urged her forward. Jenny was not amused and already exhausted both mentally and physically by the days' many activities. What could they possibly want her to do now? When the uneven cobblestones beneath her feet changed to the smoother, sharp clunk of concrete she began to wonder. Plodding onwards, she tried to remember the order of the rooms before her. She knew she wasn't headed for the dungeon because even though she couldn't see the steps through her almost blinkered visage, she remembered the room was at the beginning of the concrete corridor, and judging by the number of steps they had taken, they had long since passed it. She suspected they wouldn't need the grooming room in her current state of dress, or the tack room for that matter, so they were either headed for the Red Room, the Training Room or the Exercise Room. She didn't want to visit any of them and found her footsteps dragging, the horseshoes even heavier than usual. Why couldn't they just let her slink back to the barn, where she could go somewhere private and lick her wounds in peace? Not that she'd be licking anything for a while, not with this beast of a gag in her mouth.

'We're here,' said Kyle, far too cheerfully. 'The Exercise Room. This is going to be one of your favourite rooms until you get your yellow collar. We're going to have lots of fun here, you and me.' Jenny suspected that was not to be the case, but she was too tired to argue. That and the fact that arguing was going to be nigh on impossible for the near future, anyway. When Kyle led her to one of the exercise bikes and indicated that she should get on, Jenny nearly, so very nearly obeyed him instantly and without question. Just as her foot was about to tackle the pedal of the bike fresh anger welled up inside her. Like a firestorm of volcanic proportions it demanded to be unleashed, less it remained imprisoned inside where it would consume her. So when her hoof picked itself up off the floor to loop over the bike she found an avenue in which to channel her rage and resentment: violence. Changing direction swiftly, the heavy metal hoof angled around and aimed at Kyle's nearest body part, his shin. Unfortunately her suit chose that particular moment to spring into action. Her nether regions all of a sudden came to life and everything seemed to vibrate at once. The stimulator hummed, and it wasn't a gentle purr of movement but more of a full blown earthquake. She could feel her body shaking with some impressive contractions, and if she had to put a number on the seismic activity going through her, she'd go with a force seven major quake. It wasn't just the stimulator; the two dildos were also pulsating inside her and her backside wasn't at all sure it liked the sensation of things jiggling around down there. All of this served to put her momentarily off balance and she landed on the seat of the exercise bike with a painful thud. Thankfully Kyle appeared not to have noticed, studying the remote in his hand with annoyance.

'I'm guessing you don't come with instructions,' he said to the little black box in his hand. 'Too bad, but it'll be fun testing each button to see what happens.' Stuffing the remote back in his jeans pocket he concentrated on fastening her boots to the pedals of the exercise bike. There was some kind of clip mechanism, for she felt her boots firmly wedged inside the pedals, and a strap was fastened over the top of each foot. No amount of tugging on her part would release them.

'That's right, Petal. You're stuck for the duration of the ride. I think we'll start you with a ten mile ride today, and add an additional five miles each day until you've earned your yellow collar and lost a bit of weight. I like my ponies lean, mean and fighting the bit on their machines.' He laughed at his own bad joke. 'The good news is that you won't need to be fitted with an electro-shock plug, because your suit already has that covered. If you slip below a speed of ten miles per hour I'll just get your remote and play with you until you get the message.'

Kyle caressed the rubber of her hood against her cheekbone in a faintly offensive manner, before leaving her to mess around with some dials at the rear of the gym. As his back was turned Jenny struggled like mad to get her feet free of the stirrups. No such luck. She was firmly held in place and going nowhere fast, but not for long apparently. A couple of buttons were pressed, some dials were turned and the gym came to life. Bright LED lights flooded the room and the screen of her bike started beeping and flashing in its eagerness to begin her first torture session. Jenny was well aware that torture was exactly what this was going to be. She hadn't performed any type of regular exercise for years and an hour's cycle ride, even at a sedate pace, was probably going to kill her. Still, dying was probably preferable on one of your first days at Albrecht, when compared to one of your last.

As the pedals began to revolve under her feet in warm-up mode, so the red flashing lights on screen told her, she began to take notice of her suit once more. It wasn't playing fair. The vibrations had begun to tail off, thank God, but the dildos were starting to grow inside her. They were growing in both length and girth, and the feeling was more than a little unsettling. The clamps on the inside of her nipples had started to pinch quite painfully and her breasts were being sucked and squeezed in a bizarre kind of massage motion. It was both wonderful and horrifying.

'Get ready to take the strain, Petal. The warm-up session is about to end and you'll be on your own with the pedalling. Keep above ten miles per hour or I'll be forced to punish you.' Kyle grinned. He decided 'forced' wasn't quite the right word. He would look forward to watching his new pony whimper and thrash about with pain. The different forms of agony he could inflict were many and endless and he was quite prepared to make an example of her. It wasn't often that a pony at Albrecht was destined for the black and if they were, there were timescales involved. He intended to smash every record ever created. Pretty Pink Petals was going to wear the black collar in record time if he had anything to do with it.

Watching as the pedals stopped turning of their own accord, he noticed his pony's body shook as she took up the slack. The suit was already in motion, then. Directing a closer gaze at her body he detected movement from the cups that cocooned her breasts, and when he took a leisurely stroll around to the rear, admiring the tight black latex as it hugged the curves of her ass in all the right places, he noted her tail moving slightly, which was as good an indication as any that her dildos were thrusting away inside her. He was slightly jealous of them. The powers that be had bunged her up so tightly in her new get-up that he would get barely a look in for two whole days. Oh, he'd ravage her mouth all right, but it would be the only hole on offer. He'd get a brief play-date with the rest of her before they shipped her off to some zillionaire, who would probably defile her with much less precision and considerably less enthusiasm than he was capable of. Still, he'd make up for that when she was once again his to do whatever he liked with for the next year or three.

Hell, he might even want to drag her training out. If the glower on Matthews' face had been anything to go by, it would be plenty of fun to parade her around him every time he got his butt up to Albrecht. She could be made to dance right under his nose while Kyle fucked her or for that matter, fucked with her, and all Matthews would be allowed to do was watch and clap. The idea had merit.

Sinking into a cosy velvet lounge chair hidden in a corner, he propped his feet up against the wood-panelled wall and stretched his arms out over his head. All in all, he decided it had been a pretty good day. He'd got the star of the show award and his commission from her future sale would net him a sizeable fortune. Matthews didn't need the money, lucky bastard that he was, but he could sure use some. The shame of it was that he wouldn't see a penny of it until she was sold, so they both needed to get their asses into gear. Maybe he could hire her out in the meantime. He'd have to see about that.

A loud beeping sound began filtering through the room and he was startled from his pleasant daydream. Looking at his watch, he was disgusted to find she'd only been on the damned bike twenty minutes. 'Get that fanny moving before I decide to shove several thousand volts up it, Petal,' he yelled.

Jenny was having a hard time concentrating on doing anything at all when her suit was playing its horribly perfect tune upon her body. It was giving her the full-works treatment this time around, and taking no prisoners. The thread-like little wires located all over the interior of her bodysuit had come to life and were firing little bursts of pleasurable current all around her. In some areas, such as her back, she could feel very little sensation. In others, such as her breasts, inner thighs and ass cheeks, she almost exploded with feeling. It was prickly at first and took a little getting used to, but as it gradually increased in intensity she could not stop herself from squirming in heat. Trying to escape the current was useless, especially when her feet where pinned into tight pedals. Add that to the pumping dildos, the boob massager, an occasional nipple tweak with one or both clamps and a vibrating clit stimulator, and you had a hell of a time focusing on anything. The orgasm building inside her was swift of commencement and quick to intensify into a thigh-trembling, full-blown, earth-shattering need. She wanted this. Albrecht had created such an incredible thirst for pleasure inside her that there was little else she could think about. It couldn't be slaked, no matter how many times she was granted an orgasm. Knowing she would be denied such a release made the pain and imminent denial of such hedonism all the more powerful. Why did you always long for that which you could not have? And she hungered.

Each second that ticked by, each slow, dragging turn on the pedal by her hoof increased her anxiety. The screen flashed instructions to her and beeped out obscenities, but she barely heard them. She could only listen to the concentrated whimpering of her body as it cried out for release. The dildos began to vibrate in both her ass and pussy. She tried to suck in air. No air. She could barely breathe through the tiny hole in her gag and her nose was not cooperating. The beeping became louder in both volume and pitch. Her eardrums protested the sound. Kyle shouted something, but his words sounded slurred and broken inside her head. Her suit was too tight and far too hot. Her hooved hands pawed helplessly in mid-air. Her mouth wanted to shout 'get me out of here!' but all she could do was suffer in silence as the suit consumed and suffocated her physique.

There was another shout from Kyle, angrier this time, but no more intelligible to her addled brain. Her feet could not move any faster even though she tried her hardest to pummel the pedals beneath her.

With no warning the device shocked her body into bone-jarringly rigid submission. One of her hooves smacked her hard in the face as her body did its best to escape the pain being shot through it. It felt like a thousand rubber-band slingshots had been aimed at her body and snapped. Every nerve-ending screamed, each hair stood on end and every muscle contracted with agony. Her eyesight disappeared for a second before everything began shaking. Then Jenny realised it was her shaking, rather than the room around her.

Unsurprisingly enough, when comprehension of her surroundings dawned and she heard Kyle yelling in the background, her feet began to move again. They were shaky circles her ankles were making, but they were adequate. On the plus side, all thoughts of her impending orgasm and desperation to climax had been abruptly forgotten. With her lungs breathing fire she began to dwell on the thoughts of her own fragile mortality.

By the time they'd reached the forty minute mark Petal was getting a regular shock every five minutes or so. Whilst he enjoyed administering the dose of current, watching as it spiralled through her body, making her twitch and jump spasmodically, he realised he had much more work on his hands than he'd initially thought. The girl was so out of condition that a lazy thirty minute walk might finish her off. He'd never seen a pony so out of condition, and it was galling to realise that they were going to have a hell of time catching up to the others, even on the fast-track programme he had planned for her.

'Faster, Petal, faster.' Kyle kicked his feet out in front of him and watched disgustedly as Petal once again faltered on the pedals. The bike sprang to life with flashing lights and alarms. Goddamn. He was officially annoyed and they hadn't been in partnership more than an hour. This wasn't a great start to their relationship. Trying a different button along the bottom of the remote, which had faithfully doled out pain in different measures up until now, he hoped he'd hit the mother lode this time. The girl needed to learn a lesson. He was in charge and if he said cycle, she'd better cycle her little backside off or risk the consequences of frying it big style. As his finger punched the tab he heard an almighty shriek before Petal's body stiffened in shock and then slithered over the side of the bike. If her boots hadn't been locked in she'd have toppled over headfirst. *Oh shit.*

Flying across the room, nearly tripping over his own feet, he tore the gag out of her mouth. He was supposed to have removed it before she got on the bike. Unbuckling her feet he lowered her to the floor. She was a bit heavier than he'd expected and they both tumbled rather abruptly. Feeling around for a pulse, he breathed a sigh of relief to discover she was indeed still alive. Phew. Then he looked at his prized gold Omega watch and clucked in annoyance. He'd promised she'd be back in the stables in ten minutes' time. She had five cocks to suck to completion as penance for yesterday's failure in the paddock, including his own, and she was supposed to spend an hour with Mistress Lupine and the dildos. That might have to wait until tomorrow. By the looks of her they'd need to be quick as she'd need a feed straight after he got her stabled up for the group session bedtime spanking. She could suck at the same time. Semen could be classed as food, too. There were fifteen calories per teaspoon, apparently, although she'd have to be a very busy girl to make a decent meal out of it.

Grabbing a bucket of water from the low wooden shelf behind Petal, he tipped its contents over her face. Hopefully some would make it past the latex. It took two further buckets of cold water before she spluttered into life. 'Come on, Petal. There's no sleeping on the job. We frown on that kind of thing here. You've also successfully pissed me off because now I've covered you with water I'll be unable to shock you until tomorrow morning. We take health and safety very seriously here at Albrecht.' Kyle formed a growl in the back of his throat. 'Get on your hands and knees and follow me out to the stable. If you're a good girl you get to move on two feet but if you misbehave, you'll be crawling. Trotting upright is a privilege round these parts and you'd do well to remember that, horsie. OK, you've got cocks to suck and a bottom to be spanked.' Kyle sighed. 'I'd better not hear a sound out of your gob, either, or I will shock you, the water trickling around your body be damned. It would be a shame if you ended up in medical on our first night together, though.' He gave her a sour look to drive his point home.

Striding on ahead, he didn't bother checking behind him to make sure she followed. Why should he bother, Jenny thought acidly, when she'd been chipped and wired up to blow? Seething, she barely had the energy to get up on her hands and knees, much less crawl, but somehow she made it out of the room and followed him towards the barn. She was speechless, but not because Kyle had ordered her to be. She simply could not form one coherent word in her head after the day's events, which weren't finished by a long shot by the looks of it. She had no idea how she was going to make it through the next five minutes, let alone complete the antics her new trainer had planned. If she'd thought things were bad before, she had no idea how bad things were going to get. Speaking of all things bad, her suit chose that moment to wake up and the dildo in her ass began to inflate with eye-watering pressure. The one in her pussy quickly followed suit and she wondered if there was any chance they might burst, what with all the air being pumped inside them. She could only be grateful that there was no vibration as yet.

Crawling with her legs as wide as they could go, to relieve what pressure she could, she swore silently as the rest of the suit gradually came to life. So much for there being no vibration, now she practically trembled all over. Disgustedly she found her mouth drooling with need, even though she had not been gagged. Wiping away the spittle with a plastic hoof she crawled onwards and thoughts of vengeance overtook her once more. She wondered if Kyle would help her, given the right incentive. If not, Mark's previous offer for the position of a lifetime submissive slave suddenly seemed a whole lot more appealing.

Yoo-hoo Darling

Tapping sharply against the glossy screen of a smartphone, a bright red talon poised over a list of contacts before choosing one that read *The Boss*. Lifting the phone to her ear with extreme caution, it was clear that the woman did not wish to do damage to her elegantly-styled blonde waves, which had been tamed in beautifully long tresses that rested in perfect glossy order upon her immaculate leather jacket. Listening to the dial tone as the call connected, the woman smiled to herself. It had been a good day - a very good day, in fact.

'Darling,' said a refined male voice, 'I trust you've seen the CCTV footage?'

'Exquisite. Just the tiniest glimmer of pain as he exited the building, but it's the most expression he's allowed us to witness in a very long time. I think you might have nailed it. Who would have thought? The girl might very well be his Achilles heel and we'll be there to exploit that weakness to the fullest, won't we, dear?'

He chuckled. 'I certainly hope so. I've been waiting a long time to bring him down and my patience was beginning to wear thin. No one seems to inspire any kind of emotion within him and I was beginning to despair.'

She purred into the handset, 'You think he might drown, hook, line and sinker with this one?'

'You never can tell, but there's a chance. It's been a long wait.'

'Do you really think you'll get him to agree to what you have planned?' The blonde pushed her lips into a delicate moue as she considered the question.

'There are no guarantees, but that's half the fun. Now he's taken a bite of the apple, I suspect he'll be back for more. If we see him back at Albrecht within the week, we'll know we've nailed it.'

'What then?'

'Then, we let him have another little taste of her, to whet his appetite and up the stakes. Kyle's the perfect trainer with which to achieve that. I couldn't have picked a better one had I done it myself.'

'Don't you feel in the least bit guilty?' The blonde already knew it was a stupid question before the query left her lips, but she wanted to make sure this man was almost as inhuman as he seemed.

'Not even the tiniest bit, darling.'

'So you're going to let Kyle do his worst?'

'Yes, my dear,' he said with absolute conviction, 'although I don't think it will be necessary.'

'And when you get Matthews right where you want him, you'll let me do my worst?'

'That's the part I've been looking forward to the most.' Michael Redcliff did not smile, but he allowed himself to get lost in a rather pleasant daydream of Mark Matthews, kneeling naked, prostrate at his feet and begging for mercy as the whip came down.

Research

Immediately cancelling his hotel reservation for the evening, Mark headed straight for the chopper and got the crew to file a flight plan straight back to London. Good job he'd had the forethought to keep them on standby. He didn't fancy the long drive home in the fired-up state he was in. Stepping up into the AW139, the two blondes from earlier greeted with him garishly bright smiles and looked crushed when he told them to fuck off. Too bad. He wasn't in the mood for anything even remotely resembling sex, and wasn't that a first? He was beginning to wish he had never laid eyes on Jennifer Redcliff. Now he had a head full of questions that probably wouldn't find answers and a throat full of bile. Buckling himself into the deeply cushioned cream leather seat at the rear of the craft, he let his thoughts tumble about while he tried to piece together the puzzle.

He should probably think himself lucky to have lost, and count his blessings. It wasn't as if he needed any additional distractions in his life right now. Training Petal would have been a large undertaking and one he really didn't have the time or resources to be taking on. His plate was already overflowing and there were plenty of seconds to be had with the merest wave of his hand. *Let it go. You don't need this kind of aggravation in your life.* Hah! His cock was screaming, oh but you do, and because it rarely screamed such things, on the rare occasions it did, he listened. What was so damned special about this one? He growled.

Pulling out his cell phone he quickly began to bark out orders to poor unfortunate Khalil, the head of Intel for Zystrom and his numerous other holdings. 'I'm sending you a voice recording. I need you to analyse it. I want to know whose voice it is. Yes, I am well aware there are a lot of people in the world but I also know you're the best. There's a pay rise in it for you if you come up with the goods. Twenty-four hours. No. That's a maximum of twenty-four hours and there'll be a bonus involved if you can get the info to me in less. While you're on the line, I want everything you can get me on a Miss Jennifer Courtney Redcliff, daughter of Michael Redcliff, owner of Synstyte Petroleum.' There was a brief pause. 'I pay you enough to do both at the same time. I do not pay you to be funny. Yes, I want bra and panty sizes, favourite ice-cream flavour, if she's ever had lesbian sex and whether she does threesomes. I also want bank details, parentage, siblings, previous boyfriends, store card debts, the works.' Another pause. 'No detail is too small. If the girl likes picking her toenails while watching *When Harry Met Sally* every Saturday evening, I want to know about it. Oh, and get me all you can on a Kyle Levison while you're at it, and I can tell you now it won't be pretty. When you find out something, call me immediately.' Another lengthy pause as Mark digested some chatter before he interrupted, 'Then what are you waiting for? We're on a timescale here.' He terminated the call.

Tapping his foot upon the cream carpeted floor, he let out a pent-up breath. At least that was one item on his agenda dealt with. He'd know who the owner of Albrecht was shortly. Toying with his cell a moment longer, he wondered whether to have Marianna ready to serve him when he arrived back at the office. Whilst not in the mood to play now, by the time he'd replayed Jennifer Redcliff being fucked by Dirty and Bastard, he'd probably need to take the edge off his hunger and cheer himself up. He decided to make the call. He would probably need to release a few endorphins if he had any chance of sleeping tonight.

'Hello Cecilia. Is Marianna still in the office? No, don't tell her I require her, but make sure she doesn't leave her apartment this evening. That will be all.'

Deposited back at his apartment a mere two hours after his brief round of telephone calls, the first thing Mark did was shed his clothes and jump into the shower. His bathroom was more of what was termed a 'wet' room and there were no cubicles, just lots of elegantly modern chrome taps and dark slate tiles. Turning on the faucet to max, he ran large quantities of steaming hot water over his body, as if it might erase the stink of his God awful day, before stepping out onto the heated floor and towelling himself off.

Quickly running a razor over his jaw, he applied moisturizer and cologne. All he needed to do now was slip into something a little more comfortable and he was good to go. His eyes flared as the image of Jennifer Redcliff, sitting on his lap in her rubber suit and squirming madly as she succumbed to the suit's first real attempt at playing with her came to mind. She had smelt of polish and sex, and bizarrely, the combination was intoxicating. He would have loved nothing more than to have been granted the honour of training her body and mind to within an inch of its life, but sadly, that was not to be and he'd do well to get over the fact.

Pulling a black cashmere sweater over his head and dragging on a pair of expertly tailored black trousers, he grabbed the keys to his Mercedes and began to contemplate his next move. It was clear he needed to get her out of his system and Marianna would be the obvious choice. At the very least she would slake his thirst for the female sex and it might be enough to appease his anger at the day's events. Stopping briefly in the kitchen to avail himself of the use of his coffee machine, he decided caffeine would be a good precursor to the evening ahead. He could certainly use some 'rocket fuel' inside his system to get him motivated. Although he could survive on just a couple of hours' sleep a day, it wasn't a particularly pleasant experience.

Flipping the switch to heat the water and grinding some fresh coffee beans, he took slow even breaths and planned his surprise date down to the very last detail. It was the control freak inside him. Every 'i' needed to be dotted and every 't' crossed. Would his blood run as hot for her as it had Miss Redcliff? He doubted it, but time would tell.

The light on the machine flashed green and he pressed the button to hear the satisfying roar of the coffee percolator come to life. Spewing forth steaming, inky black liquid into his espresso cup, he cooled the strong brew with a dash of cold water, but added nothing more. Firing the shot down the back of his throat in one gulp he banged the cup back down on the table and made for the door. Showtime.

Would the lovely Miss Morreau be wearing panties? He hoped so. He had an all-consuming need to mete out various types of punishment, and a little pain on her behalf would be a delightful end to his rather unpleasant day.

Marianna had not been expecting any callers, so when a knock rapped at her door she was immediately suspicious. She was not concerned for her safety as she knew the security around the little 'harem' Zystrom had stashed here was tight, but generally a caller would make themselves known via intercom, which would sound in her kitchen and they would ask for admittance. It was probably one of the girls then, after a cup of sugar or something. They didn't normally knock at her door, but perhaps after the recent office activities she had moved up in their esteem. Wow, things were looking up. Before she knew it they'd be round for supper and girlie gossip. She'd better brush up on her kitchen skills, which had become almost non-existent during the last year. The salads she existed on weren't much fun, but they were easy and when there was only her to cook for, she couldn't be bothered with much else.

Striding over to the large pine door, her toes curling in the beige shag-pile carpet, she peered out of the small window as her hand grasped for the handle. She got the shock of her life. There, on her doorstep, was Mark Matthews. Her first reaction was to run and hide, even though she knew he'd seen her. She wasn't ready for him. Her hair was a mess, her feet were bare, nail varnish chipped and half a dozen other reasons like the fact that he scared her senseless. Her hand hovered over the steel lever of her front door and began to shake.

'Let me in, Marianna.'

His voice was a gentle, seductive purr and whilst it might have calmed a skittish pussycat or two, it didn't do much to calm her.

'Just a second. Be right there.' Oh hell, Marianna thought, running her fingers halfway through her hair before losing them to a pile of Medusa-like writhing snakes, all of which refused to be tamed. Trying to extricate them, she almost lost a fingernail in the process and yanking her hand back out again she decided he'd just have to appreciate the ruffled 'bed-head' look. Hey, some people paid a lot of money to get their hair looking like that. Marianna just happened to be able to achieve it for free.

'I'm waiting.' The voice was cool, collected and faintly amused.

Marianna was searching the room for a pair of shoes. Any shoes would do as long as they matched and covered her toenails. Spying a pair of fluffy pink slipper-booties she rapidly worked them over her feet with one hand, while the other was pretending to open the door.

'I can break it down if you prefer? You girls like that type of thing, right?'

'Wrong.' The door opened and Marianna witnessed her boss trying desperately hard to cling on to his deadpan expression. Giving him a dark look, she said, 'Have you ever heard of a thing called *the telephone?* It's a really handy gadget. It allows you to warn people in advance of...'

'I'm well aware of what a telephone is used for, but thank you for the reminder, Miss Morreau. I wanted to surprise you.'

'Congratulations, you've succeeded.' She pulled the door open wide and stood back to allow him entrance. Her heart rate had already accelerated up 36,000 feet in the air and her stomach was on its way up to meet it. 'I thought you were away on business until tomorrow evening, Sir.'

'Change of plans.' Mark strode into her spacious modern apartment as if he owned the place, which was only slightly entertaining, considering that he did actually own the block of apartments. 'Oh, where are my manners? I've brought you a present.' He held out a shiny black rectangular gift box which sported a giant red bow and grinned at her. Mark was entertained to find that Marianna's fingers shook somewhat as they gently pried the box out of his hands.

'Thank you, but you really don't need to buy me presents. You pay me more than enough as it is.' Placing the box on her smooth pinewood dinner table and using the opportunity to catch her breath, she eventually turned to ask, 'Can I get you a drink?' She wanted a chance to escape his assessing all over gaze, put a dash of make-up on and apply another fresh coat of polish to her feet.

'No, thank you. The present isn't really for you, it's for us. We'll open it together, later.' He moved into the lounge and took a seat on her large faux-suede sofa. Crossing his legs and sinking into the soft padding, he looked quite at home. His assessment of her body continued, quite happily, until it reached her feet, where it stopped abruptly. He pursed his lips. 'Love the boots. Did you wear them especially for me?' His eyes twinkled with mirth.

'Would you like me to remove them, Sir?' She stood perfectly still, facing him, and her long black lashes batted over dark green eyes already smouldering with heat.

'Actually, Miss Morreau, I'd like you to remove everything. You'd better hope you've remembered to forgo wearing your panties and bra or you're in for a rather unpleasant start to your evening.' This time he raised both of his eyebrows in challenge, the look he was wearing one of pure devilment.

Marianna just managed to stop her face from crumpling into a look of despair. Her look would have read: *oh my God, of all the rotten luck in the world, how can this be happening to me, fuck it.* This thought was followed by: *there must be some way I can extricate myself from this mess.* Toying with a very cute and cuddly pink bootie, before flipping it off with her foot and kicking it behind her, she decided to play it cool. There was a good chance that the situation was not lost. If she could strip off her skirt and the waistband of her panties in one movement, keeping the latter hidden inside the former, she might be able to save her ass from some serious carnage. It had to be worth a try. It didn't matter that she had been told he was out of town on business or that he had never visited her before - or any of the other girls, to her knowledge - in her apartment, if she had been given a direct order to wear no panties, he would expect it to be immediately obeyed, without question, and at all times. How could she have been so stupid? In her defence it had been an automatic reaction to pull out a pair of panties as soon as she had finished her half-hour soak in the bath tub. *Arrgh.* She was going to have to bin the contents of her panty drawer to make sure she was never tempted to make such a mistake again.

Kicking off another bootie she bared her chipped 'Jungle Red' toes and wiggled them into the carpet in an effort to hide them. She needn't have bothered. His eyes were already working their way up her body for the main event.

Starting at her neck she began opening the buttons of the soft, buttery, chocolate silk shirt she had donned only moments ago. Amazingly, her hands were steady and the little brown discs almost flew open of their own accord. She let the material hang over the soft 'V' of her bared breasts before shrugging the fabric backwards, over her shoulders, and letting it drop elegantly to the floor. Her nipples immediately peaked and the aureoles surrounding them deepened in colour.

Mark's eyes had darkened. His easy, relaxed posture remained the same, his hands in his lap and his back folded into the chair behind him, but something had changed. There was the scent of danger in the air. 'Congratulations. No bra, Miss Morreau. This is a promising start.'

Marianna could feel tiny little beads of sweat beginning to form behind her ears and at the back of her neck. Oh, why hadn't she thought of the panty thing before she opened the door? Worrying about her hair and chipped polish seemed rather silly in comparison to the mess she might shortly find herself in, if her performance did not go to plan.

'Is there something you wish to tell me, Miss Morreau?' Mark had a smug grin on his face and if she didn't know better she could have sworn the man had x-ray vision, feeling his stare melt through the delicate satin of her oyster-grey skirt to reveal the white wisp of lace panties below.

Marianna shook her head firmly, put on her best coquettish smile and let her hands caress her naked torso as they made their way down to her skirt. A bead of sweat trickled down her back. Thank god he couldn't see it. Concentrate, Marianna, she berated herself, and smiled. Gripping the waistband of both skirt and panties at the same time, her hands did not give themselves away in the slightest. There was no discernible tremor, no tell-tale wobble as they slid down her delicately perfumed flesh. If she was honest, she would have to admit that she was looking forward to getting naked. There was no embarrassment to be had in revealing her body, not an ounce of fat graced it and not a single blemish dared to accost the expanse of subtly tanned flesh that covered her both front and back. Although Mark's visit had come as a shock, her body was already looking forward to being used and worshipped by his. So there was only one last obstacle standing in the way of a night which could be painful, pleasurable or a decadent mixture of both. She was not entirely sure which option she preferred.

Feeling moisture begin to bubble between her legs, she tried to summon her thoughts together to complete her striptease. It was one simple move, one mere flourish of her hands and then the offending items could be tossed into a corner to be forgotten for the evening. Her thumbs hooked under the waistband of both skirt and panties combined and, with a deep breath she pushed them deftly to the floor, before one lithe, long leg kicked the offending articles away from her. She did not risk a glance backwards to check upon the landing position of her wardrobe. Instead she moved forward, towards the man who had been the object of her desires for so long and asked seductively, in her soft, breathless voice, 'How may I please you, Sir?'

That and her near-nakedness should have been enough to distract any normal man from perusing the discarded items of clothing in too much detail. But of course, Mark Matthews was not in the least bit normal.

'You may please me, Marianna, by fetching me your lovely skirt. I wish to inspect its contents.'

Marianna's face dropped faster than a skydiver with no parachute. Trying to quickly repair her blunder she plastered on a bright smile and brought her eyes up to meet his. It was too late, though, for he had spotted her mistake and his grin became an awful lot wider. She had no choice but to run and fetch the offending article of clothing for his deliberation. There was no question that she could get rid of the panties inside the skirt without a great deal of rummaging about, and that would simply mire her deeper into the land of immense trouble she had created for herself.

With a heavy heart she walked the few paces needed to pick up her skirt, examined the landing spot and found that no hint of her panties was visible from within its fallen folds. How on earth had he known? Bending down she clutched the floaty fabric in her hands and made short work of delivering it to her Master. Her fate would be decided in short order, and due to her error and the lie, albeit of omission, she would probably be in for a trying evening - to say the least.

Passing the lightweight ripples of satin into his awaiting hands, there was a discernible tremor that ran right through her. Needing something to do she knelt in front of him and clutched her hands behind her back before dipping her eyes to the floor.

Even though now focused on the carpet she still managed to catch a glimpse of her skirt as it was gently unfolded. The material was then shaken vigorously and her traitorous panties fell to the floor, almost invisible on the beige carpet before her - almost, but not quite.

'Well, well, what have we here?'

There was a lengthy silence, and in the end Marianna decided he was waiting for her to break it. It took some effort to pry her tongue from the roof of her mouth, and further effort to make it articulate intelligible words. Finally she managed to utter, 'My panties, Sir,' in a broken sort of whisper and added, 'I'm sorry.' It would not be as simple as an apology though, and her thoughts began to run riot as to what torments might befall her shortly.

'Oh, I suspect you are, Marianna, but not half as sorry as you will be.'

A Spanking Goodnight

After an exhausting crawl back to the stables Jenny found herself smartly lined up with all the other ponies. Squirming in the prickly hay, a long line of bare buttocks were mounted in the air, quivering with apprehension. Thankfully she couldn't feel the annoying spikes of the bedding beneath her, but that did not mean she was at all enamoured of the thin cocoon of latex which protected her. She had been in the suit less than two hours and she could honestly say she would have happily traded her soul in order to escape it. Gearing up to torment her further, the incessant vibrations increased and with shocking intensity.

Similarly on all fours, the girls in front of her had been stripped of most of their tack and given a good rub down. Their bodies displayed the tell-tale marks of a good grooming and every single inch of skin on display had pinked in colour, some more than others. Each ass cheek, without exception, had blossomed from the pale white hue upon awakening to the colour of brilliant fuchsia.

They had obviously been waiting for her and none of them looked particularly pleased. Ah yes, that would probably be because they were all getting a few extra spanks due to Lyle's nastiness yesterday. It was hardly her fault and what was an extra ten spanks between friends, anyway? It wasn't as if most of these weirdo's didn't enjoy it, was it? To be honest, Jenny had even decided she was looking forward to a little heat on her backside, because the damn vibrating dildos were beginning to drive her mad as they twisted and drilled inside her. The suit had taken its time with a slow build-up of sensation and it was now beginning to get nasty, employing all of its nefarious devices in perfect unison. Still, it hadn't managed to get to her yet and she refused to let its continuous pestering affect her. Mind over matter, she told herself. She could beat this. She could beat them. The only question was time.

'Have all the grooms got their spanking hands ready and primed?' Kyle was wearing a sickening grin as he faced them all, and his wide-legged stance with his green crocodile boots pointed in opposing directions meant business. He rubbed his hands together as if to confirm his obvious glee, before he continued. 'We'll start with a warm-up hand spanking, to get the fillies used to the idea, and then we'll progress to paddles. When I think we've adequately prepared these asses we'll finish up with our final ten additional spanks of the evening, which have been provided courtesy of Miss Redcliff, and these will be delivered by your belts, gentlemen.'

The long line of ponies treated this news, on the whole, as bad. There were a few gasps, some lip biting, some excited whinnying, some head tossing and more than a couple of dark looks directed at Jenny. She sensibly kept her eyes forward and on the floor. She was in enough trouble already.

'To make things a little more interesting and challenging for our lead pony, Petal, she'll need to suck five cocks to completion before we begin the final ten. So the length of your warm-up is entirely dependent on her abilities. Let's all hope she's a good little cocksucker, shall we? If not, you're all going to be bedding down to sleep on your stomachs, ponies.'

Due to Jenny's field of vision being severely limited with her tiny little eye slits, she didn't see Kyle's nod of the head which indicated the proceedings should begin. When Daniel slammed his hand into her backside, offering little sympathy for the day's previous abuse, she shrieked out a vehement protest. He paid not the slightest bit of attention to her and when the next slap of his hand landed on her buttocks she almost wished for the gag to be back in her mouth. At least she would have something to bite down upon. Even though the initial spanks of his hand weren't particularly fierce, they stung with a fervour that was unholy.

Twin tears trickled down Jenny's cheeks. Thankfully they were obscured from view, although she was beginning to wonder if she cared. What started as tears could well end in screaming and all around her would hear those, she would make sure of it. Her previous stripes from the cane at the auction were going to make this new ordeal the worst she had endured yet. If she was crying at a few handprints, by the time Daniel had unleashed his belt she would be screeching. The thin rubber coating which covered her from head to toe did little to lessen the severity of the smack and only served to be a hot, sticky annoyance. She squirmed. Daniel grabbed her tail, which thankfully was not now embedded in her ass, and wound it carefully around his free hand as the other continued to do damage.

'Stay still, Petal,' he said softly. 'You've got to try and set an example for the herd.'

An example for what? Her ability to withstand ridiculous and nonsensical discipline? She was going to set an example all right. First, she was going to test the powers of her newly corseted lungs by yelling the place down. She opened her mouth to do just that when she felt something press against her lips and shoot forward. She did not have to peer down to ascertain what it was that had just filled her mouth. It was soft, it was silky, it was delightfully fragranced with a sweet, citrusy, lemony soap, and it was by far the best thing she had tasted in the last three days.

When it sunk straight to the back of her gullet and started swelling in the hot confines of her throat she nearly came on the spot, but the suit had other ideas. All of the thrusting dildos stopped in mid-stroke and at the same time the vibrations cut out. That in itself wouldn't have stopped her orgasm, but unfortunately two twin nipple clamps bore down on her very tender teats and the pressure was excruciating. That took care of the impending explosion. She cried out in pain, but due to the thick cock now filling her mouth, there was little sound to be heard.

'Goddamn, she's tight. You said she was good, Kyle, but hell, the back of this throat is heavenly.'

'I'm looking forward to sampling the delights after you lot have finished, Dino, so get a move on.'

Jenny heard Kyle's voice to the rear of her, muted somewhat through her hood, but didn't pay it much attention. She was more intent on sucking the long spear in front of her clean of all its deliciously zesty sweetness. After three days of mush anything with a modicum of taste was appealing. What she wouldn't give for a single square of chocolate at this moment in time was anybody's guess. Trying to ignore the way her pussy clenched around the now silent and still sentinels buried deep inside her, she made herself busy slathering the cock in her saliva, before sucking at it as if she were taking part at the national lollipop slurping championships, if there were such a thing.

The thought of doing the member in her mouth some damage didn't even occur to her. The suit had fired her body up to boiling point and the spanks still descending from Daniel's hand kept her pleasantly simmering, with the added stimulus of a cock inside her. The tears were long gone, the pain was manageable and her appetite took on an insatiable demeanour. She loved the feeling of being filled in every available hole, she wanted sex and lots of it, and most of all she really wanted a large, juicy, biggest-orgasm-in-the-world type earthquake. Which she was well aware she was not going to get, for at least the next two days anyway.

So to kill time until then, Jenny sucked. And sucked. And sucked. Number one must have spurted in record time because she felt she had barely begun before her mouth was filled with the salty taste of semen. She was so thirsty she welcomed any kind of liquid and greedily lapped the goo down.

'Hungry little beastie, isn't she?' Dino watched appreciatively as Petal devoured his present, her lips smacking together as she savoured her tiny meal.

'Aren't they all?' Kyle drawled the question lazily and indicated that the next man should take his place in line. Jenny was ready for him. Her mouth was already open and eager to receive the next contestant. Number two was big, hairy and smelt of pine forests. That was when the paddles came out. Even through her hood the sound of vigorous smacking echoed noisily against the brick walls of the barn. The air was filled with cracks, bangs and noisy squealing. She barely noticed, so focused was she on the impressive rod in front of her. The man now standing before her was a bit bigger and a good deal more forceful than the last. In order to accommodate the large girth of his member he used his hands on either side of her face to slam his cock repeatedly to the back of her throat. She didn't care. The suit had just started up again. Things began thrusting and jiggling very nicely. The paddle upon her backside was only a minor inconvenience. Heat was spreading all over her body and having her mouth impaled on the large monster was an impressive challenge to conquer.

The girls around her were becoming far more vocal in their cries as the smacks of the paddle increased in both strength and volume. They were also shuffling around a lot more and even through her hood she could hear continuous rustle and crunch of hay as it moved around underneath them. It was a good thing she was made of stern stuff if this was to be her lot from now on. Concentrating on the long hard strokes as he plunged his cock back and forward, Jenny needed to do little but sit back and enjoy the ride. She kept her jaws carefully clamped around his member and sucked when she was able, drawing as little air in as necessary. With an explosive roar the man came in a gurgling fountain of fluid and she was two down, three to go.

The suit was beginning to come into its own as number three, a rather slim and pathetic affair, nudged at her lips. This one smelt a little sweaty and tasted particularly salty, and she guessed it belonged to one of the stable hands. Her eye slits didn't get to admire faces, just stomachs as they were thrust in front of her. That was probably a good thing. As her tender nipples and breasts began to enjoy a soft massage she almost purred as her face twisted this way and that, trying to get the perfect angle with which to suck. This one lasted barely three minutes inside her talented mouth.

'She's good, Kyle. She'll do you proud.' There was the sound of a zipper being refastened and a heavy thump on her head. 'Well done, filly. You'll get that black collar in no time.'

Jenny would have growled at him, but another cock had already begun to fill her. Enormous, minty and rather frisky, it gave her plenty to think about. Especially as the stimulator had buzzed into life which in turn caused her to wiggle her ass to and fro, making Daniel have to work a little harder than his colleagues positioned around him. The blows rained down a little slower, but there was more force behind them. The grooms were getting tired. Jenny was oblivious to the pain her backside was experiencing but her fellow ponies were not. Snuffles and sobs of distress could now be heard down the line and it was obvious that more than a few backsides were suffering. There was more than one anxious whiney that flew through the air on a pained squawk.

Hey, I'm doing my best here, Jenny thought, with a mouth stretched to its absolute limit and a body once again suffering the delights of intense arousal. At least the other girls only had a spanking to contend with. She, on the other hand, had the works. Her mouth was now dribbling with a mixture of saliva and semen, and her jaw was becoming tired. The effort of bobbing her head back and forth was taking its toll and her head felt heavier and stiffer with each passing thrust. Luckily number four had an agenda all of its own and managed to erupt with little effort on her part. As he came he kept his balls pressed tight into her chin and she couldn't breathe for the whole time it took him to climax. When he finally withdrew she had to quickly intake a big gulp of air and this had her choking upon his offering. Her eyes were watering yet again and there wasn't a tear in sight.

'My turn,' said a familiar voice. 'Suck it up, Petal. It's time for the finale.' Kyle didn't even wait for the choking to subside. His hips thrust forward and his cock speared her throat in a single lunge. Jenny found herself unable to breathe yet again. The latex was becoming insufferably hot, her body was swishing and swaying in the throes of intense pleasure and her plastic hooves were pawing at the floor in panic. She needed air. Trying to pull her head back to suck in a breath, he countered her move by pushing forward and placing his hand on the back of her neck to keep her in place.

'I know you can't inhale,' he said, even as she struggled to free herself from his captivity. 'I hold that power over you now. I can withhold the very air you breathe. Scary isn't it?'

Jenny couldn't summon enough energy to nod her head, which was spinning and dancing with black spots due to her lack of oxygen. Kyle slid his member out of her throat slowly and watched as she gasped and spluttered.

'I hold so much power over that body of yours; you'd do well to remember to please me.'

Taking big, wheezing lungful's of air, Jenny managed a small nod. He patted her head as his cock rested carefully on her tongue.

'So far you've managed quite well, but I can see you flagging, Pet. Let's put a little bit of enthusiasm into this, shall we?'

The air all around her was now rife with gasps, whimpers and moans. The paddles were being thrown with some force and only Jenny still remained impervious to the agony her backside was receiving. Deciding to get her one final task of the evening over with, so she could get some food and rest in short order, she took a deep breath and dived forward, impaling herself on the mean monster before her. As she took him to the back of her throat she had the strangest suspicion of déjà vu. He smelt familiar. He also had a familiar taste and felt like he was trying to split her jaw in two. Trying to place together the tastes, smells and sensations in her head, her mind tried to piece together the puzzle. The trouble was, it was almost impossible to think with dildos thrusting about everywhere, a clitoris nearing the point of no return and a backside that had just started to feel like a ball in a ping-pong tournament. The pain was now beginning to bite and she let out a whine as Kyle began slowly thrusting back and forth inside her. She did heed his warning, her mouth tightening around him as hard as it could, making sure her tongue twisted its way around the head on each upstroke. Her jaw ached so badly that the effort of holding her mouth open was agony, but there would be no excuses with this man. She knew that instinctively. With each heavy stroke that passed along her tongue she began to regret her decision. Mark hadn't been this rough and at least he'd had a sense of humour. This one, although he had the look of an angel, appeared cruel and thoughtless in his actions. Time would tell, she guessed. Her backside stung. Her body felt like a shoal of fish were beginning to nibble and slurp at each nerve-ending. She was at sensory overload, and unfortunately it appeared that Kyle was in no hurry to spurt.

The pony-girls around her were wiggling and writhing in desperate attempts to avoid the paddle. When Jenny managed to catch a glimpse of them it was to see tormented eyes, labouring breaths and several agonized looks of suffering, directed her way. I'm doing my best, she thought, as Kyle dragged his cock through her mouth yet again.

In an effort to speed up the process and save her own ass, which was now a throbbing, raw mess, she took matters into her own hands and thrust her head forward to push him as far down her throat as she could manage. She let her lips compress around him as she squeezed him with her mouth. He moaned. Finally they were getting somewhere. Letting her head do all the work now and ignoring the pain she devoured him in long, hard strokes. She cared not that her throat would be bruised and sore after the event; she just needed him to end this. Back and forth he ploughed on, but by the looks of his hands, curled into tight fists by his side, he was close. Thank God. She couldn't last out much longer. Another heavy thrust forward with her face, and another. Please come, she begged inside her head. Then the sound that they had all been waiting for bellowed through the room.

59

'Yesssssssss,' Kyle yelled out as he twitched and thrashed about inside her, pumping madly into her throat. Jenny's head wanted to fall off the face of the earth she was so damned tired, but Kyle's cock pinioned her in place. Gurgling around it, trying to swallow the sticky goo before it congealed in her throat, she heard the rustle of buckles being unfastened and the swish of leather as belts were removed from waists.

She didn't think she could take any more. Kyle had not softened inside her mouth. She hoped to hell he was not waiting for round two while her backside got a taste of Daniel's belt. Still, if he wanted to be cut in two she would happily oblige. He must have read her mind for his next words were:

'If your teeth touch me in any way during your next ten strokes I will double them personally, and I won't be half as gentle as your little groom. Giddy up, guys!'

The sharp sting of the belt shouldn't have taken Jenny by surprise, but the speed in which it was delivered was astounding. The grooms must have been lined up, belts in hand and ready to attack at his command. The shock managed to get her past strokes two and three, which landed in quick succession, but stroke four felt like someone was trying her slice her backside open. She could feel fresh tears welling in her eyes and prayed that Daniel would get this over with quickly. There was no way in hell that she could withstand ten of these and she pulled her sagging jaws open as wide as they would go in an effort to make sure she did not touch the forbidden fruit inside her.

She felt Kyle's eyes boring down upon her. She knew instinctively that he was someone who would enjoy watching her suffer. He had a mad look about him now. A look that said he wanted to crush her, every last piece of sinew and bone, from the inside out. She'd seen that look before, and on her father no less.

The rafters of the barn filled with the noise of sobbing girls. Bottoms jiggled and wriggled, trying to avoid the sharp bite of the belt, but not a one escaped their vicious trajectory. The grooms were far too practiced in their task. As the fifth and sixth strokes bore down Jenny joined them in their cries, but barely realised she had been sobbing until the latex of her hood began to stick to her face. The seventh stroke fell and she felt a moment's pride, knowing her teeth had sat perfectly still and that her mouth hadn't moved a millimetre. Her backside was on fire. It was swaying and bouncing with the rest of the rounded rumps, but it did little to lessen the pain.

Only three more to go, she consoled herself as she kept count of each stroke in her head. As the next slap of the belt hit her she could feel her teeth trying to snap together in agony. Just two more to go - two more and this was all over. Her body was nearing the point of no return and she knew that any second now the suit would stop and leave her cold turkey, sweating, panting and crying. That might actually hurt more than the belt. She had no idea how many times she'd neared the point of no return, only to be summarily returned and each time made her a little more despondent than the last. It was hard to retain focus when your body was shooting hormones and endorphins all over the place. Revenge was beginning to take a backseat and self-pity could well win the race for supremacy.

The ninth and penultimate stroke had the stables in fits of hysterics, and she was no exception. It was all she could do to ensure her teeth didn't dismember her trainer. Feeling the familiar quickening of her body as the dildos drilled and pumped, she braced herself for the final stroke but hadn't counted on how hard it would be. All of the girls shot forward as the last slam of the belts hammered down and some of them landed nose-first in the hay, their bright red buttocks quivering in dismay at the unpleasant treatment they had just received.

Jenny did not have the option of falling over. As she surged forward she managed to impale herself upon Kyle, and when the thrill of it all sent her body tumbling into the land of climax her suit gave her clit a vicious nip. Crying tears of agony, not even able to let forth a scream, shock had her biting down automatically. Even though she quickly pulled her jaws apart she knew there would be trouble by the dark look in his eyes.

He glowered at her dangerously and withdrawing swiftly, let her drop to the floor with the rest. 'That's two marks towards a dungeon visit, Petal. You have yet to impress.'

Rolling over, coughing and spluttering, she got to her knees to find Kyle's whisky-coloured eyes devouring her in a most unpleasant fashion. They were angry beacons of flame and they signalled trouble. 'I think you can spend the night in one of the stalls to contemplate the error of your ways, P.' Clipping a long silver chain on the front D-ring of her collar, he directed her towards the back of the barn with a series of vicious tugs.

Trying to crawl, but discovering that every last semblance of energy had fled from her body, Jenny had to be content with a half drag, half crawl type motion. The latex appeared to be made of strong stuff for there was no snagging or tearing as she made her way, mostly on her stomach, across the large expanse of prickly hay and through a solid oak door to one of the small stalls at the rear of the sleeping quarters.

It featured four brick walls and a floor strewn with straw, much like the outside barn. There was a high wooden shelf that ran around the room and items such as rope, cuffs, chains, clamps and crops were residing on its benign surface. There were no windows and a single light bulb, otherwise unadorned, hung from the ceiling. Its light blinded Jenny for a moment, before she got her bearings.

Two long tubes fell from the middle of the rear wall, one grey and one red. It took her a moment of puzzling to discern what they were. When Kyle came at her with the ball-gag she remembered the earlier comment the vet had made. '*You will be fed and watered through the hole in your gag.*' Marvellous, the food at Albrecht had just managed to get worse, if that were at all possible.

She was so deadbeat she barely even cared about food at this point. Sleep was calling and a yearning for blissful unconsciousness was her only need, want and desire at this moment in time. As usual, though, her wants had little to do with anything. Her face was pulled upwards and her jaw gripped tightly in Kyle's capable hands. The rubber ball was then slotted back into her mouth and fastened tightly behind her head. Her jaw felt like it had been sawn in two and split apart. Wasn't much point in moaning either, because little sound was going to get through the rubber ball that now completely filled her oral cavity.

'What would you like for dinner, Pet? A nice juicy steak? Fried chicken and chips? Probably not posh enough for the likes of you, is it? How about *duck a l'orange* or *lobster thermidor?*'

Jenny did moan then; she couldn't help it at the thought of savouring anything that had an ounce of taste or crisp texture.

'No thoughts on the matter, huh?' He grinned evilly at her. 'Guess you'll have to make do with delicious vitamin goo.' Then the awful man came at her with one of the long tubes on the back wall and Jenny simply didn't have the strength to fight him.

When Kyle inserted the feeding tube through the hole located in the front of her gag and fed it down into her windpipe, a whirring sound could be heard before the liquid burbled up the tube and trickled slowly down the back of her throat. It was tepid and tasteless. She'd have rather eaten mush, and that was saying something. Having no option but to swallow the awful stuff down, after ten minutes or so she felt her stomach begin to swell due to the volume of water now inside her. She had no idea how long it took for the tube to stop pouring its sludge into her stomach, but she was very relieved when it finished and Kyle unthreaded the tube from her lips. It left her throat sore and scratchy.

Curling up into a little ball, she wanted nothing more than to close her eyes and drift off to sleep. She could barely keep her eyes open after the day's rigorous events and the machinations of her suit. That one small privilege was not to be hers, however. Kyle began fastening metal ratchets around the base of her limbs. Jenny was only half comatose as he did so, but she could hear the sound of the handcuff levers as they secured each ankle and wrist.

'I think we'll leave you with a hogtie for your first night under my gentle command.'

Jenny did manage to hear that and snorted her thoughts on the matter.

'Quite,' Kyle agreed, entirely without humour. He pulled her wrists and ankles back behind her prone body and connected them at a point in the middle of her back. It would not be a comfortable position to sleep in, but then, she guessed that was why he was doing it.

'I shall leave you in your stall to contemplate your new life as my trainee, and can only hope you manage to perform better, tomorrow. I'm sure that with the right encouragement you'll be zooming towards that black collar in no time. Isn't that right, Petal?'

She knew he was waiting for a response, and as she was gagged the only thing she could do was nod her head awkwardly in response. She hoped that would suffice.

'I'm glad we understand each other.' There was a soft rustle of hay, a jangle of his spurs as he turned to leave the tiny cell and the rapid snick of a key in a lock. He obviously wanted to make sure she wasn't going anywhere. She was trussed in more metal than the average police officer carried, and with the addition of her four hooves, escape was currently the last thing on her mind. What was on her mind, and rather frighteningly so, was the fact that she'd recognised the jangling noise of his spurs. Where had she heard that before? It was important. As her suit fired into life for the umpteenth time that day and the dildo in her ass began inflating in earnest, she had an epiphany. The pyramid plug. Oh God, that really hadn't been Mark. It was him! Levison was her sadist. *Oh crap, crap, crap.* It appeared she'd just gone and made yet another colossal fuck-up. What on earth was she going to do now?

Marianna's Fashion Statement

'I think it's time to unwrap the present, Marianna.' Mark's eyes travelled towards the large box that sat unopened on the dining table. 'You may crawl and fetch it for me, sweetness.'

Jumping around to do his bidding, faster than the proverbial cat on the hot tin roof, she sashayed her pert backside in his direction as she raced to complete her task. Realising she was skating on already heavily cracked ice, she wished to give him no reason to find further fault.

'There's no hurry, take your time; I rather enjoy watching your ass,' he drawled provocatively.

Marianna dug her fingers into the heavy wool pile of her carpet and slowed her body down. She wanted to race about. Her heart rate was thundering and there was plenty of nervous energy that needed to be burnt off, but alas, she had been issued with instructions and they needed to be followed. Letting her fingers wallow in the soft strands of the wool carpet, she wiggled for him. Giving him a chance to look his fill, she made a meandering path towards the pale legs of the dining table and wondered what might greet her in his fancy box. She levered herself upright on her knees and pulled the shiny black rectangle towards her. The red satin bow that adorned it was almost as big as the package itself. It screamed 'expensive!', but then she suspected everything Mr Matthews bought hailed under that tag. He had little need to worry over the cost of living.

Taking her present in two hands, a little surprised at how light it was, she lowered it to the carpet and wondered how she would deliver the thing back to him. He had not ventured off her sofa and she had not been given permission to stand on two legs. Looking up to find his aquamarine eyes staring down at her in an amused fashion, she cursed inwardly. If Matthews hoped to best her so early in the evening, he was bang out of luck.

Placing the box on the floor in front of her, she used her nose to gently push it forward in little bursts with as much grace as she could muster. Marianna was well aware that he was laughing at her, but needs must when the devil drives. With her head dipping and diving and her flyaway hair dragging along the carpet and picking up an awfully impressive static charge, she hoped he put his hands on her and got the shock of his life when she reached him.

'Just leave it on the floor in front of you. By the state of your hairdo you can keep well away from me for the time being.' He bit his lip as she accidentally touched the bow in front of her and a crackle of electricity shot through the air. 'Ouch,' he murmured. 'Perhaps we should hurry this along, considering we have a long evening ahead of us. 'Go ahead and open it, Marianna.'

The box loomed large and dark on the beige carpet. The fact that it weighed nearly nothing should have been enough to calm the worst of her fears, but with Matthews nothing was ever that clear cut. She had no idea what could be horribly dangerous, weigh next to nothing and reside in a reasonably sized box? Trying to breathe normally, she gently swore at herself for overreacting and then swore again as she got another shock from the sparkly red bow. Damn.

Ignoring his laughter she tore at the ribbon, which thankfully came away easily in her hands, allowing her to remove the lid.

She was greeted by a mound of pink tissue paper and an elegant black sticker bearing the expensive motif of Chanel. He'd bought her something to wear? Intrigued, she gently tore away the tissue paper to reveal an item of clothing nestling snugly beneath its folds. The colour of the garment was a beautiful bright teal green and it begged to be touched. As she suspected, the material was as smooth as silk, and strangely rope-like. Scrunched up in the box it was a solid block of colour, but as she picked it up she was surprised to find it almost fell apart in her hands. Long woven strands of material clung together, inlaid with miniature sparkling sequins only slightly bigger than a pinhead. As it was stretched wider tiny glistening diamond shapes appeared and her fingertips ached to caress them. What on earth was it? Unravelling the see-through material to its fullest, she discovered she was holding what appeared to be a dress. Her eyes widened.

'Beautiful, isn't it?'

'Yes,' she whispered, 'but what on earth would you wear underneath it?' Judging that the dress would fall only a few scant inches past her backside, she guessed that a simple slip with fine spaghetti straps would suffice. It might spoil the gorgeous effect of the dress somewhat, but if worn in its current state it would be positively indecent, and people had been arrested for a whole lot less in these parts.

'Well, normally you would be allowed to wear something to cover up those obviously amazing charms of yours, but seeing as how you've been such a naughty girl this evening, you're going to wear it as it was meant to be worn. As you can't seem to follow instructions I feel the need to spell that out to you, so here goes: you are to place that dress over your head and you will be allowed to wear nothing else upon your body bar a pair of earrings and, perhaps, a necklace.'

It was Marianna's turn to smile. He wanted to play naughty, then? 'Should I go and model it for you, Sir?' She had no qualms wearing the dress indoors. She was surprised he wished her to dress up in order for the evening's proceedings to begin, but who was she to question her Master?

'Go and model it for me now, Marianna. I have a feeling you're going to knock my socks off in that outfit, if you hadn't knocked them off already with your delightful nakedness.' He smiled down at her and nodded, which indicated she had permission to leave his presence. Placing the dress in her teeth, which was the easiest way to carry it whilst crawling, she wiggled her bottom once again for his pleasure. Having not received permission to walk, she arrived at the open door of her bedroom and quickly hid herself in the corner. As soon as she had manoeuvred herself safely inside, where his prying eyes could not find her, she got to her feet and rushed to the mirror.

When Marianna tried the dress on in front of the floor to ceiling art deco mirror, it wasn't quite as opaque as she'd feared. It clung to her body like a second skin, with a tenacity that surprised her, and covered up all of the important parts. That was, until she made a move. Then the diamonds quivered, stretched, sparkled and revealed naughty glimpses of skin as they pulled this way and that. As it shifted around her the dress became a walking advert for indecency. Twisting this way and that at the mirror she caught a flash of nipple, watched the curve of her breast as it moved softly against the material, and if she moved her legs, well, that was another story.

Standing with her legs shoulder width apart the mound of her naked, hairless sex was clearly revealed beneath the delicate triangles. Turning around to view the back, she could see the outline of her toned backside and, if the material was stretched further, the valley between her ass cheeks was clearly revealed. It felt sinfully invigorating.

Taking a few practice steps around her bedroom, she smiled as the tiny threads of rope rubbed against her nipples, breasts and sex, and she found that the faster she walked, the more exquisite the sensation. As she moved the dress slithered in tiny stimulating whispers all around her body. It would make her acutely aware of her nakedness with every step she took, which was the idea, she guessed. Mark Matthews was indeed a master tormentor. No foreplay would be necessary with an outfit such as this, if foreplay had been necessary - which it wasn't.

Deciding to humour the boss she sat down at her dressing table and reached into the top drawer for a thin strand of freshwater pearls, which she fastened carefully behind her neck before pinning the matching earrings in place. Picking up her wooden hairbrush she began taming her long brunette locks into a semblance of submission, before fastening them up in a sleek chignon. Holding a can of hairspray she used it to subdue her flyaway ends and in this particular exercise, she maintained complete control. Her hair didn't stand a chance. Before long she was elegantly garbed, coiffed and with a quick lick of paint on the errant toenails, ready to present herself to Master.

Wiggling her toes around rapidly to dry them, she wondered if she should don a pair of high heels to complete the look. Even though they were not going anywhere, it would give her a few extra inches of height, slim down her legs and elongate her calves. She had a pair of stilettos in just the right shade, too. It would be a shame not to give them an outing with one of Chanel's finest creations. Opening the doors of antique oak armoire, she quickly found what she was looking for. They were still in their original shoebox, as they had never been worn. She'd bought them at the beginning of her career with Zystrom, hoping the statement colour might attract the eyes of her boss the day before she had learnt that only blonde hair would achieve that miracle. After that her wardrobe had remained dull, staid and boring, so she could blend into the background and shadows, attracting the least amount of attention possible, for Marianna wanted Mark and Mark only. She had little wish to be a plaything or toy for his colleagues. Entertainingly enough, that would change now she had his attention. He often enjoyed watching the other girls as they were used by his colleagues and friends. The thought scared her a little. She didn't know whether she would like being the object of another's hands, tongue and lips. She suspected it wouldn't be long before she was put to the test, though, and as she would have little choice in the matter, she would be wise to do exactly as he asked.

Plucking the shiny green stilettos from their box, she inhaled the wonderful scent of new leather and took a moment to appreciate their shiny curves and lines. She loved shoes, she loved shoe shopping, but most of all she loved standing tall and proud in them. Slipping them on her feet she took a few tentative steps around her room, to get used to the feel of them, before summoning up the courage to go outside and display herself before the boss. It took a few deep breaths before she had managed to achieve the brave frame of mind she was looking for. Puffing her chest out and holding her head high, creating the epitome of elegance in her posture and stance, she silently glided across the carpeted floor to her awaiting tormentor.

When Marianna waltzed back into the lounge, poised and almost regal in stature, Mark felt his breath catch in his throat. The Harrods personal shopping assistant, who advised him on all of his purchases, had really outdone herself on this occasion. The dress was scandalous, outrageous and damn near perfect to his mind. Each tiny flash of generously tanned flesh served to titillate his senses and the outfit managed to accentuate all her ample charms, if that were possible. It was a beautiful frame for a near perfect body. He would never tell her that, of course. He needed to keep this one on her toes.

'Not bad, Miss Morreau,' he drawled, cocking his head to one side as he appraised every inch of flesh from top to bottom. 'You have made one small error, however. I wonder if you can tell me what it is?'

Marianna's face took on the appearance of a little girl for a minute, lost and confused. It took her a moment before she remembered where she was and who she was with. Her eyes flared in understanding before she let out a strangled sob. Getting down to her hands and knees once more she whispered, 'I'm sorry, Sir. Please forgive me.'

Mark clucked his tongue. She was giving him the 'lost puppy' look and it was all he could do to stop from smiling.

'So many indiscretions this evening, Miss Morreau. We really must start addressing them.' He appeared to consider the matter, while his eyes were devouring the way her breasts wobbled slightly as her breathing quickened. His naughty little girl was aroused. So much the better. 'Hmm. I have just the thing. How about we go out for a drink? I know a lovely place in the centre of London. Fancy a gin and tonic, my dear?'

He stifled another laugh as her face dropped. He wondered if she would ask the question or whether he would just give her 'the look' and stifle it in its tracks. He decided that would be a little mean, so he waited expectantly. Marianna's mouth opened and closed several times and she looked not unlike a goldfish gasping for air. She even got to the point where she anxiously raised her finger in the air, and Mark gave her an encouraging smile.

'Something on your mind, Marianna?' Her mouth snapped shut. Damn the woman, she was spoiling all his fun. She'd obviously figured out his game. What she didn't know was that they would have been going out had she been a good girl or not. He wanted to see how she would handle the idea of being in public not only nearly naked, but with a dress that would slay the average male mortal at ten paces. It was going to be an entertaining evening.

'Before we go, Marianna, I feel that certain aspects of your behaviour need to be addressed. So you may place yourself over my knee, hands on the armrest of the sofa. I think we should make that backside take on a pleasant, cherry-red hue before we let the general public lay their eyes on it. What say you, sweetness?'

Marianna had still not come to terms with the fact that she was about to display all of her most intimate charms to any member of the public who might care to look at them, so it took a moment before her eyes connected with his. Her pupils had dilated dramatically and she was running scared. It wouldn't do her any harm.

'Now, Marianna. I am not a patient man.'

His sharp tone had her rushing to obey. She laid her slight body over his thighs and he felt his trousers crumple as she moved forward. It was probably a good thing. He'd need to look a bit rumpled if he wanted to fit in at the bar they were going to. Sliding her body forward her cheek rested on the arm of her sofa, tilted to the left, and she draped both her arms either side of her head.

He let her rest there for a moment in contemplative silence. Anticipation was the mother of desire, and he would see to it that she had more than her fair share of the fickle creature. She began squirming before he had laid even a single finger upon her. He let her wriggle. It served to arouse him as well. He watched the little glistening diamonds as they danced sinuously upon her body. His hand itched to slam into her flesh, but he waited patiently. There was a time and place for everything and he valued every last little aspect of control. Another twist of her groin, grinding into his pants made him catch his breath, but still he waited. When she finally cried out, a muffled little gasp of arousal she could no longer keep inside, he took pity upon her and slowly slid the pathetic wisps of silk covering her ass cheeks up towards her waist. Her sharp intake of breath was delightful. He could hear her fingernails digging into the soft suede of the sofa and her toes scrape against the carpet. Yes, she was ready for a little pain. She had certainly earned it.

Letting his fingers slide over the soft mounds of her buttocks he felt the taut muscle there. It was no surprise she was a little apprehensive, but he wondered if she would be wet and ready for him. His fingers walked a path down her butt cheeks. Hearing Marianna moan at even that light pressure he was pretty much assured of the outcome of his exploration, and when his fingers reached her sex they almost skidded. She was drenched. Perhaps it was a good thing there wouldn't be much dress to soak. Plunging two fingers forth into her core, he watched as her back strung itself tight as a bow and her hips bucked against him.

He whispered, 'You're ready for my hand, aren't you Marianna?' There was no immediate response. To make his point clear, his hand grasped an ass cheek with a fearsome grip and squeezed.

She gave out a high-pitched yelp and whimpered, 'Yes, Sir.'

Well, that was a bit more like it. He raised his hand in the air, palm facing down, and unleashed himself.

The first few smacks were a gentle warm-up both for Marianna's backside and for his hand. He needed to get a good pattern and rhythm going. The idea was to slowly build up the heat so each spank was a little bit harder than the last. At the end of this session both his hand and her backside would be sore, but there was no question that she would have the worst end of the deal.

To give her credit, she settled into the spanking after the shock of the first two slaps had left her and then raised her buttocks to welcome each new slap as she had been taught. She didn't move her hands or her head, and she kept her dazzling green eyes wide open even though she couldn't look at him with them.

Alternating from side to side, he admired the twin peaks of firm flesh and the first spots of colour that had just started to encourage her ass to blush rather beautifully. It would take a good few minutes to develop something half-decent and long lasting, but he was on the right path. Each slap saw a slight quiver as the orbs tried desperately to recover themselves before his hand descended again with another fresh attack.

'I've been thinking about your punishment for this evening's "panty" debacle. As you have already realised, parading you around central London in that dress will be a part of it. It should help you lose that innate sense of propriety you seem so keen to hold on to. You need to learn that when I lay down the law, I mean for my instructions to be obeyed immediately and without question. Failure to do so will result in penalties. These may be moderate to severe, depending on my choice, but I shall make sure that the lesson has been learned.'

As his hand continued to fall he increased the strength of the stroke. She whimpered in protest, but there was still little movement on her part.

'You will be pleased to know I am going to allow you the privilege of wearing panties to work.' He did not miss the puzzled frown that graced her face. She had every right to be confused but he intended to clear up her misunderstanding quickly. 'When you arrive at the office, however, you will bend over and push your panties down so they rest around your ankles. That way, I will be assured you are not wearing underwear while you're working under my roof.'

Marianna's jaw dropped in horror and he knew it had nothing to do with the effects of his spanking, even though her backside had just begun to wiggle in the most charming fashion. 'You may speak.'

Marianna did the goldfish thing again. He hadn't slowed the pace of his spanking so it was going to be a little hard for her to concentrate, but she'd get there in the end. Women were renowned for their multi-tasking skills, he'd heard.

'Isn't there some...' a rather loud squeak ensued as a particularly hard whack cracked down, 'health and safety law against that?' Her words tripped over one another in a breathless manner and her squirming increased. He could feel his cock harden painfully as he watched her body undulate backwards and forwards.

'Against what?' He raised an eyebrow out of habit, but was aware she couldn't see it.

'Against try-ing,' another squeak, 'to walk,' a yelp of pain, 'in-high-heels-with-your-panties-around-your-ankles!'

'It's a good job I speak gibberish, Miss Morreau. No, the only laws in my office are those which I set and you will ensure that you walk slowly and carefully so as not to injure yourself. If you manage to injure yourself through your own stupidity you will, of course, be punished.'

Slap, slap, slap. The metronome beat of his hand was building in tempo. She had to wait a full minute before she could summon a weak, if faintly sarcastic response to his dictate.

'Obviously.' That was the last thing she said for quite some time.

It might have been because he had one hand caressing her clit, while the other continued to see to her chastisement. It might have been because her buttocks were rather appealingly red and were probably somewhat raw and painful by now, giving her something else to ponder bar that of idle chatter or... it might have been something else entirely. You could never be certain of anything with the female sex. He would have liked to believe it was the former, though.

Bringing down his palm with short, forceful bursts of staccato enthusiasm, he let her have it. Oh yes, he really gave her a shot of the good stuff. He knew she was feeling the force of his blows, because his right hand stung like hell, but she was also in the land of pleasure. His left hand was seeing to that quite nicely. Working inside her with two lithe fingers, he used his thumb to work her clit. She was so wet that no additional lubrication was required. Her moans of pain had turned into squirms of pleasure, her breathing was ragged and her ass had effloresced into a brilliant 'chilli pepper' red. He'd put money on the fact that it felt hotter than the piquant spice, too.

'I think we're done here, Marianna.' His spanking and teasing stopped abruptly and he let his hands roam over the delicate ropes of her dress. Reaching underneath her body he felt the hard nub of a nipple bursting through the fabric and he tweaked it, purely for the pleasure of hearing her gasp.

'Aren't you going to thank me, Miss Morreau? Or do we need another lesson while we work on your manners?'

She broke free of the painful, pre-orgasmic haze that had taken over her body, shook her head and mumbled something along the lines of, 'Sorry, Sir. Thank you for your instruction, Sir.'

At least she knew better than to ask for her pleasure. Mr Entwell seemed to have managed a tolerable result with her. Some of the blondes would be begging for release right now and he couldn't help but admire her willpower. He'd make sure it came crashing down around her stilettos before the evening was out, but at this moment in time he was impressed. 'You may get up now,' he instructed, 'and present yourself for inspection before we leave.' With one last lingering squeeze of her ass he released her.

Straightening his legs in order to get his circulation moving once more, Mark remained in his seat whilst Marianna got to her feet. He noted that her beautifully long legs were shaking, and unless the sequins on her dress were dancing of their own accord she was a having a hard time controlling her breathing. Looking towards the apex of her legs he wondered if he'd be able to detect any lingering wetness there. No, there was nothing he could discern as of yet, but her pussy lips were delightfully swollen if one cared to look. Letting his gaze rise higher, he noted that both nipples had escaped the inadequate confines of her garment and were vying for attention, forming stiff, dusky-rose peaks. To add to the wonderful masterpiece he had just created, her perky full breasts quivered with each lungful of air she sucked in. 'Turn around for me, Marianna. I want to admire my handiwork.' He gave her a dark, predatory smile.

She immediately complied and tottered around unsteadily on her high heels. Miss Morreau was slightly off balance, it appeared. By the end of the evening she'd be a lot off balance, but she didn't need to know that, yet. When she turned her back to him he could see little through the fabric, as she had her legs tight together. That wouldn't do at all. He wanted to admire the brilliant colour he had just managed to inflict upon her.

'Spread your legs for me, Marianna. I want to see the damage.' Her legs moved woodenly, first the right and then the left, and her gasp was telling. Even the lightest touch on that derriere was going to sting for a bit, and every time the little wisps of fabric moved against her they'd chafe wickedly. She wouldn't be repeating her panty mistake any time soon, he thought.

Watching the material as it stretched he witnessed all of the tiny, netted diamonds opening slowly, to display the prize beneath. The vista was as breathtaking as the Alps. When she walked and the dress strained at her movement, her red backside would be bright enough to stop traffic.

'Wider,' he ordered, for the sheer pleasure of drinking in even more of her fiery red flesh. Obediently her legs slid further apart. 'Bend over.' As she moved forward her ass cheeks filled the dress to its widest potential. He could see her glistening sex press up against the struggling cords of netting and wondered, for a moment, whether the dress would break. It held. She'd have to hope Chanel knew what they were doing. It would be a little embarrassing if the thing disintegrated upon her later in the evening.

Looking at his watch he saw the time was now past eight o'clock. Their taxi would be waiting. He almost rubbed his hands in glee at the thought of his evening ahead. Things were most definitely going his way once again.

'OK, the inspection's finished,' he said. 'You're allowed a quick toilet break and then we must be off to meet our eagerly awaiting public.' As his back was to her he couldn't see the look of absolute horror on her face, but knew, without a single doubt, that it would be there.

The BDSM Bar

Marianna walked into the lift with the manner of one who was about to receive their last supper. Even though she walked tall and there was an air of grace and elegance about her that most females would die for, there was a look in her eyes that was a cross between fear and defeat. Defeat, because she knew she could not escape this - without losing her job at any rate - and fear as to whether she would manage to hold herself together until the evening had finished. Time would tell.

Mark was facing the evening with an air of delicious anticipation. He had plenty of ideas beating at the grey recesses of his mind, and although most were somewhat depraved, they were also rather fun. Money brought certain privileges in life, and he enjoyed them to the fullest.

As the lift doors pinged open on the ground floor he watched Marianna's body tense. It was an instinctive reaction that she had no control over. She was preparing herself to do battle with an audience. As the doors glided silently apart she tried her best to appear unconcerned with the prospect of baring all her most intimate charms, but her telling hesitation to move as the doors peeled back in their entirety said it all.

'After you, Marianna, I insist.' Mark gave a long and gentlemanly flourish with his hand to indicate she should precede him. Marianna gave him a rather petulant, unpleasant look, and he could have likened her face at that moment in time to a bulldog chewing a rather crunchy and most definitely unpalatable wasp.

Knowing she had little choice she took a cautionary step forward, followed by another and then another. Sweeping her head around from side to side, she found the brightly-lit foyer of Sandringham Apartments blissfully empty. Not even the receptionist was in sight and her previous averseness to move dissipated swiftly. Her high heels practically ran through the building at breakneck speed, and spotting the glossy black taxi that was waiting patiently just outside the automatic glass doors of the entrance, she nearly dived into it headfirst.

Mark watched her antics with interest. Public humiliation was obviously not something she was happy or familiar with. He wondered just what she had learned under the careful eye of her tutor. They would probably find out tonight, one way or another. Little did she know it, but they were venturing out to visit a very special bar, located just outside Knightsbridge and populated by some extremely wealthy people. The bar catered to those with 'different' sexual tastes and would feature plenty of BDSM style activities. He would make sure it would be a night she would remember for quite some time to come.

Sauntering his way outside into the refreshing, cooling night air, he opened the car door which she had slammed abruptly shut, and indicated she should move up the seat. He was teasing her, knowing she would have to move her body past the watchful eyes of the driver in his rear-view mirror. She was quick to accomplish her task.

'Had I any idea how eager you were to parade yourself around central London nearly naked, I would have dispensed with your earlier spanking.' Mark pursed his lips together as Marianna's face took on an alabaster hue. Reaching up to grasp her seatbelt, he buckled it into its awaiting receptacle and let his hand brush the underside of her breast. She jumped. 'Don't look so frightened, pumpkin. If they see fear where we're going they'll eat you alive. Actually, they'll eat you alive regardless, but the difference will be whether you enjoy it or not,' he added. Marianna did not relax her rigid stance in the slightest.

As the taxi hummed into life and pulled away from the curb Mark studied Marianna, noting she was taking slow, deep breaths and that her eyes were slightly unfocused and obviously far away from the situation at hand.

'Meditating, my dear? At a time like this?' He rested his hand on her thigh and let two of his fingers poke through a shimmering diamond to draw a pattern upon her flesh beneath. She shivered and offered the faintest of curses.

'Naughty girl,' said Mark, waggling his finger at her. You know language is not tolerated in my presence. You've just added another punishment to your list. His fingers pulled at the flimsy dress and dipped below to search out sweeter, wetter pastures. Marianna immediately clenched her legs together, without thinking, and he raised a single eyebrow at her. 'That's two punishments now. Care to make it three?' Having realised her mistake, she spread her legs wide for him and wisely kept a tight lid on the expletive she would have liked to air. 'Good girl,' he consoled her. 'Don't feel too bad; I know you've been out of the loop on all things submission for the last year or two, but it will all come rushing back to you soon enough. The golden rule of thumb is to obey. Obedience is rewarded, bad behaviour is punished.' His finger stroked the silky flesh of labia and she whined petulantly.

'Define "good behaviour" and "rewards",' she said testily, as it took all the willpower she had not to pull her hips up from her seat and grind her clit into Mark's clever fingers.

His lips twitched as his free hand reached up to stroke his jaw. 'Good behaviour is doing exactly what I tell you to do. If you can figure out what I'm going to ask you to do before I've said it and act accordingly, you get bonus points.'

'Fantastic,' was her clipped reply.

'As to rewards, I'm open to suggestions. What would you like, Marianna?'

She appeared to consider his question thoughtfully. As his fingers swirled over her clit and her tongue caught in her throat she finally managed, 'To catch up on a year's worth of fucking.'

He laughed. 'Tut, tut, my dear, three punishments and counting! I hope you have lots of energy for the night ahead. I think you're going to need some.' He then concentrated his attention on exploring the easily accessible portals of her dress. His fingers worked themselves through the fine trellis of holes until they were able to caress her most intimate parts. He took his own sweet time. Car horns bleeped, passers-by hurried to their next destination and the taxi meter, along with Marianna's pulse rate, continued to rise. Her face was that of the condemned prisoner, but at least she was only awaiting the 'little death', rather than ill-famed road to perdition.

'You can't fight this, Marianna.' He continued to edge her towards the point of orgasm, slipping inside the wet, wanton core of her body, feeling her hips tilt towards him of their own accord.

'I can try.' Marianna's eyes flicked back and forth, from the taxi driver to her tormentor.

'Try all you like. I guarantee you'll fail.' He began to spread her slick heat generously over her clit before proceeding to nudge the little nub into life once more. 'Twenty minutes ago you'd have begged me for an orgasm, given half a chance. You women are contrary animals.' He watched her body stiffen and struggle to retain control. It was a battle she couldn't hope to win. 'Before you know it you'll be enjoying the art of exhibitionism and begging me for more of the same. It's an adrenaline thing.' He saw her eyes dart to the rear view mirror and knew she had caught the taxi driver looking at her by the shocked expression on her face. His fingers continued to plunder her body, pulling her dress this way and that across her body, chafing at her nipples and making them peak into beautiful, rosebud points.

'Come for me now, pumpkin. Show me and our driver just how much you're enjoying the ride.' He knew she was close. He could smell the resentment and arousal through her tortured breaths.

'Speaking of rides,' Marianna managed to bite out through the fast onset of her rushing hormones, 'why didn't you use your limousine? Surely that would have been more comfortable?' It was a timely comment as they hit one of London's many potholes, which rocketed both the car and herself into orbit.

'I like to live life on the edge,' was his reply.

When the taxi pulled to a stop not ten minutes later Marianna had almost managed to restore her equilibrium, such as it was. When she took this career path she had known what would be expected of her, but putting it into practise was another matter entirely. Where had her poise and grace fled to? The other side of the continent, she suspected, if not further. Glancing through the window to see what sort of fate awaited her, her eyes were met by darkness. The journey had taken close to forty-five minutes and the thick veils of night had now firmly descended upon the inhabitants of London. It was a relief of sorts, because no one would be able to see as clearly as they would have in daylight, but the drawback to that was that the interior of some of the bars littering the streets were brightly lit. If she were to be 'showcased' inside somewhere with glaring bright lights, life was going to get a little difficult for her, to say the least.

To be fair, an evening with Matthews was going to be a hell of a lot more 'difficult', but hanging off his arm was a reward of sorts. How could a face that was so handsome hide a mind that was more corrupt than the average politician's? If the man had morals, she had yet to discover them.

He had shown some compassion towards her, she thought grudgingly. At least he'd allowed her a moment of release before they embarked upon this next journey or she would probably be at his feet, dribbling and begging for a moment of his time, pretty much like any other sane female on the planet.

Watching as Mark placed a wad of bills in the driver's hand and offered a kind word of thanks, her hooded eyes followed him as he opened his door before walking around to pull open hers. He was playing the gentleman this evening, then. What a laugh that was. Bracing herself to absorb the horrified stares of the general public, she gripped hold of Mark's proffered hand and let him propel her upwards. The sound of the taxi speeding off into the distance did not even register. There were people all around her, chatting, walking, pressing buttons on their cell phone and delving inside their handbags. London was alive with the soft sounds of jazz music and the hum of neon.

Although Marianna's legs were unsteady at first, her stiletto heels not helping to maintain her balance, she found the sheer indifference of the people around her, who whizzed past on either side lost in their own little worlds, served to soothe her somewhat. Most were dressed a good deal more conservatively than her, but one or two could have been near rivals, with skirts so short they revealed lacy panties and almost transparent plastic tops which displayed Victoria Secret's finest creations. There was plenty of leather to be seen, and black appeared to be the colour of choice. Studded, spiked collars were on proud display (with chains attached!) and piercings through tongues and nipples could also be spotted, if one cared to look carefully enough. Had they just entered the twilight zone? This was an area where there should have been Dior dresses and Hermes handbags.

'We're going to an "alternative lifestyle" bar, in case you're wondering,' Mark offered.

No kidding, thought Marianna, as she tried to summon up enough courage to stand a little taller and walk a little straighter. Every ten seconds she had to resist the urge to try and place her hands over her chest and crotch. Rolling her eyes, she consoled herself with the fact that she didn't have enough hands, regardless.

'Don't worry, you're soon going to see more naked people than you are clothed, so before long you'll feel almost fully dressed in that outfit.'

He winked at her. If he was trying to be reassuring, Marianna thought sourly, he was failing miserably. The paving slabs clipping under her heels stopped abruptly as he led her through a stuccoed portico, featuring some very grand ionic columns, dwarfing her with their sheer height and making her feel even more insignificant than he already had. Glancing upwards she witnessed a series of beautiful frescos, which must have been painstakingly painted by hand, adorning the ceilings.

That was just the beginning. When they entered the ornate iron doors Mark was greeted by name and the concierge, if he could be called such a thing, immediately began to lead them off to the left where they entered one of the most amazing rooms Marianna had ever seen.

Curiosity taking over, she tried her best to peer around the concierge's uniformed back, who was standing directly in front of her. To say there was a lot to take in would have been the understatement of the century. At the rear, a floor to ceiling fish tank took pride of place in glorious aquamarine blue and housed a collection of the biggest, brightest tropical fish she had ever laid her eyes upon. There was a bar directly in front of it and liveried serving staff scurried around pouring drinks and completing orders. Huge cream vases, decorated in delicate, swirling patterns, sprung out of the floor erupting in tall, leafy green potted palms. The floor was glass, it was backlit and it was clear there was a series of waterways underneath her feet, this time in turquoise green. Goldfish swam in busy shoals beneath her. The movement set her off kilter and her heel would have folded beneath her had Mark not tightened his grip on her arm.

Tables were set beneath the floor-line and you had to descend small glass steps to reach them. Bright blue, velour cushions were provided to soften your landing if you were lucky enough to reach them unharmed. While the lighting was dim, there was a mass of scented candles on raised transparent pillars, which were dotted about the floor and smelt heavenly. She couldn't place the fragrance; vetiver, citrus and maybe some kind of spice? It was tantalising and made her mouth water. And that was just the décor.

London's glitterati had assembled in droves. Some had dressed up and dripped money in the form of designer clothes and diamonds at every turn of their elegantly fashioned heads. The men wore anything from double-breasted suits to tight leather trousers. The women, for the most part, wore considerably less. Many sported collars around their neck, some of which were subtle and consisted of delicate gold or platinum chains fastened together with a tiny padlock. Others were made of thick leather with bold buckles and decorated with spikes, studs or sparkling gems.

About half of the women assembled were completely naked, whilst others were paraded around in little more than stockings and underwear. A few wore pathetic excuses for clothing, much as she did, in either shockingly transparent fabric or easily accessible body-stockings. It didn't ease the pressure on the constant urge to cover her most intimate areas, but it did lessen her sense of vulnerability. Although why that should be the case was anybody's guess; the men here were sexual predators and with Mr Matthews' permission she could be used by any of them. The attention she had courted for so long was now hers, but it came with demanding consequences. She had been prepped for all of this, of course, but that had been two years ago. Since then she had become a virtual recluse, head buried in her computer screen at work before she reburied it in television soaps when she returned home. She spun around the room to try and encompass everyone and everything. All of this was too much and too soon.

'Impressive, isn't it?' She jumped as Mark's voice breathed into her ear. 'They're about to serve up the main course if you're feeling peckish.' He captured her chin with his finger and directed her gaze, which was still slewing left and right with no anchor in sight, to a long rectangular banquet table. In keeping with the transparent theme it was made of glass, and clear, cylindrical perspex stools circled its base. He began leading her towards it. 'They call this place *Atlantisse*. A nod to the depravities of the Greek Gods, no doubt, not to mention the fact that most who enter here are lost beyond all redemption.

That was one way of putting it, thought Marianna. The sound of traditional Asian music began to gently seep through the air and made her skin prickle.

Twanging strings performed an intricate dance with the soft, reedy sound of the flute. Her ears strained to hear it at first, but the ballad was so beautiful she could not resist its lure. The volume increased slowly by small degrees and the crowd assembled looked towards the entrance of the room in silent anticipation of the main event. They were not to be kept waiting.

A long, rectangular stretcher was carried into the room by six naked, oiled male slaves and atop the wooden slats laid a young, lithe, Japanese girl, bound hand and foot to it with thick, hemp rope. Technically she was naked but in actuality her body was clothed in a myriad of different types of Japanese cuisine. Sushi rolls decorated her stomach, and raw and brightly coloured scraps of sashimi fish were patterned over her legs and adorned with little slivers of green condiment. Fragrant noodles danced upon her arms and the air was redolent with the scent of spice, making Marianna's mouth water.

The girl was more than worthy of being a feast for the Gods and she was exquisitely adorned from head to toe. Parcels of rice wrapped in banana leaves were stuffed between her legs and tempura prawns were arched over her breasts with an array of colourful vegetables, none of which Marianna could put a name to. As she was laid gently down on the centre of the table, it became clear that there was even more on offer. Her mouth was stretched wide open, filled with tiny bright pink pickles, and around her neck rested large cubes of pineapple, decorated with mint, coloured sugar and dribbling strawberry coulis. Her sex was full to bursting with tiny, bright orange pearls. Marianna found her jaw hanging in amazement.

'Would you like to be devoured, Marianna? We can come back next week and your body can feature as the entrée of your choice. You can keep with the Asian theme or perhaps you'd like to try something a little more traditional. We could have you trussed up like a turkey and suitably stuffed.' Mark raised an eyebrow at her and she thought he was teasing, but couldn't be absolutely certain. Finding something the size of an average tennis ball stuck in her throat, Marianna took a moment to clear it, her eyes never leaving the prostrate culinary masterpiece.

'I think I'd prefer to be sucked and nibbled, preferably in private.' She tried for an even, assertive tone, but everything came out in a horrible rush. Taking a deep breath she tried to voice the question, 'Is this a usual feature to the evening?' This time she sounded rather squeaky, but she was suitably impressed that she managed to talk at all.

'Features change from week to week, but this is a regular activity. We've had all sorts paraded before us. Intricate human desserts from chocolate profiteroles decorated with spun sugar to a living and breathing cream cake - and yes, it gave a whole new meaning to the words "squirty cream".' Mark winked at her. 'There have been exhibits for seafood platters, paella, loin of lamb with crushed apples and on occasion, simply a round of canapés and caviar. Can you guess where the caviar goes, by chance?'

Marianna was afraid that she knew exactly where it would go. As Mark ushered her forward to take one of the simple stools, she placed her simmering backside down on the cool perspex and sighed.

'Still a bit raw?' He laughed and plunged straight back into the previous conversation. 'Can you imagine a hundred, softly rounded knives dipping inside your sex and seeking to taste its nectar? A little bit of your essence being spread on the lightest and fluffiest of blinis, to be savoured by all around you?'

The tennis ball had not really moved in her throat, but Marianna found herself just about able to dislodge it when politeness was required.

'I'm not sure I can imagine that, Sir,' she whispered, her eyes focused on the attentive male slaves, who were now handing out elegantly patterned bamboo chopsticks to the dining participants. Accepting hers gracefully she had to resist the urge to run her fingers over the man's superbly muscled, glossy chest. Suspecting her backside would get another pounding for such a slip, she gripped her chopsticks as firmly as she could between trembling fingers.

'I saw that moment of temptation, my sweet.' Mark gave her a lingering, knowing smile and then nodded towards the food, giving his permission for her to begin her meal. He then focused his attention on doing the same and deftly picked up a tuna roll as if chopsticks were second nature to him. Why was she not surprised? The man had confidence oozing out of every pore in his body. It was infuriating, disturbing and, strangely, arousing. There was no question that he was in control. It wasn't bluster or arrogance, either. He had a presence that demanded attention and respect, both in the bedroom and in the boardroom. Mark would be a fearsome opponent if one stupidly decided to go head-to-head with him. She was not that opponent, however. She intended to obey him to the letter. The panty incident had been enough of a warning and she suspected the mistake would be rued more than once before the night was over.

Flexing her chopsticks a couple of times to get the measure of them, she gingerly picked up a sliver of salmon from the girl's leg. A thick dollop of green paste was dotted in a corner and she didn't think very clearly before placing the morsel into her mouth. Ooh, wasabi. Fire instantly exploded and her first instinct, which was to spit the offending offering out, wasn't really an option. Keeping the fish on her tongue and the wasabi, which was liberally smeared on the top of it, well away from the roof of her mouth, she sat there for a few seconds in utter panic. She couldn't eat the thing. She hated hot food and this was hotter than most. What on earth was she going to do? Because of the damn dress she didn't even have a tissue she could use to whisk the unsavoury item away.

'Wasabi, or Japanese horseradish, has quite a strong flavour, does it not? It's used by Japanese chefs because it helps preserve the flavour and kill the bacteria which can develop on raw fish. I wouldn't hold it in your mouth too much longer though; the fumes get rather painful after a while.' He waited for her to swallow.

She looked at him helplessly. It would take the threat of a good caning in order to get her to swallow this fiery green lava.

He sighed and rolled his eyes. 'Come here.' Pulling her head towards his mouth he took her lips deftly in his and sucked the small sliver of fish into his mouth, where he swallowed it with little effort. Marianna's pulse had just gone nuclear and at that point in time she could have bitten into a bird's eye chilli and been unaffected. His eyes bored into hers and his tongue gently traced a slick path on her bottom lip. Unlike her, he was not breathing hard.

'Lucky for you, I like hot things.' He was trying hard not to laugh. 'Now may I suggest you leave the Sashimi alone and stick to the noodles or sushi.' Picking up another piece of fish, this time in a more conventional way by using his chopsticks, he guzzled more of the blistering condiment down without a moment's unease.

Even though the aftereffects of the wasabi had lessened somewhat, Marianna was still feeling the heat. The stray stares of the men gathered around the table, admiring her form in the barely-there dress were obvious, as was their hunger for pleasures not in the least bit related to food. Mark's immediate proximity had wetness seeping between her thighs as his kiss, brief though it was, performed its magic. She squirmed on the now sticky stool and gasped as her backside protested being rubbed on the unforgiving plastic surface.

'I'd sit still and eat if I were you,' said Mark, reaching up towards the Japanese lady's breasts for an elegantly curved tiger prawn, wrapped in batter. She watched as he tormented the poor girl first, squeezing a soft pink nipple between his chopsticks before he released the devilish pressure and lunged for his original prize. He bit into the succulent, soft, juicy flesh and sighed in appreciation. 'They even spice her skin. Furikake, seaweed flavour by the looks of it, has been sprinkled just beneath her breasts. You can dip your rice in it.'

Marianna cautiously picked up a parcel of banana leaves tied neatly with string. She was careful not to touch the woman's sex as she grabbed her snack, which was getting a lot of chopstick attention, and concentrated on getting the item back to her plate in order to unwrap it. When she'd managed that she almost groaned in despair. Rice. How on earth did she eat that with two little wooden sticks?

'Japanese rice is sticky and glutinous. It's easy to pick up with the chopsticks, but by all means use your fingers. I have a feeling you'll be very popular around here if you start licking things.' Mark had reached for a similar parcel of rice, which he deposited on his plate, but his chopsticks returned to her sex and delved inside. Marianna looked at him curiously when he pulled out something spherical and orange. 'It's called *Ikura*. Open wide, sweetie.'

She looked at the small orange ball with mistrust, but opened her jaw obediently. It wasn't like she had a choice. If he'd had a tube of wasabi in his hand and demanded that she eat it, that would have been her lot unless she decided to risk angering him and then she would still be required to suffer, albeit in a different way. Rolling the ball around on her tongue she detected little taste. Biting into it released a distinctly unsettling 'popping' sensation, which made her jump. The taste was not unpleasant, slightly salty and almost - dare she say it - semen-like.

'Salmon roe. I'll have you know it's an excellent source of omega-three fatty acids.' Marianna sucked in her cheeks and nodded. She wasn't quite sure how she felt about eating fish eggs, but was well aware that he was having fun with her. Popping a few more into his mouth and savouring them with the look of a seasoned connoisseur, he said, 'Would you like some more?'

She shook her head so quickly and forcefully she nearly dismantled her chignon. It wouldn't do to send pins flying everywhere. She pursed her lips and whispered, 'No, thank you, Sir.'

'I didn't think so.' Placing his hand over his chin thoughtfully, he studied Marianna carefully. She couldn't help another squirm and yet another squeak as her ass slid painfully on the plastic. Shaking his head in amusement he said, 'They are going to need some volunteers to serve the wine in a moment, so why don't you make yourself useful at the bar?' With that he turned his attention back to the naked girl's sex and continued his thorough exploration.

Marianna did not miss the fact that most of the men's chopsticks resided there and spent as much time pinching and nipping the folds of her labia as they did actually acquiring the delicate morsels of food. She was most grateful it was not her body plated up as the *plat du jour*.

Excusing herself from the table and her now somewhat gooey stool, she slowly made her way over to the bar. Her heels clicked loudly on the transparent floor and the sight of moving ripples of water and swimming fish unnerved her somewhat. Getting her balance and maintaining her eye-line above floor level, she made it without a stumble.

The bar was lined with row upon row of little ceramic flasks which were neatly stacked on the counter. A line of girls, mostly naked, had gathered in order to help serve the beverage. She guessed this must be sake, although she had never actually tried it herself. The sound of a door slamming abruptly caught her attention and a bald-headed man with a fist full of leather strips cleared his throat sharply.

'Right ladies, hands behind your backs because you won't be needing them.' His voice was deep and guttural and she, like the rest of the women assembled, obeyed instantly. He was a big, portly fellow and had a gold front tooth that wouldn't have looked out of place on a gangster. The tattoos that littered his forearms and disappeared into the rolled-up sleeves of his bleached white shirt screamed 'do not mess with me!' A team of helpers quickly followed in his wake, and she found herself pressed firmly into the counter by one of them. Her arms, now gracefully pressed behind her, were arranged fingers to elbow in a box-tie, and this was secured at the wrists in a figure of eight knot. They were yanked tight together and the result was that her breasts and shoulders were thrust forward in a rather painful manner.

'Right, you can all turn around now and 'ave your trays fitted. Face forward,' the large man bellowed, and she whipped her body around smartly. Her assistant stood directly in front of her and even though she had known he was behind her, seeing him in the flesh still made her jump. He was in his early twenties, either Spanish or Italian in origin, and obviously worked out. Muscles popped out of his shirt in all the right places and he had a sly look about him that spoke volumes. He did not have to work to get women; they fell in a heap at his feet. She wanted to run her fingers through the soft dark curls that rested on his collar bone, and taste the essence of man he was parading around him so boldly. She wouldn't, of course. For one thing, Mark would have his eye on her and it would be more than her life was worth to dishonour him in that fashion.

For another, she had her hands tied behind her and any leaning forward on her part would probably cause her to fall flat on her face.

Something cold pressed against her stomach. She'd been so lost in her daydream that she hadn't spotted the clear plastic tray he held in his hands. He was buckling it behind her and as his face leaned over her shoulder to check the fastening, he pressed his lips to her neck. She shivered and hoped to hell Mark's attention was still focused on his meal. His hands lingered on her waist and when his fingers had managed to complete the simple belt fastening, they slid up and down the contours of her spine.

'Stop that,' she whispered, but only half-heartedly, feeling her body tremble beneath his youthful fingers. In response to her command the man playfully nipped her buttock, making her jump.

'Stop horsing around!' bellowed gold-tooth to his staff, unimpressed with their slow progress. 'Fit the trays, gentlemen, and then gag the ladies if needs be.'

As her assistant stepped back Marianna wondered idly how they would manage to fix the trays upright. At the moment hers was hanging over her stomach and the inverted 'V' of her legs. Chains dangled from two points on its outermost rim and if she followed them towards the floor she could just make out the twin jaws of two metal clamps. How on earth would that work? Surely they weren't going to attempt to attach them to her dress? It would fall apart in a matter of seconds.

'Querida, you are going to look muy beautiful when you serve like this,' said the smiling young man, who had proved himself to be Spanish. Marianna raised her eyebrows. She failed to see how going about with a large plastic tray on her stomach was going to... and then realisation dawned. The clamps were for her nipples. That was how the tray would be anchored. One clamp for each nipple and the tray would rest at a forty-five degree angle to her body. Any weight placed upon the tray would be borne by her tender...

The first clamp came at her before she was ready for it and the tight metal jaws bit into her flesh with a bite that would have rivalled a bull mastiff's. Pain immediately lanced through her, only to be made worse by the fact that it was soon going to be repeated on the other side. Marianna held back the sob in her throat, but only just. A couple of seconds later the second clamp was headed in her direction. Marianna's first thought was to run but she quelled the reaction. Most people here would find a running, howling submissive highly entertaining and she didn't intend to grant them that pleasure or give them the opportunity to punish her. She wasn't entirely sure she would be able to contend with the extra pain coming her way, and when the second clamp bit she sucked in her breath on a sharp hiss.

'Ah, yes, that is a beautiful look. I was right.' The Spaniard winked at her and ran the tip of his index finger around her right nipple. Marianna whimpered. The tiny portion of nipple left poking out of the clamp was extremely sensitive and even his small caress was enough to make her gasp. 'A little sore, right? You wait till you start serving. It is going to be a very sweet agony, I think.' He caressed the underside of both breasts, whilst pretending to straighten out the tray. She moaned and her pussy clenched tightly. Pain hadn't dulled her arousal in the slightest, it had just reinforced it. 'Now, how many jugs would you like start with?' He gave her a questioning look and reached for one of the pretty ceramic jugs that had been delicately patterned with brush strokes, depicting Japanese characters of some sort.

'Can I start with one?' Marianna raised her eyebrows and gave her best pleading expression. She could barely contain the pain flowing through her body, a jug of sake would double it and two jugs... well, she might decide to run screaming after all and damn the consequences.

'Of course, but you are going to make things hard for yourself. Each waitress has to serve ten jugs. You take one at a time and you're going to be the slowest serving girl here.' He gave her an unimpressed look, but Marianna was beyond caring.

'I can walk quickly,' was all she said.

'Suit yourself,' he said with a dark frown. Marianna had managed to get a hold on the initial pain and her breath evened itself out, but she knew that would all change with the additional weight and braced herself accordingly.

The Spaniard held the jug above her tray several seconds longer than necessary. He was enjoying her discomfort. The marks of a sadist were already evident in his sharp, caramel eyes. They hungered for pain. The jug finally landed on her tray with an audible click and as much as she would have liked to disguise the look of immediate agony that appeared, it was impossible. Tears instantly sprang to her eyes and she witnessed his smug look of satisfaction, albeit through miserably blurred vision.

'If you break a jug I get to play with you for a bit as punishment. Would you like that?'

Marianna declined to reply and began walking towards her Master, but she was yanked back by his hand upon her arm. 'Uh, uh, uh,' he said, waggling his finger. He held up a red rubber ball-gag with a leather strap.

'But I haven't made a sound,' she protested, aghast at this unfair treatment.

'You just did.' He pressed the gag to her lips and she had no choice but to accept its presence. The large gag filled her mouth completely and the unpleasant taste of rubber infused her tongue. The leather strap bit into her lips and she knew it would not be long before she began to dribble.

'Get to work, querida. The gentlemen are waiting.' He slapped her backside, making the sake jug wobble precariously, and laughed as she winced at the sting in her raw ass cheeks. She didn't need to be told twice though, and her feet sped along the floor.

It took only a couple of steps before she realised the intensity of the pain would increase with each move she made. The tray wobbled and bounced with each click of her stilettos, thus causing the chains to pull painfully at her nipples. Although it would be only a short journey to return to Mark, it would undoubtedly be challenging. Concentrating on making her progress as smooth as possible she glided elegantly along the smooth plastic floor. The jug did not wobble again. There was no way her Spaniard was getting a freebie, gorgeous though he might be. As faint wisps of steam rose from the jug and teased her nostrils with their light scent she was taken aback for a second. Sake was served warm? Surely not?

'Ah, Marianna, here you are.' Mark smiled and, turning to face her, plucked the jug quickly from her tray. She moaned with relief as the painful weight was lifted. 'They had to gag you, hmm? We'll need to work on your pain tolerance then.'

If Marianna could have made a grimace at that statement she would have. Instead, a long sliver of drool chose that moment to drop with a splat upon her tray. The corner of Mark's mouth rose. He slowly picked the white linen napkin up off his trousers, shook it out and proceeded to dab at the corner of her mouth with it. He then very gently wiped her tray.

'You're going to need to try to carry at least two at a time. The weight hurts but the jarring motion of the tray as you walk will be the killer. He sucked a single finger into his mouth and circled a drop of saliva around her left nipple. The strain in Marianna's face as she took the caress was exquisite. 'A little bit sensitive, aren't we?' He raised both eyebrows in challenge and smiled. 'Off you go, Marianna. Come back and see me when you've completed your task.' He returned his attention to the meal and scooped up a line of noodles, tipping his head back to eat them.

Groaning silently in frustration she made her way back to the bar and her new challenge of carrying two jugs at a time.

Walking back to the table for the second time in her new role as a drinks waitress, Marianna politely positioned herself between two gentlemen as they ate their fill. Her nipples were on fire with the increased weight and her jaw strained around the gag in silent anguish. She had no choice but to await the gentlemen at their leisure, however, and stood in the correct submissive posture with her body erect but her head and eyes dipping slightly downwards. Even though her vision was somewhat reduced, she still had an excellent view of the girl and judging by the amount of naked flesh on display, she ascertained that the diners were over halfway through their meal. One of the men had even stretched over the table to begin sucking and lapping at the bared flesh of her stomach, in order to enjoy some of the trickier titbits and crumbs that had escaped from the main dish.

'Her skin has been coated with something, any idea what?' The gentleman in front of her, with dark hair greying around his temples, turned to his colleague in a questioning manner. He licked his lips in pleasure. The other gentleman, a little younger in years, stood up from his seat to complete his own taste test.

'Miso, I think,' he said, as his tongue worked its way around his mouth, savouring the flavour.

'That's it. Fish. There's a different taste to her legs. Salty.'

'Might be that someone's got carried away with the soy sauce.' They both chuckled at the remark. Her body was dribbling with the popular Japanese condiment and it ran down the sides of her body and legs in little rivulets. 'I think it's time for a drink. What say you, Stephen?'

The younger gentlemen nodded and both turned their attention to Marianna and the contents of her tray. Stephen frowned. 'She's clothed. Shouldn't she be naked?' He urged Marianna forward with his hand, which cupped under her buttock.

'This one isn't your run-of-the-mill submissive. She's the prized pet of Mark Matthews.' He smiled and shared a knowing wink with his friend. 'For all intents and purposes, though, she's mostly naked. We can still have a little fun with her.'

'Thank goodness for that,' came the dry reply, 'because she looks almost as delicious as our little Japanese lady, Dev.'

Dev had picked up his flask of sake and poured it into his friend's tumbler. 'Why don't you have a little drink? You can watch and learn.' Picking up his napkin he dabbed at his lips before twisting his body around to face Marianna. Studiously ignoring the choked spluttering of his colleague he directed her down with a single swipe of his finger and said, 'On your knees, slut.'

Marianna knew an order when she heard one. With a pained grimace she tried to lower herself to the floor as smoothly as possible. There was no easy way to complete her task with the tray anchored to her nipples, and as she set to one knee before the other there was an awful yank. Her left nipple felt as if it had been wrenched from her body. Looking down, expecting to see carnage or at the very least bloodshed, she was surprised to find everything intact, if not throbbing somewhat ferociously.

'You're a beauty, aren't you?' Dev put his finger under her chin and lifted her eyes to meet his. 'Only the best for Matthews, I expect.' He pulled the tag from the back of her dress and examined it. 'This dress probably cost more than my car,' he commented thoughtfully.

Stephen took a sip of sake and said, 'Don't tell me the green-eyed monster is upon you?'

'Hardly,' came the reply, 'she'd be one hell of a handful, don't you think?'

Stephen could only murmur his agreement.

Dev arched his head forward to suckle upon her temptingly erect nipple and the clamp that surrounded it. Warm flesh surrounded by hard, cold steel. It was a surprisingly pleasant taste, made even more pleasant by the fact that his little servant mewled pitifully at his touch. Reluctantly he drew his mouth away from the luscious peak and addressed her.

'Has Master not serviced you this evening, slave?'

Marianna had no choice but to nod and tell the truth. If she was caught lying a mere spanking would look very tame to the ingenious punishments Matthews could dish out, she suspected.

'Ah, so you're a greedy little slut who needs constant attention. I bet you're already dripping wet for me, isn't that right?' His mouth hovered over the other nipple, his warm breath caressing the tortured flesh and sending heat spiralling through her body. Marianna tried to shake her head, humiliated that she should be so aroused for a stranger she had only met several minutes ago, but he took hold of her chin in a vicious grip and forced her to look at him. 'It's easy enough to find out if you're lying, sweet slut, and I wouldn't want to be in your shoes,' he looked down at her expensive footwear, 'stylish though they may be, when Matthews finds out. So I'll ask you one more time. Are you ready to be finger-fucked, slut?'

Furious heat flooded Marianna's cheeks, but she nodded her acceptance of the fact. There was no question that he would check and, sure enough, his hands had already begun to snake up both her inner thighs. The dress melted in his fingertips and rose gracefully above her buttocks, settling there quite happily. The whole of her nether regions were now on display for public perusal. It was mortifying. She watched several pairs of eyes turn around to watch Dev at work and wondered how she would be able to endure this.

The first touch of his hand was a lot kinder than she expected. It was a silky-soft caress of her labia. She sucked in a painful breath. Immediately wondering if she'd be allowed to orgasm she then cursed herself, because the thought of climaxing in front of this crowd sent shivers of horror racing through her. The taxi driver had been bad enough, but there was always the chance he hadn't actually been watching them. In this room there would be no question that she would be a focal point for onlookers.

'Widen those legs for me,' he demanded, as a long finger searched for the entrance to her sex. She whimpered, but did exactly as he asked. The awkward shuffle of her legs caused the tray to drag painfully at her teats and blood to pound through her body. Marianna's frantic eyes scanned the room quickly, searching for Mark, hoping he would give her an escape route of some sort.

'That's right, search for Master,' said Dev, his voice dripping with sarcasm.

When she found him it was to find he was already occupied with a serving waitress of his own. He appeared to be quite busy with his hands and his eyes did not stray from the girl in front of him. Rescue was not on the cards.

Dev's finger sunk inside her easily. Her hips bucked of their own accord. 'She's wet, all right,' he confirmed. One finger swiftly became two and he used the pad of his thumb to roll her clitoris back and forth. Marianna choked around her gag. It had taken seconds for her body to become aroused to boiling point and the desire to explode for these people was frightening in its intensity.

'Does Matthews take your arse, princess?'

Marianna spluttered and was almost grateful for her gag. She decided to keep moaning her little moans and hope the question would go away.

'Shall we find out, Stephen?' Dev pulled his empty dinner plate towards him and ran his free fingers through the liquid which remained. It was a combination of grease and soy sauce for the most part and Marianna knew exactly where his hand would be headed. Her nipples ached terribly, her clit was close to bursting and the evil man in front of her was about to introduce food residue to her back passage. She directed another helpless glance at Mark, who was still completely immersed in doing something similar with his serving wench.

Dev drew his slimy fingers along the line of her butt cheeks. He took his time with the journey, but when they reached her sphincter they were still well coated with the grease he had dipped them in and he began to spread it about liberally. 'I'm waiting, Marianna. Does he fuck you here?' His finger popped into her backside and she shot forward unthinkingly, cursing her own stupidity as the tray she was wearing followed suit. The question that she didn't want to answer needed to be addressed. She shook her head to get the message across. Dev looked at her incredulously as her words sank in. He grabbed her chin and eyeballed her. 'Are you telling me Matthews has never taken your ass?' Marianna shook her head miserably, embarrassed at the confession. Now they would all know she was a new addition to his fleet of women.

Dev's eyebrows managed to float back down to earth as he considered that little snippet of information. His finger worked its way inside her slowly. It had been so long since she'd had anal sex that the penetration felt quite alien to her. Working his way deeper and deeper he watched as her desire-drugged eyes fluttered open and shut.

'You like this, don't you?'

She nodded helplessly. She didn't merely like it, she loved it. Tilting her head to one side in breathless anticipation she gave a loud moan as he began to play with her, thumb on her clit, finger in her backside. Seventh heaven did not begin to describe the sensations floating through her. The brutal ache in her nipples was long forgotten as he worked his magic. Her hips shuddered from side to side, the tray shook and the tight muscles of her stomach were vividly outlined as her body tensed under his onslaught.

'Would you like to come for me?'

Marianna had to think for a minute. She was almost lost to reality, caught in a thick haze that threatened to overwhelm her. Her tormentor was aware of the thrall he held her in. As his tongue snaked out again and began to tease the clamped tips of her nipples, the spectacular bolt of pleasure and pain that accompanied it was nearly her undoing.

'Do you want to come, slut, in front of all these people?'

Her eyes flew open to acknowledge his question and she was about to nod when her eyes caught Mark's, who now appeared to be very interested in her serving skills. She wanted this, but she wasn't at all sure she could go through with it, not with all these eyes upon her. A quick scan of the room told her she was attracting the lion's share of attention. Her head was torn in indecision. She wasn't sure if it would shake or nod, or plead for mercy to have the decision made for her.

'I'm waiting. Do you want this?' His fingers had her gurgling in breathless excitement, but then her eyes caught Mark's again and they looked dark and thunderous. Oh no, what had she done now?

'I'll take that as a "yes",' Dev murmured, and she shook her head in panic.

'No?' He threw his head back and laughed as the fingers of his left hand worked furiously. The fingers of his right threaded through the pins at the nape of her neck and with a sweep of his hand he tore her neat chignon to pieces. He gripped a handful of hair and pulled it sharply downwards, so his head hovered above hers. He whispered dangerously, 'Whatever made you think you had a choice?' With that her body tumbled into the dark but joyful abyss of pleasure and the many eyes of the room devoured her.

When Dev had finally finished with her she was sent back to the bar with her dress still up around her waist. That wasn't the worst of it by far. Two empty sake bottles and two heavy plates rested upon her tray and she thought her nipples might explode under the pressure. She was openly crying and her feet couldn't move fast enough. Add to that the two sets of chopsticks that were protruding from her ass and Marianna was beginning to wish she had never laid eyes upon Mark Matthews.

The Spaniard had obviously seen it all before. He pulled the chopsticks out with an elegant flourish and proceeded to unload her tray for her, agonisingly slowly. 'You had much fun out there, bonita, si? I saw you playing with the rich boys. They all have small cocks.' He snorted as if to emphasize the fact. 'You need a big man, like me, si?'

Marianna nodded politely. It wasn't as if she could smile. Right now the only man she needed was Mark. She had been left deep in a pot of very hot water, and it was sink or swim time. For some reason he felt the need to test her. She'd show him. These people would not get the better of her.

'How many jugs you want this time, senorita? Two again?' Marianna shook her head. 'Three? Four?' She shook her head. 'All of them?' He wore a look of awe. She gave him a nod. There was no way she was doing another three trips if she had to endure more men like Dev and Stephen. She'd make it one. Tears would be a small price to pay.

The Hot Walker

Jenny had no idea what time it was, but the blackness surrounding her would indicate it was somewhere in the small hours of the morning. She had thought sleep would overtake her almost instantly when she hit the straw floor of her cell, but that hadn't been the case. Although her eyes had been quick to close nearly as soon as the wooden door slammed shut, she had only been able to nap fitfully. That was solely down to the device which had no concept of night or day and plagued her incessantly with its ridiculously irregular timetable. Sometimes the build-up would be rapid and she would be allowed a half hour of peace. Other times the machines would work their magic in an excruciatingly slow fashion before they stopped just shy of the main event, and she would only just manage to get her heaving gasps of breath under control before the antics repeated themselves.

Things proceeded to get worse the longer the night drew on. Being tied up tightly had taken its toll upon her limbs and they ached bitterly for freedom. Her jaw protested in a similar fashion from the ball-gag. Pussy, rectum, clit, nipples, skin, and eyes - everything was beginning to hurt, itch, ache, rub or burn. She was hungry, thirsty, tired, grumpy and mad, but little good did it do her. Tonight had brought her to an all-time low at Albrecht and it didn't look like it was going to improve any time soon.

Rocking back and forth like a seesaw she tried to ease some of the discomfort created by her distorted body. It provided momentary relief and was of little benefit, making the ache all the more potent when she returned to her stomach. Tears of frustration tracked down her cheeks and burned like acid down her stretched lips, which were now chapped due to the lack of their staple diet of lip gloss. She wished someone would burst through the door and knock her unconscious, for that was about the only thing which would ease her suffering right now.

A few minutes after the thought had crossed her mind Jenny thought she heard a rustle of hay. She was probably going crazy and had made the noise herself. Her eyes had been slipping restlessly into sleep before being wrenched open by the attentions of her bodysuit, but she could have sworn the noise came from outside her stall. It was difficult to hear accurately through the latex hood and she tried desperately to still her body and strain her ears, to see if the noise repeated itself. Nothing but silence permeated the air around her, and after several seconds of inactivity she relaxed as much as she was able and began to try her seesaw move again. She wanted to flip over on her side, but it was going to be a near impossible manoeuvre, trussed as she was.

'You have a fairy godmother, angel.'

Jenny almost jumped out of her skin. The voice was elegant and spoke in perfect, lilting English, and although there was a faint trace of some other origin in the accent, it was cleverly disguised. She must be dreaming again. She began to wonder if they'd put hallucinogens in her feed...

'You're not dreaming.' The tip of a booted foot lifted her face and Jenny saw the blurry outline of a woman, dressed from head to toe in black latex, much like herself. 'I'm on a mission of mercy; apparently you have friends in high places,' came the sultry whisper. She moved to the far wall and dragged one of the small tubes over to Jenny's face, feeding it slowly through the small hole in her gag. 'Drink your fill and nod when you're done. There's no rush. Thankfully there are no cameras in here.'

The woman leant against the wall and it was clear by the sleek silhouette of her body that she took good care of herself. Why was everybody at Albrecht so damned slim? It was another gripe to add to an already very lengthy list.

Jenny didn't waste any time questioning her good fortune, if it could be called that. Thirst had been at the top of her list of woes and as soon as the water pipe entered her mouth she began to suckle at it eagerly. There was little point trying to examine her fairy godmother in the darkness, so she greedily drank her fill and awaited her opponent's next move. She didn't have to wait long.

'I can't stay. If they catch me in here I'll be of little use to you and very little use to myself once they get their hands on me. Disobedience, as you have gathered, is punished rather harshly inside these walls. So I'm here to give you one option and one option only. Would you like a couple of sedatives that will knock you out for the next few hours? Nod if the answer's yes.'

Jenny's immediate nod clearly came as no surprise. 'OK. They come in tablet form, and thankfully they're just about small enough to fit through the hole in your gag. I'm going to take the tube out now, pop the tablets in and then feed them back through with the hose.' The woman was as good as her word and two tiny tablets fell onto the back of her tongue, where they were promptly swallowed. She washed them down with plenty of water.

'I'm sorry I can't untie you, but that's more than my life's worth,' she whispered. 'This should at least offer you some relief. If you want my advice, you'd do well not to anger Kyle. He's got a reputation around these parts that leans towards the mean and nasty. Why you didn't pick Matthews is a question that will continue to bug me for some time. Unfortunately you won't be able to tell me. Kyle likes his ponies mute at all times and will ensure you are constantly gagged. He will also work you so hard you'll come into these stables each night and flop down in exhaustion. The man has something to prove and he's intending to use you in order to do so.'

Jenny groaned. The device had started up again inside her and a solid wall of miserable depression came crashing down all around her. There was no way she could suffer this for another whole day. As far as torture went, there was no other pain like it.

'You'll be asleep in ten. Keep your chin up.' The woman laughed softly at her own joke. 'Remember my warning. I'm not here to save you. Behave around Kyle or face the consequences.'

With that she departed as silently as she had come and Jenny's mangled body had to suffer and tremble through yet another round of the device before sleep finally overtook her and her mind collapsed into oblivion.

When Kyle entered the stall the next morning he was incensed to find his new trainee was snoring soundly. The alarm had been blaring off for several minutes, the noise was deafening, and yet here was his new charge sleeping like a baby. She should have been awake all night. She should have been in tears, begging for his mercy. She should have been hungry, thirsty, exhausted, with her body tied up in miserable cramping knots. His mood instantly soured and he clenched his jaw in annoyance. Using the tip of his boot to roll her over he was rewarded with first one groggy blue eye blinking through the glue of sleep, before its twin joined suit.

'Good morning, princess. Hope you had a fun night without me?' His tone of voice was not in the least bit sincere. 'Time to get your sleepy butt out of bed and have it spanked a beautiful shade of ruby red. I think we'll give Daniel the morning off because I have a feeling he's a little bit soft on you. I will not be.' When Petal's eyes widened in horror he felt slightly better. Unfastening the ropes that held her tight he devoured her face as pain filled it. Her circulation was going to take a little while to return, and nothing would coordinate very well within her body until it did.

'Right, that's enough dallying. We're already late so you'd better get a move on. His large hand connected with a satisfying crack upon her backside to get the proceedings started, and she made a reasonable effort to move forward. Another smack and she stumbled a little faster, her coordination all over the place, and with the third heavy-handed spank she was almost crawling. He began to feel a little better. He had a morning of activities planned that would bring Joan of Arc to her knees, and unfortunately for Jenny, that was how she was starting her day. How she would end it was anybody's guess, but it wouldn't be pretty.

Jenny looked longingly at the sticky mass of gloopy porridge in her trough. It taunted her. Her gagged mouth could do nothing but salivate at the prospect of food, no matter how unappealing. Grumbling in protest, her stomach also made its feelings known. But it mattered little; even had she not been gagged there would have been no possibility of her eating anything.

Kyle had set about her chastisement almost as soon as she was secured in the stocks and he showed plenty of enthusiasm for the task. He administered several stinging blows with a heavy leather flogger, and the latex of her suit provided little protection against the onslaught of his hand. Her backside had not recovered from yesterday's bedroom routine and it took no more than ten swats before her bottom was wiggling vigorously of its own accord. But although Kyle's spanking was intense, it wasn't anything she hadn't managed to cope with before. He could do his worst.

She had decided upon awaking that no one was going to get a single tear out of her today and she meant to keep to her word. Her tears were going to become a precious commodity. She would make sure they were rarer than six carat diamonds. Mark's words were coming back to haunt her and they echoed painfully in her head.

'Never let them see you cry. No matter what they do, refuse to let them have your tears. That is all you have left here and some days, that might be all that keeps you sane.'

As the blows continued to wallop into her ass she spluttered around the ball-gag and did her best to tense her body in order to lessen the sting. She could be thankful for one small mercy; while the other ponies were getting a good scrub down with the evil smelling soap, she had been left alone to wallow in the sweaty heat of her latex suit. Whilst she would have happily committed murder for a bath, she was not at all disappointed to miss the harsh rubbing down of the grooms as they set about making sure each pony-girl was squeaky clean - both externally and internally.

Listening to the squeals and gasps of her fellow cohorts as their grooms' hands dipped anywhere and everywhere, Jenny was not going to become jealous of those noises. Fine, she was horribly jealous and each tiny squeak served to remind her of her wretched predicament. These were ponies who stood a chance at an orgasm, when she was guaranteed a day of misery. As if to confirm the fact her dildos began inflating simultaneously and blew themselves up to their biggest diameter yet. Her eyes began to water as her body felt like someone was trying to insert a water melon into her back passage. Oh Lord, she might have to break the tears promise and after only ten seconds of having made it. Then the inflation suddenly stopped, and for that Jenny was almost pathetically grateful. It was bearable. The tears would hold.

Kyle finally remembered that she hadn't had any breakfast and brought the feeding tube around, slotting it into her gag. He didn't stay to watch, so eager was he to return to the spanking. Jenny had no option but to guzzle the fluid down her throat as quickly as possible, while he continued to set her ass on fire. It was almost comically difficult. Like trying to pat your head and rub your stomach at the same time. She found herself hiccupping, gulping, spluttering and gasping as the flavourless fluid sloshed around in her mouth. Trying to tense her body and swallow at the same time was nearly impossible.

When the spanking finished and Mr A did his rounds, he pulled out the feeding tube for her and directed her to drink some water from the grey tube beside her. 'You'll be needing lots of fluids inside you today; I hear you have quite an exercise schedule to complete,' he said in an amused tone, before slapping her rump and moving on towards the next pony. Jenny did not find his words comforting.

When the other ponies began filtering out of the stable she was led away with them. To be fair, Kyle practically had to drag her due to the dildo's putting her body ridiculously off balance. They had begun the familiar vibrate and pump pattern, the breast massager and clit stimulator had also come into play and Jenny wondered if she had shelved her tears too quickly. How many hours did she have left to endure this kind of torment? Her body was hypersensitive and as she thought the words electrical current began to run down the wires that enveloped her skin, sending shivers of pleasure through her. She felt like a dog in heat. Given half a chance she would have happily rubbed herself upon the nearest tree until she obtained some kind of relief, and she wouldn't have given a toss if an entire football team had sat around her to watch. She was in agony and her anguish was inescapable.

She barely noticed when they left the barn and the cool morning air hit her face; her body was too busy feeding upon the pleasure that the suit was generously dishing out. Her breasts felt tender and swollen, her nether regions felt like she'd been sitting on a horse for the past twenty-four hours and her jaw was going to spontaneously combust if someone didn't take her gag out soon, which according to all accounts, was extremely unlikely to happen. Oh, how many days had she been here now? Lost and alone with her woebegone thoughts, Jenny could already feel her mind slipping away into the distant lands of mush. Could these people really turn her into a human pony? Mute, restrained and spanked on a regular basis, she had the horrible suspicion that they stood a fighting chance.

She and the novices were being guided towards one of Albrecht's exercise yards. The first thing she noticed was that there were actual horses, or bio-equines as she'd heard them called, in the yard. Several hot-walkers were stationed on the grass and the horses were already being led out to them. While Kyle directed her towards the walker at the rear of the yard, she saw that two stallions had already been hitched up and were awaiting their morning trot. There were a couple of spaces left. A chestnut and a beautiful bay were snickering and snorting with glee to the right of her, while pawing at the ground with their hooves. Good for them, Jenny thought rather sourly, wondering if they'd had a morning spanking before they were led out of the stalls. She suspected not, and she also suspected they managed to dine on a far better breakfast than the pony-girls had been allowed. This was what her life had become now, reduced to a lower status than that of an animal. The horses probably got to graze all afternoon. That would not be a luxury she could look forward to. Her lot would be a fun session in the training room with Mistress Lupine and the multi-coloured plastic stalagmites.

She wondered, for a moment, what exactly they were doing out here. Was this some kind of 'watch and learn' session, where they'd be expected to copy the actions of the horses afterward? She wasn't sure exactly what use it would be, as they couldn't really be expected to replicate the exact gait of a four legged animal. Kyle chose that moment to yank her bridal forward and as he marched her towards one of the waiting arms that had yet to be occupied, she quickly realised this was not about to be a fun morning watching from the side-lines. They expected her to exercise with the horses! Another pony-girl was led across to the final empty arm of the walker and they were both hitched up to the machine by their bridles.

It took Jenny a moment to comprehend exactly what was about to happen. She was facing a horse's butt, there was another horse behind her and she would be expected to trot around in a circle with them. They must be joking, she thought in horror, but as the hot walker purred noisily into life and the arm began to pull at her bridle, there was no escaping her predicament. She was being exercised exactly like livestock.

'Raise those hooves nice and high,' came Kyle's voice from behind her. 'I want to see some enthusiastic trotting this morning. If I see those knees drooping I've got a nice surprise waiting for you.'

Jenny suspected it would be anything but, and speaking of butt's, hers prickled in the aftermath of the morning spank. She was already hot and sweaty after the brisk trot outside and they hadn't even started moving yet. If the large fly swatter Kyle held in his hand was any indication, things were going to get a whole lot worse before they got better.

As the arms of the motor began to turn she stared helplessly to the front, and as her bridle yanked her forward, giving her no option but to move, she could barely comprehend what was happening to her. She was being exercised and trained exactly like the horses would be on her father's estate. She would be forced to walk around in a circle until someone saw fit to stop the machine. As her suit began a new frontal attack, with the clitoral stimulator and thrusting dildo's being brought into play, Jenny mewled her frustration through the unforgiving confines of her gag. She pleaded with her eyes, but Kyle's were hard and unforgiving and they did not connect with hers. The man might be drool-drippingly gorgeous but he did not have an ounce of compassion in his body. Stumbling forward, as her body went into orgasm alert mode, his voice rang through the air unkindly.

'Let's get the party started, P. Knee's high in the air and hooves up in a begging position beside those tits. Head up, back straight and feet shoulder-width apart. I want to see a nice gait and I'll be providing some additional encouragement if I don't get it. I said hooves up, P!' His oversized fly swatter took aim at her backside and Jenny nearly ended up hanging off the arm of the walker as she tried to escape the blistering swipe. She propped her hoof mitts up in the air as told and began to lift her knees as high as she could, thankful that the pace of the walker wasn't too fast. It was hard enough just keeping her balance in the preposterous boots; having her heavy plastic hooves dangling up in the air did not help matters.

She watched as Kyle stroked the horse in front of her. He clearly had an affinity for horses that he did not share with the girls. The trainee across from her chose that moment to utter a loud squawk as he lashed out at her. 'Push those tits out, Dew Drop, there's a reason your arms are tied behind you.' The girl hastened to obey.

As the pony-girls continued trotting around their endless circle, Kyle became a little more unpredictable and considerably more spiteful with his blows. A stumble was rewarded with a smack to the back of the upper thighs, knees dropping below waist height earned a swipe across one or both breasts and any errors in regards to posture would provoke one between the legs. Jenny's ass might have been grateful for the respite, but the rest of her body sure as hell wasn't.

'Let me see those hooves paw at the air,' Kyle shouted as his swatter found her rear once more. 'Prance for me, princess. Keep those knees high, and your fore hooves higher.'

Jenny didn't manage to catch the command. Her body was at maximum capacity for pleasure, tightening in anticipation of the mother of all orgasms, when her clit was miserably pinched with a ferocity that took her breath away. She stumbled forward and the hot walker dragged her around by the tips of her boots for a quarter of a circle, her body straining painfully as it was yanked forward by the leading arm. Whilst the walker was relatively forgiving as soon as she had managed to regain her balance, Kyle was not. He sent short, nasty shocks through both of her dildos which caused her to plummet forward once more, but she learnt to recover quickly. The strain of compressing her windpipe against her collar wasn't pleasant, however.

'Hooves in the air, Petal, both sets or I'll work my way through the nastier controls on your suit, *capiche?*' He made his point clear by demonstrating the shock feature of the entire suit, all at once. Jenny gurgled and hit the ground, knees first. Bouncing back up she managed to get to her feet but it was nothing short of luck. Her whole body felt limp, dazed and disorientated. Pawing madly at the air with her hooves, she brought up her knees as high as she could in order to prevent another misdemeanour on her part and the dreaded punishment that would ensue. 'Now that's what I'm talking about, Petal. Much better movement. Keep that up.'

It didn't take long for the ground to become churned and slippery as the horses' heavy hoofs cut up the grass beneath them. Finding herself slithering about on the metal horseshoes, it took all her concentration to keep herself upright and moving forward. When her suit cut off abruptly in the middle of yet another almost-orgasm, she nearly strangled herself with a perilous skid of her hooves and the gurgling, choking sounds she emitted were not pretty as she clung to her balance for dear life.

'A baby hippo at her first ever ballet class would have more grace than your newbie, Levison.'

Kyle had just delivered a rather vicious swat to Petal's inner thigh and the sarcastic comment that came from directly behind his ear made him jump, nearly throwing him off balance. The laugh that followed set his teeth on edge.

'Katrina. Do you have to creep up on people like that?' Kyle cracked his neck and turned to face her, his hands on his hips. 'And aren't you supposed to be on vacation? Can't stay away, huh?'

Ignoring his comment she gave him a splendidly vicious, blinding smile. The only reason she had entered the stables this morning was to rattle his chain. She'd be back home with her feet up in approximately an hour's time, but he didn't need to know that.

'The odds of you getting her to wear the black are about three hundred to one in the stable stakes,' she purred. 'It's laughable that she's the only trainee who hasn't managed to earn her yellow yet, and that's by far the easiest colour to manage. Judging by the enthusiasm in her brisk trot she'll do well to make it to the green.' Katrina compressed her glossy red lips together and gave him a playful look. 'Matthews was the favourite. Why on earth she picked you is beyond me. You're untried, wild, lack experience and have a short attention span. I didn't realise you have yet to prove yourself. You've not managed to qualify even one of your trainees for the coral, yet alone the black collar. Did you know the owner was unaware of your previous history at Albrecht? Now he's had a chance to look through your stats, I've heard he's reconsidering giving the position back to Matthews, to ensure Petal's success.' She watched Kyle's face drop in horror.

Katrina nodded to herself with quiet satisfaction. She had successfully managed to bury the knife deep into what little brain matter Levison possessed. By the looks of him, the knife had come away bloodied. He was all ego. Now faced with the seeds of doubt, liberally scattered all over the ground, he would endeavour to make sure they did not take root, and if Katrina was not much mistaken, he would do that by taking out his frustrations on Miss Redcliff. He was predictable, if nothing else. After her taunts he would put Petal through hell and back to ensure she wore the black in record time, and wouldn't that be just peachy? The filly known as 'P' would be gracing her dungeon before the day was out, Katrina was sure of it. The shame of the matter was that she would not be there to witness it.

Information Overload

The phone's shrill tone drilled a hole inside Mark's head the size of the Grand Canyon, made even worse because it was one of the more ridiculous hours of the morning. He rolled over on his king-sized divan, let his hand search about groggily for the phone and managed, by some amazing piece of luck to hit the right button to accept the call.

'Who the hell is this?' His mouth was bone dry, the after-effects of alcohol no doubt, and he felt a moment of fierce anger. For the first time in ages he had been exhausted enough to sleep soundly. Being rudely awakened from such a rare slumber was not going to induce any friendly conversation on his part.

'Mr Matthews?' The guy on the other end of the phone did not sound at all sure of himself after his abrupt greeting. 'Err, maybe I should ring back later?'

Mark did not give him the chance to put the phone down. 'Now you've successfully woken me up I suggest you get on with the purpose of your call,' he said in a deceptively calm tone that had 'danger' stamped all over it. 'If I find out you're wasting my time I will make it my mission in life to ensure that your life is as miserable as I can possibly make it for the foreseeable future. So talk. Now.'

'Yes Sir. Err, you did say to call you as soon as I found out anything. Immediately, you said.'

'Khalil.' Mark sighed. He hadn't recognised the man's voice through his sleep-filled haze. 'Next time I say "anytime" that does not include the hours between midnight and five a.m.,' he clarified, 'but seeing as you're on the line and I'm awake, you might as well fill me in.'

'Well, I've managed to find out quite a bit. Where should I begin?' Khalil huffed out a breath of air as he considered his question.

'At the beginning?' Mark's answering tone was curt with a touch of sarcasm. Khalil got the message.

'Surprisingly enough, your voice recording was pretty easy to match. Ever heard of a Michael James Geoffrey Redcliff? He's an oil tycoon. Made his money...'

Khalil continued to bring him up to date on the finer points of Mr Redcliff's illustrious career path, but Mark was too stunned at that little snippet of information to take anything more in. Not that it mattered; he was well aware of the way Redcliff had made his fortune. Could this be true? Not only was the man the owner of Albrecht stables, but he had sent his only daughter there to be trained and disciplined as a sex slave? He'd suspected it was Redcliff all along, but to have it confirmed was even more shocking than the initial suspicion. The man was sick. What was this all about - money? If she earned the black she'd be worth a fortune and then he could sell her, but goddamn, even so. He began to pay attention to the conversation once more, but his brain cells were working overtime.

Khalil had got him bra and panty sizes, just as he'd asked, as well as dress and shoe size. He'd also managed to find out a brief life history, details of her education, travel, social life, friends, regular pastimes and fitness regime - or lack thereof. Disappointingly, she did not appear to engage in lesbian sex, but on the plus side she did not spend her weekends in front of the TV. Unfortunately, what she normally did on a Saturday night was a whole lot more unpalatable. He could understand why daddy dearest had become rather annoyed, but the fallout was nothing short of nuclear. Did Redcliff intend to wash his hands of her entirely?

That gave Mark pause for thought. He'd remembered her tears in the surgery as she'd been given over to Levison. At the time he'd thought it was because she had finally come to terms with her predicament. That hadn't been the case at all, had it? She recognised the voice over the loudspeaker; the voice of her father, casually endorsing her life sentence in a world of debauched sexual slavery without a shred of emotion. The poor girl wouldn't have to be overly bright to deduce that all hope of rescue would most probably die with that revelation. Redcliff had the money and resources to bury nearly anyone who stood in his way. Mark's gut clenched at the pain he knew she would be suffering. She would be feeling betrayed and abandoned. She was a strong little brat, but a blow like that would knock her sideways, and being paired with Kyle was a disaster waiting to happen. Having successfully managed to distract himself yet again he snapped to attention when he heard Khalil mention Kyle's name.

'Kyle's history is pretty ugly, I'm afraid. You sure you want to hear this?'

'Oh, I'm sure,' said Mark in a dangerously quiet tone, and decided that if it was anything really unpleasant he was going to scrape out Kyle's innards with a spoon - preferably while he was still alive, but dead was almost as good - stuff him with fluff and mount him on his mantelpiece.

'Levison has been interviewed by the police in connection with more than one crime towards the female sex. The crimes were committed in the US, which might explain his fondness for the UK at the moment. I believe the Feds haven't finished with him yet. He messed up a couple of females pretty badly, and whilst his stand is that they enjoyed that kind of thing, their take on the matter is somewhat different. Both girls signed disclaimers to his "edge play" treatment, but both claim the documents were signed under duress.'

'Are you able to access pictures of what he did?' Mark had his face in his hands and his eyes were closed in disbelief. This was worse, much worse than he'd been anticipating. Sadists were allowed at Albrecht, of course, but they had to know when to draw the line. This idiot clearly didn't. How the hell had he slipped through the net? There should have been checks run on the man, and lots of them, before his foot could even cross the threshold. CRB checks, references, previous training details... something didn't add up.

'Kyle Levison isn't his real name, is it?' Mark tasted the familiar burn of bile in his throat. Jennifer Redcliff was giving him an unwanted addition to antacids, dammit.

So, he had a problem on his hands. A girl had been abducted against her will and given to someone who would immensely enjoy every ounce of torment he could wring out of her. He would not have his trainee's best interests at heart. He would be looking out for himself and his pleasure. Jennifer Redcliff was a firecracker. All she needed to do was light the touch paper and Kyle would go off with a bang. There would be no second chances. If she got injured he'd simply spin some fanciful story. The man appeared to be rather good at it.

'No, we haven't managed to get access to the pictures, although we're still trying. As to your second question, you are indeed correct. His real name is James Miller. He's in the UK with fake documents.' Khalil clucked his tongue on the line, disapprovingly.

Mark wanted to do much more than the odd spot of tongue clucking, but held himself in check. There would be plenty of time for that later. 'So, that means if we could get our hands on him outside the security of Albrecht we could have him deported,' he said thoughtfully.

'Good luck with that,' said Khalil. 'He has a digs on the compound and rarely leaves the base.'

'Great,' said Mark darkly. 'Well, my thanks to you, Khalil. You've given me plenty to think about. Keep on the case and see what else you can dig up.'

'Oh, before you hang up there's one more thing you should know.'

'Go on,' said Mark, thinking that whatever Khalil had held in reserve till the end couldn't trump the information he'd just divulged about Kyle.

'Michael Redcliff isn't Miss Redcliff's biological father.'

Cleaning Duty

Jenny was not upset when the session upon the hot walker abruptly ended. Kyle was unpleasantly rough as her bridle was unfastened and when he dragged her forward by her reins, he used so much force she thought she'd been fired from a catapult. It was clear that the blonde lady was up to no good, again. Unfortunately, Jenny hadn't been able to catch a word of the conversation; her hood and the sound of plodding hooves had seen to that. One thing was for certain, though, the lady looked like she had a mean streak in her at least a mile wide and it could easily rival her new trainer's...

Marching her forward with his lethally long strides, Jenny had to trot three steps to keep up with his one. Even though they were now on grass, her balance did not improve due to the awful pace he was setting. No quarter was to be given for her 'trainee' status, it appeared. She was breathing heavily in seconds, having not yet recovered from the light exercise session of the hot walker, and when Jenny finally spied her Louis Vuitton luggage and a small cart in the distance, she wanted to stamp her hooves in protest. Surely they were not going to go through this farce again? There was no way she would be able to pull around her eight suitcases without giving herself a hernia the size of a beach ball.

'Right, you've had your warm-up, now it's time for you to get down to the main event. You need to earn your collar. You're the only trainee who hasn't managed to achieve her yellow collar and I am not going to look like a second-rate trainer while you drag your heels around. Get your butt into that cart and get ready to pull for all you're worth, P.' Kyle gave her already smarting backside an extremely good wallop with the flat of his hand and wasted no time in securing her to the one lonely cart which appeared stranded on the practice field.

When the arms of the sulky were threaded through her corset, the strain of the cart was almost crippling. Her body already felt sluggish, tired and weary beyond belief, so there was little chance she would be able to accomplish the same task that had proved impossible on a freshly rested body just a couple of days ago.

'Pull!' Kyle was standing in front of her brandishing a mean-looking, whippet-thin crop. Jenny's bruised body, still smarting from the flogger, shuddered at the thought of what the whip might do. Her feet stumbled for purchase on the dry earth and she sunk her heels in with purposeful intent. How hard could this be? 'If I have to say move again, P, your ass will regret it.'

Jenny would have liked to mention that he had not actually said 'move' the first time, but getting that little snippet past the gag would be nigh on impossible, not to mention stupid. Kyle lacked a sense of humour gene. He certainly made up for it with the mean and nasty gene, which was more than a little disconcerting. She wondered if he was conscienceless enough to rival her father. Suspecting she did not want to delve into that thought too deeply, she braced herself to take the strain of eight impressively-sized leather luggage cases.

After contorting and straining her body into every position imaginable in order to get enough traction to enable her to pull her cart forward, Jenny was coming to terms with the idea that the thick, white, uncomfortably high collar she wore might be hers for life. Straining this way and that with all her might, the thing would not budge an inch. She even grunted under the effort of trying to move the unwilling beast behind her, and she had been carefully taught that ladies did not grunt. Ever. The whip connected with her backside and she howled.

'Pull!' Kyle was visibly agitated after his conversation with Katrina and it appeared Jenny's backside was going to provide the means of lessening his frustrations with the world. The spitefully hard blows of the crop should have burned like fire into her tenderised skin, but the latex suit had woken up again and was doing its thing. The dildos were quickly expanding, and this time she felt no pain as both channels were dilated, just a hot rush of pleasure and sticky fluid settling at the base of her crotch. How humiliating. Her body obviously loved this kind of treatment.

The blows, which Kyle was trying to permanently embed into her ass, were only serving to excite her further. As the ovals of plastic grew they began thrusting with renewed vigour. It was almost as if they knew the heightened state of arousal her body had now achieved. The stimulator buzzed with a cruel pace that could have shaken her eyes out of her head, whilst the wires all around her pulsed with a delicate whirr of electricity. Her body was on the cusp of orgasm in less than thirty seconds. The pain of the crop had fuelled it in both intensity and speed and she surged over into the land of pleasure with a fierce thrust of duelling dildos, burying themselves deep. She screamed out her pleasure, the sound actually managing to make itself heard around the gag before the suit realised what was happening and put a stop to the proceedings. The stopping mechanism was brutal. Both her breasts were squeezed in a vice-like grip and her nipples were pinched excruciating tightly and pulled sharply forward. A short sharp shock ran all the way through her body and her clit was nipped in such a way that tears rolled helplessly down her eyes. So much for her promise. The pain brought her to her knees but her mind rejoiced. She might have received only the tiniest kiss of pleasure, one that had barely surfaced before it had been savagely snuffed out - but it was, she felt, a victory of sorts.

Kyle, of course, didn't see things in the same light. He came at her backside with the crop as if it was a machete and he was trying to scythe down half of the Amazon jungle. Unfortunately for him his actions backfired miserably. The acute pain of the continued blows overrode all of Jenny's brain circuits and she tumbled quickly into another short sharp climax. Her latex-clad knees buried themselves in the grass below her and she choked mindlessly around her gag. The suit didn't know what to make of it, having stopped an orgasm only seconds before, so it remained eerily silent and still while it tried to work out what to do next.

'You good-for-nothing, worthless piece of horseflesh,' Kyle yelled as he slammed the riding crop against the sulky, which promptly broke the tip off. Throwing it down in disgust he turned to face the source of his displeasure and growled at her. His predicament was somewhat similar to the suit's, because he didn't know what to do with his trainee either. She seemed to enjoy pain, which was going to anger him no-end and put a stop to most of his fun, at least for the time being, until he discovered a way to work around the problem. For now, he guessed the best thing to do would be to get her moving around the track with her cart, which would hopefully restore plenty of misery and despair back upon her face.

Throwing two of her heavy cases to the ground he barked, 'Move!' She went nowhere, though he could tell she was putting her back into it and trying her hardest to get the thing started. He threw another suitcase on the grass and yet another before the wheels started rolling underneath her. They didn't roll particularly fast and she didn't keep a straight line. Her balance was off and she was breathing hard through her gag in a matter of seconds. Kyle was pissed. Why on earth had he bid for her? She was currently the worst performing pony-girl in the stables. Yelling directly into her eardrum and smacking or pinching her ass cheeks, he managed to get her to complete a single circuit of the track before she collapsed in exhaustion.

Kyle was furious and for several reasons. One, he'd have to get special dispensation to get rid of some of her suitcases. There was no way in hell the girl would ever manage to lug eight of them around. Two, she'd had an unauthorised orgasm and he rarely allowed his ponies pleasure unless they had greatly pleased him - and she most definitely had not. Three, he couldn't punish her by walloping her backside into the next century because she seemed to enjoy that kind of thing. And four, now he had to figure out a way to punish her that didn't involve his favourite subject - pain.

Jenny had a few moments of perverse pleasure in managing to succeed where all the other girls had failed. Now she had achieved one orgasm in the suit she was sure she could chase another one, given the right incentive. Kyle seemed intent on parading her around the perimeter of Albrecht stables, as if showing off some new and wondrous prize, but unfortunately he seemed to have lost his taste for revenge. Typical. Even the sadists were out to screw her, and whilst on the subject of screwing... Jenny needed sex. She needed dirty, rough, messy, nasty sex. The suit, having been in a quandary for a few minutes, had taken the maximum half an hour break before it revved up its engines for a rerun. Within seconds of its renewed attack she was hyper-aroused and her previous orgasm seemed like a distant memory. Her movements, as she was led along by her bridle, were stiff. She was sore in all the wrong places and walking as if she had been riding a horse for several days, let alone having become one. This was still an impossible dream, wasn't it? But she knew with absolute certainty that she was living it and that she would need all her wits about her in order to escape these stables with some semblance of her life still intact. She needed Mark. One way or another, he would help her. She was sure of it. The trouble was the man was nowhere in sight.

'Ah, here comes the hotel. This is where we're headed, Petal. I figure you're due a spot of cleaning duty. It might teach you some humility and that pleasing me really is in your best interests, if you're intent on surviving your stay at

Albrecht, that is.' Kyle ran a hand through his sandy blond hair and smiled to himself. The day was beginning to improve. For one thing, he'd just remembered that her suit featured several volts of electricity to reach the places other types of pain could not, and that humiliating this spoilt little rich brat could be a lot of fun if he set his mind to it.

As the hotel loomed into view he spotted Petal's head twisting this way and that, as her eyes anxiously sought out avenues of escape. She'd be crazy to try it. She was tagged and they would hunt her down and teach her a lesson she'd never forget if she put a hoof out of place. For that reason alone he hoped she'd run. He'd love to be the one who found her.

Hauling on her reins and watching her stumble forward, he led her up the gravel path towards the hotel's side entrance, which was reserved strictly for staff. Leaving her facing the door he let her bridle trail on the floor and gave her an opportunity. The question was, would she use it?

Jenny's feet itched to run, as far and as fast as they could, but although the thought of escape was uppermost in her mind she was not as foolish as Kyle thought. For one thing, she was wearing stupid high-heeled boots that made a quick getaway virtually impossible, and for another he was right behind her. If she was going to make it out of this place she would need to pick her time very carefully, and she wasn't foolish enough to believe she would make it on her own. She needed a helping hand from someone on the inside.

'Going to open the door for me, Petal?' Kyle asked the question from directly behind her and she jumped, the hood having shut out her peripheral vision. Immediately she moved forward and her hooved mitt pawed at the door before she realised her mistake. He laughed. 'You're not going to need hands in your new vocation, P. Just think of yourself as a bunch of juicy wet holes that will constantly beg to be used and abused. You'll be pleasing the patrons of the stable by allowing them to watch those lovely tits bounce up and down, when they get a chance to sit in your cart, as you prance about prettily and take them for a ride. You're officially a plaything, P. Your only mission in life is to obey every single word directed at you. Get used to it.'

He opened the door, issuing the command, 'Follow me.' As he grabbed her reins and pulled Jenny had little choice but to obey.

He led her through the empty restaurant, with its sparkling wine and water glasses, and pristinely polished crockery. Yellow English roses spewed forth from fluted vases and knives and forks glistened. Cutlery! How many days had it been since she used the ubiquitous utensils? A fresh wave of anger swept over her at the petty detail and her eyes threatened to leak fresh tears. She stoppered them. Kyle would enjoy them, and the fewer pleasures he received the better, in her opinion.

'Good morning, Grace.' Kyle winked as the secretary who had greeted Jenny a few very long days ago walked past.

'Morning, Kyle. If you're here for cleaning duty they're starting in the lobby. There are some onlookers today, wanting a bit of fun, so you've been warned.' She winked at Jenny and gave her a pleasant smile.

If Jenny had been able to she'd have bitten her head off. The ball-gag sat thickly in her mouth as she fumed. Her wants and needs mattered for little though, as she was dragged to the entrance of the lobby. When they reached the door Kyle let go of her bridle and placed his booted foot in the small of her back, before pushing her forward. Her hoof-mitts shot out to break her fall and she landed heavily on her knees.

'We always enter the lobby on all fours, to show respect for any guests who may be present.' Kyle sauntered past her and as the door swung closed, Jenny had little choice but to shuffle forward if she wanted to avoid getting her backside squashed. Following swiftly behind him, her view obscured by the back of his legs, she nearly had a heart attack as soon as he moved out of the way. The lobby was filled with naked pony-girls, but the sight of them wasn't where the shock lay. She was almost inured to bare-fleshed women and pony tack by now. The shock was wholly in what they were doing.

All of the girls were gagged without exception, and all of the gags had various cleaning attachments. There were feather dusters, mops, scrubbing brushes, brooms - and even a squeegee for cleaning the windows. If that had been the worst of it, Jenny might have sighed and accepted her fate, if not with equanimity, then with a sense of subdued resignation, but as usual Albrecht had gone a step further in its depravations.

There were several guests milling around in reception and it was clear they were there for a show. An array of pony-boys and girls had been tied up with white bondage rope in a number of different positions, all of which left them spread open wide and allowed easy access to their various orifices. Some had been tied together, male upon female, while others suffered to be hogtied and a couple were suspended mid-air by their ankles from ceiling chains. That didn't concern Jenny overmuch, although she didn't particularly want to be in their place, remembering the fierce pain of cramped muscles from last night. What did concern her, was that some of the gags she saw on the girls' faces featured butt plugs and dildos and it was clear what the trainers had in mind for them. Please God, no, she thought in horror. They couldn't force her to do that, surely? But she knew with a fatal, sick kind of inevitability that they could do exactly that and the more she showed her disgust, the more the twisted patrons of this place would enjoy it.

Jerking out of the way as one of the girls swept a wet mop back and forth with her lips, diligently working at the parquet floor with her mouth, Jenny sucked in air and cursed as her suit began to hum. The added calculation of her arousal would take the edge off this room, and that was a bad thing because she was sure she would need all her wits about her in order to survive the experience. Crawling a little faster behind Kyle as adrenaline spiked in her system, she tried to not to watch as one poor pony who had soft cloth pads attached to her hands and knees, polished behind the mop. Looking with dread towards her mouth Jenny saw a black rubber butt-plug gag anchored firmly within her jaws, and she shuddered.

Meanwhile, Kyle had been exchanging various pleasantries with the guests and charming the lady patrons with his friendly banter. Jenny wondered how he could chat about inanities such as the weather when there was a room full of naked sex-slaves on display, wiggling their asses and polishing the woodwork. The twilight zone wasn't a patch on this get-up, that was for certain.

The buzzing on her suit became more insistent and her body tightened into its pre-orgasmic haze of pain. Mind over matter, she thought, as she felt her ball-gag being roughly unbuckled from her lips. Maybe she would be able to orgasm if she concentrated carefully. The pounding dildos had her body rigidly anchored to the floor for balance and her swelling sphincter had her gasping with the heady combination of both pain and pleasure. She let out a sharp squeal just as she was about to jump off the edge of oblivion before her suit gave her a short, intense shock and nipped her clitoris cruelly. Jenny would have squealed again but Kyle stoppered her mouth with another rubber gag as her eyes nearly burst out of their sockets.

'This is called a butterfly gag,' he informed her. 'It will anchor itself in your jaw a bit more firmly than that of the ball variety and will enable you to perform your duties with a bit more finesse.'

Jenny wanted to growl as the sharp taste of rubber invaded her mouth yet again, harsh and unpleasant. The gag was fitted into her mouth by means of a head harness and leather straps were buckled tightly behind her head, with a vertical leather strap forming a triangular shape over her nose. Kyle attached a pump to the gag resting over the lower portion of her face and began inflating the rubber butterfly inside her mouth. It didn't take long for her to realise that this was a much more unpleasant way of silencing her than the ball-gag. The tighter he pumped up the orb inside her, the harder it would become to breathe and as the thing began to stretch her jaw she pawed at the floor in helpless agitation, choking around it.

'That snug enough?' Kyle's face wavered into view as her two eye slits looked around the room in panic. 'You want it tighter?' He raised an eyebrow to indicate that he wanted an answer. She shook her head madly and gave a couple of paws to the floor for good measure. She was rewarded with a smile. 'Didn't think so. Now, let's see. What shall we start with?'

Jenny felt her lips swell to double their normal size under the pressure of the gag and her eyes locked upon the screw fixture which protruded from her mouth. What would Kyle choose? Please don't let it be the plug, she pleaded silently. Her hands were trying to form fists within her mitts and failing miserably, and the feel of her heartbeat trebling was none too pleasant.

Kyle looked at her, assessing. 'Hmm, how about a position as chief boot-cleaner?'

Jenny was, unfortunately, all too aware that it wasn't a question. He squatted down before her and began rummaging around in a cardboard box. 'Ah, perfect,' he said, pulling out a stiff-bristled shoe brush attachment, holding it up to her eye slits so she could see his chosen instrument of humiliation up close. After she had taken a look he nodded to himself, and wasted little time in screwing it onto the front of her face.

'You look gorgeous,' he said, and his eyes fairly twinkled with malicious glee. 'Now how about you go crawl around and find some boots to lick. When you've cleaned all the shoes in the room you can report back to me. You'll find the wax in a tin next to the trophies. Remember to beg for the privilege of cleaning their shoes and for God's sake don't look at any of the guests. Keep your eyes to the floor and your nose busy just above that shoe brush. Annoy me any further today and you'll find your delicate little backside getting a roasting in the dungeon and maybe even a spell in the pit.' He slapped her ass hard to indicate that his pep talk was over and Jenny was sent scurrying over to the wax tin, with more eagerness than she would have thought possible.

She put her enthusiasm down to the fact that it was just a shoe brush and not a butt-plug or dildo that would be adorning the front of her mouth. She could not deny the relief she had felt when he pulled out the brush. Just three days ago she would have been horrified at this type of activity, now she was accepting of her lot in the lowliest of low positions and ready to serve.

Reaching the tin of wax she pointed her mouth downwards and ran the brush across the tacky surface, liberally coating the bristles with the clear polish. The smell of coconut infiltrated her hood and was actually quite pleasant. She savoured it for a moment, having smelt nothing but sweat, muck and musty straw for most of her stay at Albrecht. It took a moment before she realised what she was doing. Inhaling wax? These were to be her little pleasures in life? She wanted to roar, but Kyle's boot up her backside was an indication that her spell of daydreaming was up.

'Get to it, Petal. My temper's on a short leash today, remember?' His voice was laced with venom and it was clear he was unimpressed. Jenny wanted to rub her hindquarters, sure that the cowboy had left a bruise with his swift kick to her flank, but she didn't dare stop until she reached the nearest patron to service.

She chose a pair of women, sitting side by side and resting on two white chairs. They were middle-aged, perfectly groomed and dressed to impress in knee-high boots, leather skirts and sheer blouses which left little to the imagination. The underwear was lacy and racy. As their gazes bent down to examine her she wasted no time in showing off her efforts to please, getting to her knees quickly and begging with her hooves in a gentle pawing motion. She was rewarded with laughter.

'Aren't they adorable?' It was a woman's laughter Jenny heard and she was given a pat on the head for her troubles. 'Yes, you may clean my boots,' the giggling voice continued. Helpfully placing both feet shoulder width apart on the floor, she waited patiently for the novice to begin.

Jenny swallowed thickly, aware that she should be dismayed at what she was about to do, but the dildos were drumming away inside her once again and the knowledge that worse things awaited many of the other ponies allowed her to accept her new position with more grace than usual. She lowered her mouth to the supple leather of the left boot and began to scrub away diligently. The ladies completely ignored her as she worked.

'I come here for my two week vacation every year,' said one.

The other chuckled. 'My hubby thinks I've booked myself into a health farm.' They both then had fits of hysterics, which made life very hard for Jenny who was trying to clean the ankle of a boot which was trying to slap her in the face.

'I bet you lose weight after the two weeks, though, so he'd never know,' continued the other. 'All those orgasms...' There was a long sigh. The boots twitched but this time they managed to remain on the floor and Jenny continued to scrub vigorously up their sides, craning her neck in a way that would have greatly impressed her yoga instructor, had she made it past the first lesson.

'Sylvia, why have some of the girls got butt-plugs strapped to their mouths?'

The boots wobbled as Sylvia snorted. 'Oh, it's an incentive to make sure that those who are given cleaning duty do a thorough and careful job. If they don't, well, let's just say it gets quite entertaining around here.'

It was the other lady's turn to snort and they dissolved into yet more laughter. Jenny nearly gave up her cleaning job, as trying to get anywhere near the boots was proving difficult.

'Lavinia, I think my boots are just about finished. What say we ask our pony to give them a shine?'

Lavinia clapped her hands together, and although Jenny didn't dare raise her head to look at the woman she knew there would be a wide smile upon her face. 'What an excellent idea, Sylvia. Go and fish her gag out. I do hope she tries to talk to us. Remember what they said, in orientation? We can slap them if they try to talk to us. Imagine that.' Lavinia peeled off into more of her extremely irritating laughter.

When Sylvia unbuckled Jenny's gag she tried to wrench it forcefully out of her mouth before realising she would have to let the air out of the vent. Kyle came to the rescue and quickly depressurized the gag before pulling it from his trainee's mouth.

'I hope Petal is pleasing you, ladies,' he said in a particularly smarmy voice.

'Very much so, Sir, but we're a little curious. Why is she in the latex get-up? We were hoping to have a little fun with her,' pouted Lavinia.

'Ah, well this kiddo here is a very special pony. She's going to be trained to be the best of the best and knock spots off the rest.' He winked at them. 'Petal, here, is destined to wear the black collar and she'll need to endure lots of rigorous training in order to make herself stand out from the crowd. The suit she's wearing is designed to bring her to the peak of orgasm again and again over a period of two days, but not allow her the luxury of release. It's intended to make her hungry for the smallest touch, or the lightest little caress of her trainer's hand, and it will help to soup-up her sex drive.' He looked at his watch. 'In around twenty-four hours we get to see if it's done the job, don't we, P?'

Jenny could do little but nod her head miserably in response. Her lips were covered in sticky drool and her hand came up automatically to swipe at it, before she realised the hoof-mitt wasn't really designed for such a thing. Kyle slapped her face, hard. As his handprint bloomed on her cheek, leaving a hot and throbbing mark of fire, Jenny wondered what on earth she'd done wrong now.

'Ponies do not touch their faces with their hooves. Your groom will clean you up later. The ladies have asked you to shine their boots and here you are messing around. Get your tongue out, slave, and attend to these boots! You're not to stop until they're sparkling under the weight of your saliva.' He gave her backside a pinch for good measure, yanked her head up by her hair and smothered her nose to the boot in question. He did not let go of her until she began to lick.

Jenny did not like the taste of leather. She didn't think much of the coconut wax, either. At least there was some kind of taste to it, she supposed, rather than the bland mush and liquid she had been forced to endure over the past few days. Lapping at the leather and keenly aware of her subservient status, she felt heat pool in her loins. Hopefully it had something to do with subtle electric current running through her suit, which was starting to tickle and excite the places that ordinary clothing could not reach. She had the nasty feeling, though, that it might have something to do with crawling around on the floor and obeying orders for the delight of brutal individuals who had no thoughts whatsoever about tormenting an innocent young lady. The electric current unfurled through her body slowly, and built up a steady anticipation that could be felt across every nerve-ending she possessed.

When she had finished the set of boots before her she was aching with need and desperate to be used, although she knew she had little hope of her wish being granted. She pawed at the air, begging for attention, to indicate she had finished her task.

Sylvia examined her boots slowly, twisting them this way and that, before deigning to give Jenny a pat on the head for her troubles. 'Good job, P,' she said, before turning to Lavinia and adding, 'How on earth do we reward her, if she's got all of her holes bunged up?'

Lavinia shook her auburn curls in puzzlement before taking a single ringlet in her index finger and pulling at it, obviously deep in thought. Her face screwed up in several different unexplainable expressions before she came up with an answer. 'Her mouth's available. How about we get one of the other girls to fuck it?'

Sylvia laughed and clapped her hands excitedly. 'There's a reason we're best friends, darling,' she purred.

'You, you there, yoo-hoo,' called out Sylvia, waving frantically to a pony-girl who was sporting a pink dildo from her mouth-gag and currently trying to thrust her jellied instrument of insertion inside one of the ceiling-suspended participants who was swaying in the air. 'Can you spare a minute?'

The pony-girl scuttled over obediently, as they knew she would. Jenny couldn't help but stare at her jaw. The dildo drooped slightly as it was suspended horizontally and must have been a good eight inches in length. It had an impressive girth and her lips would be stretched to their fullest if they wanted her to accommodate the beast inside her mouth.

'We want to see you take it all, P. Swallow it up like a good little horsie and we'll tell your Master you've been a wonderfully obedient little thing who deserves a treat or two.' There was a chorus of amused sniggers before Sylvia managed to calm herself enough to continue. 'Fail in our little task, however, and we'll have to *complain*.' The emphasis on 'complain' and their shared look made it very clear to Jenny that their threat was not an idle one.

Taking a deep breath and facing her new challenge, Jenny wondered how her aching mouth would cope with the large offering that was slowly working its way towards her. She'd only been gag-free for about five minutes today and her jaw would start cramping at the slightest provocation, she was sure of it. Watching the large pink abomination come straight towards her as the naked pony-girl crawled forwards, she licked her lips and lubricated her mouth with as much saliva as she could. It looked like she was going to need it.

'Come on, Honey,' said Lavinia. 'Stop all this messing around and fuck her good. We want a show. Make it messy.' They stomped their boots in enthusiasm and disintegrated into raucous laughter, watching the long pink dildo gag wobble up and down as the pony-girl crawled. Jenny rolled her eyes around in her hood, safe in the knowledge that the twittering twins were both laughing so hard neither would notice. Honey, her breasts swaying like heavy pendulums as their little clamps tinkled sweetly, advanced on Jenny. Giving her an apologetic glance, which considering the gag was nothing more than a softening around the eye area, she lined up her dildo and prepared her aim. Jenny got the message. She opened her mouth and pulled back at the right instant.

Whilst Honey didn't ram the thing down her throat, the size was such that it was going to take some swallowing. The plastic slithered inside her lips and the rounded dome of the head began to forge a path inside her throat. At least the pony-girl knew what she was doing. Pushing and pulling the jellified plastic back and forth she inched forward little by little, giving Jenny time to accommodate herself around the large beast.

Jenny decided it wasn't as nice as having a real cock in her mouth. The plastic was cold and didn't have the delicious salty tang of a cock, but oddly enough the sight of Honey thrusting gently into her throat aroused her. The pony-girl was gaining ground and it was clear this was not the first time she had been asked to complete this particular task. Letting her companion dominate her mouth to the best of her abilities, Jenny drank in the sight of her.

Honey wore a red collar, which meant she was much further up the pecking order in Albrecht than Jenny was. Her red collar was much slimmer than the thick white version she currently wore. Her nameplate was gold in colour too, rather than the dull silver that housed her own name. So there were perks to rising up the ranks apparently. Honey also had a full head of luscious blonde hair to complement her tail plug, which swished about behind her in great sweeps, as did most of the other girls' tails in the room. Jenny wondered if that came naturally or whether it was another aspect of the rigorous training to be found at the stables. She suspected it was the latter. Honey's big brown eyes were venturing closer and closer towards hers. The dildo was pressing regularly for entrance at the back of her throat and Jenny was gurgling at the intrusion. Trying to flick her eyes sideways she wondered what the pair of women thought of their antics, but her hood hid everything from view bar the thrusting plastic penis in front of her, and the ladies had gone very quiet.

With around an inch to go of the long pink intruder, Jenny thought it would be impossible to get any more of the thing inside her. She could barely breathe as it was, but gurgle and paw though she might, Honey did not take no for an answer and the thing moved relentlessly forward as the girl's beautiful, heavily lashed eyes moved closer and closer towards her. Jenny almost panicked. She could feel her airway constricting as the head began plunging down the back of her throat, seeking entrance to God only knew where. Honey must have read her mind though, as she gently shook her head, never wavering in her slow but forceful thrusts.

She'd seen it all before, thought Jenny. Watching Honey continue to pump at her like a well-oiled piston, Jenny concentrated on relaxing the muscles of her throat, to allow the last tiny half inch to be swallowed up inside her. Everything was now stretched to the limit. Her lips were pulled back around its thick girth, her tongue lolled at its base and her jaw was once again screaming as fits of painful cramps overtook it. She had to tell herself several times to ease her stricken jaw, breathing in deeply and letting the continued pulsations of the dildo do its work. Ignoring the pain and the tight friction in her mouth she suffered silently as Honey moved steadily, finally burying the thing deep inside her and remaining motionless as their task was completed.

The ladies applauded in obvious glee and both pony-girls, in a lips-to-lips pose, turned to stare at the couple who had clearly been enjoying themselves immensely at the show they had presented. Both women's skirts were now wound up tightly around their waists and no panties were anywhere in sight. Judging by their flushed faces, Jenny suspected they had just shared a rather nice orgasm. Lucky for some, she thought, gurgling around the eight inch plastic penis lodged firmly in the back of her throat and which no amount of tugging on her part was likely to remove.

The ladies finally took pity on their pathetic mode of coupling and began pulling the two pony-girls apart. Unfortunately the dildo had managed to connect them together in an almost permanent fashion and it took more than a few generous tugs before they managed to break the seal that had been formed. When the thing finally popped free from Jenny's mouth with an embarrassing plop, her relief was palpable, not least because she hadn't been able to breathe properly for the last ten minutes or so. Sucking in heavy gulps of air she turned her attention back to her Mistresses and felt a long sliver of saliva slide down her hooded face and land on the floor below. Urrgh.

'Do you think they deserve a treat, Lavinia?' Sylvia batted her thick black eyelashes at her friend and awaited her approval.

Lavinia's thick, rounded lips, smeared copiously with bright pink lipstick, pursed together thoughtfully. 'What kind of treat were you thinking of, Sylvia? If we're talking orgasms we can only award one and if we're talking polo mints, again, we've only got one taker.'

'Well, it's a problem that's easily enough solved, isn't it darling? We'll have an orgasm for Honey over there, and a juicy mint for Jenny over here. Splendid.'

Sylvia proffered a hand towards Jenny which contained a single, round, polo mint. Jenny's mouth immediately watered and she didn't think twice as she bent her head down to suck it up. Humiliating though it was, the mint was the best damn thing she had tasted in days. Sugar, oh God, how she had missed it! Feeling the smooth sweet slide across her tongue she savoured the intense flavour as it poured through her tired mouth, helping to return her saliva and soothe her throat. Though the humble mint was far from her favourite type of sweet, right now it felt as if she had been offered a double chocolate caramel sundae with honeycomb and fudge chips. Having said that, pleasant though the mint was, she would have killed for an orgasm and couldn't watch as the ladies worked their fingers and tongues gently over Honey's body. A mint vs. an orgasm? There was no comparison really.

Watching helplessly, while wallowing in self-pity, she observed Honey's body as it twisted and undulated beneath their talented hands. Fingers dived inside her leather harness, searching for her clamped nipples, which they then proceeded to tug gently. They flicked the little bells with their fingernails, just for the pleasure of watching the poor girl wince, and then they really got to work. The women let their lips rove over the poor girl's body, teeth nipping and pinching her exposed flesh. Earlobes, the delicate skin around her neck, and the undersides of her breasts - they ravished everything. Hands stroked, caressing, rubbing and rolling. Soft wet tongues explored her inner thighs and sex with a gentle lapping motion and they found her tail plug irresistible. Diving underneath her body and circling it, a set of teeth began to pluck it from its hideaway, amidst plenty of protest. Well, as much protest as could be offered when gagged with a giant dildo.

Lavinia got between her legs, and holding a fistful of tail hair in her hands, began to pump it up and down with enthusiasm. Sylvia got a hold on the two clamps and began tugging them in alternate strokes, watching the full breasts bounce with excitement as they swung this way and that. When Lavinia thrust her fingers into the poor girl's pussy and began pumping, Honey mewled in pleasure.

'Uh, uh, uh,' said Sylvia as she shook her head. 'Not so fast, filly. I think I would like to sample your appendage myself.' She winked at the wide-eyed pony-girl before getting down on all fours in front of her, pushing her backside up in the air to reveal a dripping wet hole. Honey's big pink dildo quivered as Lavinia brought her thumb into play, caressing the pony's clit, and she laughed as the girl began bucking underneath her.

'Fuck me, slave, or your Master will hear about it,' ordered Sylvia. That was all the encouragement Honey needed and her plump plastic penis shot forth and prepared to spear inside Sylvia's pussy. Dipping inside the rosy red flesh, Honey generously coated the tip of her cock before she began pulsing it back and forth inside her willing victim, who shook her head full of red curls in ardent appreciation. 'Yessss,' she hissed, 'exactly like that.'

'You,' said Lavinia, pointing a French-manicured fingernail at Jenny. 'Get your ass behind me and show me a good time.' Jenny was pretty sure it wasn't her ass she wanted to see, so cracking her jaw in order to try and loosen it before another heavy onslaught began she got a wriggle on and managed to position herself behind Lavinia's rather generous backside. She didn't even think of disobeying the woman. Kyle had already proved himself a mean and vicious sadist and giving him unnecessary opportunities to torment her would not be a good idea.

Nudging up the ends of the leather skirt with her nose, Jenny pushed her hooded face in the woman's backside and buried her nose firmly between Lavinia's buttocks. Her tongue began lapping at her sex. She had a moment to be thankful for her latex covering; at least she was wipe clean. Her dildos chose that moment to begin pumping themselves up to maximum proportions, while her clit stimulator buzzed into life. *Oh no. Oh, no, no, no.*

'Harder!' Lavinia demanded. Jenny employed her tongue to the best of her very limited skills, and began to pulse with a heavy pressure upon the tip of her clit, whilst her nether regions swelled and buzzed. 'Better. Keep it up, slut.'

Easy for you to say, thought Jenny, who was being rocked backed and forth by Honey's frantic pounding, as she bounced into both Sylvia and Lavinia with the frenzied thrusts of her dildo.

'Fingers on me, Honey,' ordered Sylvia. Honey immediately obeyed and her fingers dived upon the already swollen flesh of Sylvia's clit. She purred in delight. 'Harder, Honey. Show me what you can do with those fingers and your little penis.'

Jenny had no idea whether the comment angered Honey, but the next thing she knew she was nearly bounced backwards off Lavinia, who was gurgling happily beneath her tongue and the good old alphabet technique. Gathering up her hooves, she braced them around Lavinia's knees and held on for dear life as everyone begun bucking away in a mad frenzy and moaning, screaming or groaning as if they were about to explode.

Which they did... without her.

Everyone landed in a tangle of arms, legs and hooves and it was Jenny's turn to reach the peak of orgasm, before her suit fired a breath-taking shock into two rather delicate places within her body.

Honest Thoughts

'How did she do, ladies?' asked Kyle as he reached up to clip Petal's leash to her collar. There was a moment's silence while Sylvia and Lavinia shared a look with each other, before they gave him their full attention and both smiled coyly.

'Well, she got wax over my leg,' said Sylvia in a petulant voice.

'She put teeth marks on my skirt,' said Lavina, frowning, before she added, 'and her oral skills could use some work.'

'Ooh! I did not get wax...' It took Jenny all of three seconds before she realised her mistake. Her ball-gag was roughly slotted inside her mouth and Kyle pulled at her leash, constricting her heavy collar until she couldn't breathe, let alone utter a sound.

'Please accept my apologies, ladies. She's a novice and this is only her first day under my command. We intend to begin work on her inadequacies immediately, don't we, Petal?'

Jenny nodded quickly and pawed her hooves in the air appealingly. The cold look he shot her as he led her away was not at all comforting.

She seethed under Kyle's mishandling and although there was little she could do about it, thoughts of revenge began to appear uppermost in her mind. But they were quickly dashed. Honestly, what could she do to him? She was constantly tied up, gagged, humiliated and used. That was not going to change in the near future, if ever. It looked like she had exhausted her chances with both Hetty and Agnes, and Mark Matthews had probably disappeared halfway across the globe by now, leaving all thoughts of her far behind in his luxury private jet.

Why had she picked the cowboy? The worst thing about this whole façade was that she could only lie to herself for so long. She was beginning to enjoy the combined taste of pain and pleasure. Being humiliated and forced into tight bondage aroused her and, as much as she wanted to deny it, she was already beginning to crave the rough hands that manipulated and used her body to their advantage. Her body was in love with this place, but unfortunately, it appeared to have disconnected itself from her brain.

Ten minutes later she was rethinking her earlier thoughts. She was now installed inside the ladies toilets with a white plastic toilet brush spilling out of her butterfly gag, which had just been reinflated to uncomfortable proportions. But that was the least of her problems. Her tail had been unscrewed from the rear of her suit and a mop attachment fitted in its place. Kyle had a riding crop, which he wielded with both hands as encouragement for her to get the job done on time and on budget, or so you would have thought. Add to that a suit that was pumping gentle tickles of electricity around her body and buzzing away happily, and you had one unimpressed pony.

'Come on Petal, you can move faster than that.'

Jenny had already cottoned on to this game. If she moved faster each time he said it, he expected her to move subsequently faster and faster as he repeated himself. She wasn't falling for it. She kept the same pace, reserved her energy and took the fierce swats from the crop with a masochistic air of defiance. In turn Kyle swung with a heavy hand, each thrust sending currents of pleasure and pain shooting into the cortex of her brain. Sticking her toilet brush down one of the spotless pans and scrubbing for all she was worth, she managed to simultaneously mop the floor with her backside whilst slewing water by using the direction of her mouth.

Though the degrading activity should have had her blushing with shame, the pleasure the suit was awarding her and the constant swats from the crop didn't let her dwell on the activities too heavily. It was only when one of the guests entered the set of cubicles and Kyle unscrewed her brush, to have her bend down and bow her head to the woman's killer Armani heels, that Jenny felt the first unpleasant flush of heat to her face. When she then had a tiny silver tray attached to her gag and was ushered into the toilet cubicle with the lady as a 'toilet assistant' she was ready to scream. Her emotions were going up and down faster than Sylvia and Lavinia's panties. When the lady finished her toilette, blew her nose and deposited the tissue on the tray for disposal, Jenny did scream. And to add insult to injury, her body had just been denied yet another orgasm.

One extremely unappetising liquid lunch later, Jenny was being marched towards the training room door and the rather intimidating Mistress Lupine. Her stomach growled for food, her mind craved the oblivion of sleep, but her body? Well, that was another matter entirely. She should be exhausted but it appeared that surviving on adrenaline alone would not be a problem at Albrecht.

This time it was her groom, Daniel, who held the reins, but he most certainly wasn't the one who controlled them. Kyle had informed her, in no uncertain terms, that if she displeased her tutor she would be visiting the dungeon tomorrow. The thought was sobering enough to ensure her best behaviour. Kyle and implements of torture would not make for sweet dreams.

The rest of the day passed in a sweaty haze of heat. It ate at her body from the inside out and her need for release was only stemmed by pain, which she was beginning to crave as much as an orgasm.

'Enter.' Lupine's posh accent ricocheted around the large room, mainly due to the volume behind it. 'Ah, Miss Redcliff. We've been expecting you. Stop dithering by the door and come and join us.'

Jenny would probably have gulped had her mouth not been heavily gagged by the oppressive black ball. As it was, she moved forward on her hands and knees and did as she was told. Trying to keep her gaze straight ahead and on Lupine's red PVC boots wasn't as easy as it should have been. There was lots of movement in the training room. The novices had been gathered together for a session and they were currently bouncing up and down upon their allotted dildos. She was ridiculously pleased that she was already plugged and that no bouncing would be possible or required on her behalf.

'OK, that's enough vaginal stimulation, ponies,' said Mistress Lupine with a caged smile. Her long blonde hair was prised back in a stylish bun that sat at a jaunty angle on her head; the amount of hairspray needed to keep it there should have made the woman flammable. Jenny was tempted to look around for incendiary devices, but even had she found one there was little possibility that she would be able to use it. 'Today, we are starting anal practice. You may pass this tube of lubricant around and help each other out with the basics, before we start training our muscles to accept cocks in the tightest of our little holes. Anal sex, by the way, is by far the most favoured type of sex in the stables and you'll be required to show off your skills with enthusiasm and aplomb on a daily basis, at the very least. I suspect it will be a much more regular occurrence than that, which is why we're breaking you in gently, here, first.' Her smile managed to touch the corners of her eyes.

'Choose a dildo and begin to lubricate it, ponies.'

The novices began sucking diligently at their chosen rubber protrusions, giving them more than their fair share of the wet stuff. So would Jenny, had she been about to take one of the large items up her backside. The thought made her wince. Was she really going to have to do that? A shudder filled her as she recalled the details of her auction. Who had bid for her? Where would she be taken? Would there be a chance to escape, perhaps?

Lupine's sharp voice snapped her out of her three second reverie. 'Petal, as you won't be able to join us in this lesson I have another task for you. There are several gentlemen lined up along the wall that require your attention. They are visiting Albrecht for the first time and we intend to show them a good time.'

Her gag was unbuckled, her leash was pulled and her nose came face to face with a pair of leather trousers, sporting a rather impressive bulge.

Jenny looked at the long line of men and drew in the deepest breath she could manage in spite of her corset. This was going to be a challenge; but a challenge she would relish. She would show these men the extent of her quite considerable talents and have them drooling at her feet. Her bodysuit was once again priming her for pleasure and the need to have all of her holes thoroughly filled was uppermost in her mind. As the first gentleman unzipped himself and let the impressive length of his cock spring free she could have dribbled. She was going to go after her semen calories with enthusiasm and determination. By the time she'd finished with him he'd want to kneel at her feet, rather than the other way around...

'Give me your honest thoughts, Len,' said Mistress Lupine as Jenny withdrew her mouth full to the brim with creamy, salty goo, which she quickly gobbled down.

Len was quick to respond and Jenny noticed his voice had a rather bored and somewhat unimpressed tone, which did not bode well. 'Not quite tight enough, doesn't use her tongue to full advantage, doesn't go deep enough, her gag reflex is a little annoying and she doesn't twist her head enough.'

Jenny would have given him a sneer in response, had she been able to move her jaw. As it was Mistress Lupine pursed her lips and cast a disparaging glance at her. 'Hmm,' she said, and it was clear the woman was not pleased, 'isn't it a good job that you've got a further four volunteers in which to perfect your oral skills. Make good use of them, P. I'll be getting an opinion from each gentleman as you finish.' With that she stalked off to supervise the trainees currently trying to spear their delicate sphincters on the wobbling, blunt ends of their plastic phalluses. It didn't appear to be as easy as it looked. None of them were having much success and there was plenty of moaning, groaning and whimpering to be heard. Their faces were wrapped up in both pain and concentration and the look was a rather surreal one. Jenny couldn't help but feel sorry for them, for she knew that in a couple of days she would be joining them. Turning her attention to her next challenge, 'Mr Suit', she could only hope he would be more forgiving in his critique than her former conquest.

At the end of Petal's two hour session Kyle was waiting for her at the door. He was immediately accosted by Lupine, who gave him a particularly unimpressive report of her skills. She had been found lacking in every area of oral expertise and he had to endure the disapproving glances Lupine delivered his way, which clearly said why on earth haven't you got to grips with that throat yet? After enduring ten minutes worth of her evaluation his eyes darkened into dangerous slits, although he still managed to nod politely at her as she re-entered her classroom and left them alone in the corridor.

As soon as the door closed Kyle was quick to take out his ill humour on his trainee. 'Still misbehaving, after all you've been through today? Interesting. Well, I think we can iron that out with a short spell in the dungeon first thing tomorrow. As far as attitude readjustment goes it doesn't get much better - especially when I'm in charge.' The man was furious. He began to drag her and it was all Jenny could do to try and trot fast enough to keep up with him.

Her lot did not get any better as they headed back towards the barn. A long line of pony-girls were lined up and awaiting her entrance, their hopeful eyes searching her neck for the sight of a yellow collar. They were to be disappointed. Watching as they gritted their teeth and prepared their pink backsides for another ten rounds with the belt, or worse, she prepared to join them. But Kyle had other plans.

'Give 'em hell and make them count,' was all he said as he continued to drag Jenny's bridle as he manoeuvred her into the same little cell as before. The single bulb clicked, the fluorescent light glared down, and she waited with bated breath for her punishment. Her suit was just beginning to take her to the outskirts of the Promised Land, and with a good dose of Kyle's heavy hand she thought she might stand another chance of beating the thing at its own game. At this moment in time her body had the combined hormones of about fifty pregnant women and her need to climax eclipsed everything else in the world. Escape? Who the hell cared? She needed an orgasm. She'd kill for an orgasm. She'd even consider selling her soul to Mark Matthews in order to take a bite of the apple and get rid of her suit. The breast massager had just begun to shake and vibrate her cleavage, while the pincers inside the metal cups began pulling gently at the tips of her nipples. Come on, Kyle, do your worst, she silently pleaded.

Kyle moved to the wall and attached her leash to a thick metal karabiner high above her that she would have no hope of breaking. He then strode out of the room and slammed the door. The sound of a key turning in the latch could be heard, before he thumped the door with his fist for good measure.

Jenny wondered if she should be grateful he hadn't tanned her backside from red to puce. It was throbbing pleasantly at the moment, a mild stinging sensation that left a wonderful, simmering heat which worked its way through her body. Far from annoying, she had grown to love the burn as she moved, her body craving the sweet sting of the crop to fuel the fires within. No, she decided, she was not going to curl up in a ball on the floor and throw a tantrum because she had not received her evening spanking. Besides, curling up was going to be a problem. Attached as she was to the wall she would not be able to lie down. If she was going to get any sleep at all it would be standing up. There was always the possibility that Kyle was going to come back for her, but somehow she doubted it. The slam had been indicative of his mood and she guessed this was a punishment of sorts. Obey or be ignored. A little bit like corner time for children, she suspected.

Leaning against the wall she tried to rearrange her thoughts into order. The first one had flashing red lights and a blaring siren that screamed, 'You are never going to get out of this place. Be a good girl and do exactly as you're told.' She didn't much like the thought and feeling her anxiety levels increase exponentially, she moved on to the more pressing concern of food. Kyle had not fed or watered her since lunch. Her stomach was growling, but it was now a dull ache she had become accustomed to. However, it might be one she could do something about. As he'd left the light on this time, no doubt to ensure she couldn't sleep, it allowed her to see the feeding tubes hanging from the wall. Although Mistress Lupine had inserted her gag before she'd left the training room, she might just be able to manoeuvre the thin tubes between her hoof mitts in order to thread them into the single hole her gag contained.

Scraping her rubber mitts against the coarse brick she tried to prise the tube forward in order to capture it between two thick hooves. It wasn't easy, but she had all night so she figured she might as well give it her best shot.

It took her well over a half hour to get the liquid feed tube slotted deep inside her gag, but her sense of accomplishment was overwhelming when she began to feel the cool liquid food gush down her throat. Even the simplest of things were major obstacles when dressed in the bizarre get-up she had on. Movement was already becoming difficult due to the soreness of being penetrated hundreds of times over by her untiring, robotic dildos. Her body was also unfamiliar to exercise and after a couple of days of gruelling activity her muscles were tired and aching all over. What she desperately needed was sleep: uninterrupted, flat-on-the-floor, off to oblivion and beyond snoring. But it didn't look like she was going to get some any time soon. As her clit stimulator buzzed into life she banged her hooves frantically against the brick wall in a fit of mad desperation. No one heard her cries.

Kyle was in a particularly good mood when he opened his eyes the following morning to clear blue skies and twittering birds. There was only one bird on his mind and that happened to be the lovely Isabelle, who was probably already painting her fingernails in readiness for their date that evening. Even though he'd only just woken up and was still in 'morning-glory' mode, he hardened further at the thought. It was going to be one hell of a date and he fully intended to make sure his lady had a good time; preferably on the end of his cock. He reached down to fondle his glans and gave himself a few cursory strokes before wondering whether he had enough time to use and abuse the wicked stick before work called. Glancing at his alarm clock revealed very unfriendly hands positioned at 9.00 am. Fuck it. He was the one in charge and he called the shots. An extra twenty minutes wouldn't kill anybody. Tightening his grip, he began yanking at himself with a display of excitement that hadn't been seen in years.

By the time he made it to the stables, freshly showered and dressed, his Omega told him it was 10.15. He'd been given a disapproving frown from Mr A as he'd passed by his office, but other than that suffered no other repercussions for his lateness. It was great being the one in charge. You didn't have to answer to anyone, although he had to admit that Katrina's comment from yesterday still rankled. He'd better haul ass and get Petal in line right quick, because the alternative of handing her reins over to Matthews was unthinkable. He'd rather eat his own testicles.

When the door to Petal's cell creaked open he was immediately surprised to find the room was in darkness. He'd left the light on intentionally; to make sure she didn't get any shut-eye and would be suffering the torments of sleep deprivation today. Looking up to the wall where she should have been chained standing up, he found... nothing.

The Dungeon Master

It was as if she'd never been there. No indentation of her body in the hay, no soft snores, no rustling and no Petal. How the hell had she managed to escape? Opening the door fully and peering around the back of it confirmed there wasn't a soul anywhere in sight. His face creased in puzzlement. What the hell had happened here? His eyes then widened in shock as they found a pair of metal horseshoes flying towards his face with frightening speed.

Somehow he managed to avoid one but the other caught him hard across the side of his face, sending him flat on his backside and sprawling in the dirt. The black rippling bodysuit of his pony-girl jumped down from the metal restraints embedded in the wall and she didn't give him a second glance as she sprinted towards the barn door. There was no one in there to stop her, either. They'd left hours ago for their breakfast spanking sessions and various different training regimes.

Kyle swore, got to his feet and started sprinting. She wouldn't get far. Bursting out of the barn door and listening to the slam as it closed behind him, his eyes searched left and right as they scanned the area. He found her running towards the training block. Of course. She would know the hotel was tacked on to the end of it, if she could just manage to get her ass through the whole of that very long corridor. Seeing as they were headed that way anyway and the fact that he'd never seen her so enthusiastic about exercise, he decided to let her have a little fun. With his long legs he wouldn't need to run that fast in order to keep her in his sights, and she'd be on vapours anyway, having not had any decent food in the past twenty-four hours.

Thankfully there was no one about to watch his errant pony as she stumbled and skidded her way over the cobblestones towards the grey concrete corridor that she thought would lead to her rescue. As soon as her booted feet set themselves inside the building he let his fingers close around the remote control in his jeans pocket and depressed a single button. She fell to the floor instantly, and he kept his finger firmly upon the button that would deliver her compliance.

'Feel that, do we?' Kyle was furious. He had a bump on his face the size of an egg and wasn't that going to look oh-so-gorgeous this evening on his date? Isabelle would probably take one look at him and run screaming. Clenching his jaw, as well as both fists, it took him a few seconds to calm the burning rage that threatened to engulf him. Before he did something he'd later regret he managed to prise his finger off the maximum current 'shock' button and bark out one order. 'Down those stairs!'

Jenny did not need to be told twice. Though the current that had flooded her body was debilitating in the extreme, when she saw the look of fury on his face she managed to battle through the pain of twisted limbs and misfiring circuits to practically throw herself down the stone steps to the entrance of Albrecht's dungeon. Kneeling at the foot of the giant cast iron door she kept her eyes downcast and stifled the sobs that threatened to spill through her gag. She knew without a doubt that her experience in the room beyond was not going to be pleasant. Hearing the footfalls of her trainer slam into the stone, she closed her eyes and wondered what had possessed her to try and escape. Even if she had made it to the hotel she'd have never got past the staff situated all around her. It was a losing battle, but she'd come to accept the fact that the opportunities for escape were going to be so rare she would have to seize them with both hands if and when they presented themselves. As she'd already been due a visit to the dungeon, it hardly mattered that her attempt had failed.

The footsteps got louder and louder until they nearly deafened her, sounding like an elephant stampede, when in reality it was just one man with a pair of ordinary-sized feet. Well, slightly bigger than average feet, but it mattered not. When the crocodile-skin boots came to rest beside her prone form, she shivered.

'We're going to have some fun, you and I,' was all he said as he picked up the chain attached to her leash and dragged her forward.

Jenny's knees scraped along the concrete floor, but she barely noticed. Her eyes darted left to right, examining all the torturous devices and torments the room offered. The dungeon's vast floor space seemed to shrink in an instant and the room closed in around her. For some reason she had not noticed the size of the room on her introductory visit with Mark. Probably because he tended to send her hormones skittering into realms unknown and the last thing on her mind was how big the surrounding area was. Mr Nasty had her thinking about sex, and pretty much nothing else. The cowboy, on the other hand, had her scared witless, although sex was never very far from her mind in this place. Especially when dressed in the suit from hell. Only a few more hours and she would be released from its relentless grip. She was now at the stage where she would have begged, pleaded and traded vital body parts with the devil in order to be allowed an orgasm. The suit was kicking in at intervals of five minutes or less, and her pussy and ass clenched ceaselessly around their fat dildos in a state of absolute misery.

'Up on the spanking horse, P.' Kyle gestured towards the leather padded bench. She obeyed unthinkingly. Score one for Albrecht. Where had her feisty, fiery nature disappeared to? Had they knocked all the stuffing out of her already? Oh God, how many days had she been here now? Panic caused her to scuff the toe of her right boot against the rough floor and she nearly threw herself on top of the thin wooden rail, arms flailing either side of it. Her face darted up to discover Kyle's eyes were on her with a mad, incensed gleam and as he fingered the livid red mark that had sprung up in a semicircle just above his left eye, she had cause to wonder whether she would make it out of the cold room alive.

Deep breaths, Redcliff, she told herself firmly. You are made of sterner stuff than this. They will not break you.

These thoughts were all very well but it didn't change the fact that there was a maniac in front of her thumbing his way through the dungeon's library of books and none of them looked particularly appealing.

Picking up a heavy, vellum-bound title from one of the top shelves of the mahogany bookcase, Kyle waved it before her face. 'Sensory deprivation sounds good for starters.' He twisted his head and cracked his neck. 'We'll plug those little ears and blindfold you. You'll be helpless, mewling and probably

119

bawling like a baby after I tie those cuffs around your wrists and ankles. Gagged as you are, I could leave you in here for days and no one would know. I hold that kind of power over you, P. If I want you to rot, I'll find a nice quiet corner, immobilise you and leave you to suffer the torments of inactivity. That's one idea.'

He tossed the volume aside and picked up another, bearing a brightly coloured jacket which read *Figging and Salves for Ponies*. She'd seen that one before and couldn't help a shudder. 'Shame we can't have some fun with chilli oil or hot liniment pasted inside those disobedient little holes of yours. I bet they would get you trotting your luggage around the track in double-quick time. I'll put that on our list for tomorrow I think, along with a spot of figging. You won't enjoy having that ass spanked anywhere near as much if I shove a generous portion of ginger in there to spice things up. We could make it part of your morning routine, along with an ass fuck straight after.' He gave her a cruel smile. 'Pity we can't do it now, but you're an annoying anal virgin, so we'll have to wait until that's been taken care of.'

Jenny could not believe she was relieved to have all her holes filled and locked up tight, but it appeared there were definite advantages to wearing makeshift chastity belt.

Kyle hummed as he made his way from one tome to the next. He was obviously enjoying himself and why wouldn't he be, with his favourite subject of torture close to hand. Jenny wondered what the possibilities of being rescued in the next ten minutes actually were. One in a hundred? One in ten thousand? One in a bloody million? It was probably closer to the mark now she knew who ran the ship. You did not cross her father. Not if you valued your life.

'Ah, how about, Abrasion Play?' Kyle sounded relatively excited at the prospect and as far as Jenny was concerned, that did not bode well. 'Yes, that will do for starters. I think I'll rip open that latex suit of yours and do some engraving on your back. After we're finished with that I'll give you a good flogging in the Objectifier and then practice my aim with the bullwhip. We'll see how much of a pain-slut you are after I've finished with you.' He scowled as she returned his gaze unflinchingly. 'Eyes to the floor, P. Ponies do not retain eye contact with their Masters. You're so green it's shocking. Let's take care of that first, shall we? You've already soured my milk today, but thankfully there's still room for improvement. That suit unlocks itself in about two hours and boy am I gonna have some fun with you then. Those holes of yours won't know what hit 'em.'

He reached into his pocket and pulled out a small plastic packet. Ripping it open with his teeth he took out two pink, cone-shaped objects and rolled them around in his fingertips. 'I think it best if we fit these now. I haven't got anything more to say to you. He pulled the neck seal of her hood wide in his hands and rolled the rubber cones into her ears. Stuffing the wax earplugs in and twisting them in deep with his fingers, he yanked the hood back over her head. She wouldn't be hearing a thing through those and her latex covering. Petal whimpered a bit, her mouth a dribbling mess, but there was little she could do about it. He would take away her sight next, but he wanted her to see a few things first.

Walking around her, his spurs clinking merrily as his heels hit the concrete floor, he fastened each of the four leather cuffs around her ankles and wrists. He took his time about it. Anticipation was the mother of the beast in this room. He then casually strolled about and began picking up the items he would need for his scene: a toothbrush, a blindfold, an emery board, a steel wool scouring pad, a piece of medium-coarse sandpaper, and some mentholated muscle rub. Placing them all on a steel trolley in front of her, one by one, he let her imagination run riot. Her eyes had quickly focused on the odd assortment and it was clear they were not at all happy. Good. Foraging around in his pocket once again, he found a penknife and a one pound coin. Finally he laid down a heavy rubber flogger and his favourite five metre leather bullwhip. That should have her offering prayers upwards, even if none of the others did.

Flicking the steel blade of his knife open and bringing it to her face, he let the sharp edge scrape along the latex of her cheek. Her eyes displayed no fear yet, but they would. He let the blade meander down her face, dragging at her rubber covering. He moved down to her neck and then he curled it backwards, up over her shoulder blades, letting her feel the pin-prick apex of its point as he twirled it along her spine. She shuddered. Smiling to himself he picked up the blackout goggles and attached them around her head by means of a thick elastic strap. He had taken yet another sense from her and she should be feeling pretty apprehensive by now. The tell-tale hard line of her shoulders on the rail spoke volumes. You wait till I've finished with you, he thought. You'll barely be able to move.

He watched as her groin began to pump up and down upon the horse. Perfect. The suit was playing its evil game with her yet again. She groaned in acute frustration, but there was little else she could do to ease her discomfort. There would be a good deal more squirming going on soon, after he'd had his way, but this time it wouldn't be in pleasure. Concentrating on the job in hand he decided the corset would have to go. Shredding the crisscross of laces that decorated her back, he watched as it fell dejectedly on either side of the padded rail beneath her. Someone could re-lace her back into it later and he'd have a word to make sure they tightened it to its fullest potential. There were no slackers in his camp. Refocusing his attention on her back he let the knife begin to score a pattern into the thin fabric. She jumped up in shock as the pressure of the blade made itself known.

That was the beauty of the blindfold; all sensations were heightened and enhanced. Loosening his hold on the knife he began to etch his design. There were soft curves to be drawn, angular lines, and he even managed a near perfect symmetrical triangle. Humming away, almost sorry that she couldn't hear his happiness as he became absorbed in his knife play, it wasn't long before his careful project was completed. All he had to do was tear out a few key pieces of rubber and he could begin stage two, which would be infinitely more fun. It was time to make his design a little more permanent. It was going to be a new addition to her wardrobe and one she would wear for the next few days, because he was going to scour it deep into her skin.

Jenny had plenty of time to examine everything on the trolley, and she couldn't for the life of her figure out what he was up to. A toothbrush? If he wanted to clean her teeth she'd probably offer him a blowjob as a reward. What he wanted with the sandpaper, pot scourer and muscle rub was anyone's guess, but she was reasonably sure she wouldn't like it. When he got out a penknife she felt herself shrinking away from him, remembering the last time Mark had pulled one out on her in the Red Room. When the blade whispered down her cheek she wanted to run, but that wasn't going to happen, so she took deep, calming breaths and told herself that nothing bad was going to happen to her. They wouldn't be allowed to do anything permanent with her, surely?

When the blindfold came down and plunged her eyes into a world of perpetual midnight she wanted to howl. She couldn't move, hear, see or speak and her beautiful sadist held a knife in his hands. Scenarios ran riot through her head. She felt the blade coil upwards, over her shoulder, before it fell back to drag along her spine. Thump, thump, thump. Her heart thundered in panic and breathing was already difficult enough as it was. Suck in air and try to stay calm, she told herself, which was all very well but somewhat difficult when someone was running the sharpest of knife edges down your spine. Lingering over each vertebrae, it teased her with its wicked point before it moved back up between her shoulder blades and began a delicate dance upon her skin.

The blade crept over her flesh and occasionally pricked her, its cold point warning of the dangers of sudden movement. Jenny didn't know how long she held her breath for, but she did know her heart was doing flip-flops. The buzzing clit stimulator had her hips wanting to burst into song and dance, and it was all she could do to keep them in check. She allowed her body a tiny, shallow breath and clenched herself tightly as the urge to bounce back and forth in pleasure overtook her. She wasn't sure whether the biggest torment was feeling the knife casually rip her suit to shreds or curbing her body from movement. Kyle's earlier words were not comforting. Would he leave her in here, all alone? The boredom alone would drive her insane. What about food and water? He wouldn't be allowed to just abandon her, would he?

All these thoughts and more ran riot through her head as the blade tripped and fell in jagged little bursts. Locked in her own little world of terror and dread, she almost didn't realise when he began tearing at the rubber, peeling parts of the sticky fabric from her skin. Her suit chose that moment to up the ante and her hips did buck then, feeling the dildos pound inside her and bring her to the edge of the word 'despondent'. The expected shock ripped through her just before the peak of relief was achieved and left her maddened, her whole body shaking with a raw kind of rage that threatened to rival the sentiment she felt for her father. She would get out of here and she would get even.

When the toothbrush came at her the sensation was almost pleasant at first. A few mere tickles as the soft bristles were manipulated over the holes in her suit. Jenny squirmed. Her whole body was over-sensitised due to the effects of the device and her world had grown a whole lot smaller with the addition of earplugs and a blindfold. Bizarrely enough, the toothbrush sent shivers of arousal down her spine and as the pressure slowly increased she craved the gradual increments and the slight touch of pain they departed.

Closing her eyes, because there was little point leaving them open, her mind concentrated solely on the subtle shift of her breathing and the feel of the brush strokes across her skin. Kyle had begun a pleasing rhythm and she relaxed into it, letting the heat sink deep into her skin. It was all going swimmingly well until the image of Mark Matthews came flitting across her brain out of nowhere, and bam, there he was in front of her.

Kyle took a couple of seconds to admire his handiwork. Not bad, even if he did say so himself, but it was about to get a whole lot better. He'd begun gently, starting with the humble toothbrush in order to lull her into a false sense of security. The pressure he used initially would be just enough to wake her skin up. It would give her something to concentrate on in the dark little hole he had immersed her in. He worked each little piece of his pattern with careful strokes, barely pinking the flesh as he went to work on his masterpiece. She would now begin to understand what was coming and what the other items he had gathered in front of her would be used for. It didn't normally take them too long to figure it out. When she did he expected some struggling. That would aid him as he worked her over with the emery board and scouring pad. The more squirming the better, in his opinion. When the sandpaper came out she would be crying and when he finished with the mentholated oil, well, let's just say that things would be getting a little nasty.

The emery board came at her skin with a good deal more enthusiasm than the toothbrush and that was when it dawned on Jenny that the end of this scenario was not going to be a pleasant experience. From behind the privacy of her black prison her eyes opened and widened instinctively. Sandpaper, she'd seen sandpaper for chrissakes! That was going to sting. Why didn't he just flay the skin from her back with a crop and have done with it. At the rate he was going they would be here for hours. The idea of hyperventilation crossed her mind, but she thought the better of it. Could she withstand the pain? Probably. She'd had a good deal of experience with the stuff. That didn't mean to say that when the muscle rub came at her she'd be able to keep silent. She might be able to withhold her tears, but it would be a close-run thing. She knew where this was headed. Kyle had found out that she didn't mind a good spanking, so he was going to do his best to make sure her final thrashing was anything but pleasant.

The nail file was a difficult beast to wield properly and it wasn't long before he had given up his game, but he had done enough. Her skin had started a slow burn that no amount of water could ever extinguish. When the steel wool came at her she felt her body buck in agony.

'There, there, hold still, Petal. We're almost halfway.'

His words were the tiniest echo in her head, but he made sure she heard them. Halfway? He had to be joking, but his slow, repetitive strokes belied her thoughts. He was going to drag this out. Nothing less than tears and total surrender would satisfy him. So she did the only thing she could do and retreated in on herself. It was far easier than it should have been with the earplugs and blindfold keeping all other distractions at bay. She focused on the pain, isolated it within her head and let it wash over her body. It was a bizarre kind of meditation technique, but it worked, taking the edge off the pain and softening the edges to a dull ache. Her mind concentrated on nothing more than the image of a flickering candle flame, her attention glued to the black spot at the base of the flicker. It wasn't an easy game to master, but she'd had plenty of practice at it. The hardest part was keeping stray thoughts at bay.

'You're tougher than you look,' commented Kyle loudly, his mouth hovering above her latex-clad ear. Running his fingers over his angry red handiwork he hoped for a reaction. He didn't get one. Not even the slightest murmur escaped her.

Jenny could imagine him frowning, narrowing his eyes in displeasure as he wondered what to do next. She suspected that most of the girls within the facility would be sobbing by this point, and now she'd denied him that pleasure he would redouble his efforts in order to achieve it. Unfortunately, she wasn't wrong.

The sandpaper scraped across her skin and it felt like he was peeling her apart, layer by layer. In all honesty she supposed that was exactly what he was doing. Each slide of the coarse paper across her flesh felt like acid, dissolving her bit by bit. The endorphins in her body were now beginning to reach a dangerous pitch.

When the sandpaper stopped her skin felt raw and messy. It felt like the aftermath of a volcano explosion with rivers of molten lava and craters of simmering steam. The pain was unbearable and it was getting difficult for her to focus her thoughts. There would shortly come a point where the agony overtook everything and no amount of concentration or meditation would help ease it. Trapped in her black void and overwhelmed by conflagration of her body, she prayed that the end of her torment would come soon. When she heard a bottle being vigorously shaken she let out a guttural sob, barely audible through her rubber ball-gag, and trembled all over.

Kyle dragged the moment out. As she tensed and braced herself for the worst he ran his fingers over her excoriated skin. She began struggling in earnest as the smell of the embrocation cream assaulted her nostrils. Pungent and acrid fumes filled the room and she spluttered against the ball inside her mouth. She could just about make out his voice, humming away happily as he prepared to make her suffer. How on the earth did someone with such an angelic face contain the heart and soul of a monster? If there was a God she was now pleading with him, using every fibre she possessed, to get her out of this hellhole with her body mostly intact. Her mind was already gone. As her suit went into overdrive beneath her and began to vibrate, hum, thrust, pound and shake, the tiny coin came down to inflict agonies that even she could not have predicted.

Jenny would have screamed, but her mouth was too tightly stuffed, so she kicked, bucked and squirmed instead; anything to get his coin off target and away from her flesh. When everything went suddenly quiet, for a single stupid second she thought her prayers might have been heard. Her body tensed and stilled, tightly strung out in panic and her ears strained to hear the smallest sounds, but the room had gone eerily silent. It increased her terror tenfold

Where had he gone and what was he up to? The next thing she knew something tight was being wrapped around her neck. All he'd done was go for another restraining device. Cling-wrap, if she wasn't mistaken, judging by the way he was wrapping the stuff around her body, over and over. That way she wouldn't be able to move a muscle when he worked the mentholated oil into her.

Having discerned his plan she began to struggle anew, putting a lot more effort into her game this time, curling up her wrists and trying to thread them back through the cuffs in an effort to break free. The cuffs were far too small and fastened much too tightly, but that didn't stop her trying to tear her arms off in her attempts at freedom. The wrap rolled further down her body, encasing her torso and ass in an unbreakable cocoon of plastic that would make sure she remained as still as a mummified object. He'd left the upper portion of her back free so he could continue his work and made sure the rest of her had the manoeuvrability of a clamped car. She was locked down tight.

The four corners of her mind closed in and began spinning while her breathing became difficult and erratic. Jenny decided that if these were the kind of punishments Kyle employed, they were way past her endurance level and she would do everything the goddamned man said from here on in - including neigh like a horse or bark like a dog. She didn't care any more. This was all about survival and she wanted to live another day. The first thing she needed to do was get rid of Kyle. If she had to become someone's sex slave to do so, that was a small price to pay.

There was the softest of thuds, barely audible through her plugged ears, and she assumed the box of wrap had hit the floor. She tried to remain calm but it was horribly difficult when she knew what was coming next. Sure enough when the coin came down to gently stroke her upper back she had little but murder on her mind. Kyle's. Brutal anger flared brightly in her sub-conscious and her fingers curled into tight fists within her mitts. She was not going to give in and sob because she was well aware that was exactly what the bastard wanted; her complete and utter capitulation.

A few minutes later, although they might reasonably have been seconds, she was rethinking her earlier stance. The mentholated oil was trickling through her pores and it felt like hydrochloric acid. She began to wonder if she was losing her mind. Her body was close to orgasm and although the extent of her suffering had delayed the auto-correct feature of her suit for some time, it would not be long in coming. She, however, would not be coming. Not this time. As the muscle rub scoured her exposed skin she felt silent tears leak down through her blindfold and lay like sodden, wet pools in the latex of her hood. The only thing keeping her sane was the fact that she had not sobbed out loud or struggled within her plastic prison. You can get through this, Jen, she whispered as a mantra inside her head, over and over again.

'Come on, filly. Show me how much you're enjoying this. I want to see you dance.' Kyle had bent down to whisper in her ear and his voice filled her with dread. 'Don't worry, if you don't feel up to it yet you will when I put you in the Objectifier. I'll bury that head down below and take the flogger to your back's new addition before I finish up with the bullwhip. Oh, and I'm considering making my design permanent, what do you think? It would only take a few scrapes with my knife to outline and you'd have a perpetual and enduring reminder of my devotion to you and your training. It's tempting, isn't it?'

A thin, sharp object ran up the latex of her suit and pulled at the rubber. This time the reality of what was about to happen hit home and Jenny couldn't help herself; she struggled with all her might. No way was she going to have an immortalised reminder of this crazy hellhole when she got out. She hoped to God he was fucking with her.

When the knife pressed its point into the seething sea of nerves that littered her back, she screamed. The noise could be heard quite clearly through the gag, so intense was it in volume. Trying to punch her body free of the wrap was proving to be an impossibility. She was glued to the spanking rail far more efficiently than if she'd been encased in cement. The knife bit. Perhaps only a couple of millimetres, but her body went berserk. Shaking, trembling, screaming, dribbling, rearing and kicking - all to no avail. To make matters worse, the sounds of Kyle's laughter could be heard in the background, smug and self-satisfied. The knife had withdrawn for the moment, so she guessed she could be grateful that he found this kind of thing amusing. But her reprieve didn't last long and when the tip pressed at her shoulder blade again she almost begged for deliverance.

Strangely enough, it appeared someone must have heard her, for the knife stopped in its tracks and was retracted. Sobbing openly she felt her heart crashing through her body as she wondered what was going to happen next.

When the knocker to the dungeon door rang out loudly Kyle almost dropped his knife. He swore viciously as he hated being interrupted, and especially just when things were getting good. There was little option, though. He needed to answer his summons and whoever it was had better hope they had a good reason for disturbing him. He wandered over to the door in order to open it.

The cast iron door creaked noisily and he shot daggers forth from his eyes, letting his intruder know how welcome he wasn't.

'Kyle, are you OK?' Damn, it was a she. A blonde head peered around the door cautiously and stared at the mottled bruise on his face.

Fuck. It was Isabelle, and not just any Isabelle. She was dressed from head to toe in skin-tight red leather. Kyle's eyes shot out on stalks, ran two metres down the room and tried to turn the corner. He wanted to pant like a dog in heat. He hoped his tongue managed to remain in his mouth when he replied to her softly whispered question with a, 'Yes, just having a little fun.' His hand went up to gently rub the horseshoe print on his face and he winced. 'Petal was a little feisty this morning when she woke up.'

Isabelle opened her mouth and then closed it, turning her head sideways to examine the impressive contusion. As there was really nothing more she wanted to say on the matter she decided to barrel straight on with her original reason for interrupting his session. Clearing her throat delicately she said, 'I was wondering whether you'd mind if we moved our date forward to this afternoon? I've got to go babysit one of the novices in the infirmary this evening.' Isabelle did not glance in the direction of trainee, nor did she stop to admire his handiwork as most of the workers of Albrecht would have. Instead, she blinked her eyes and smiled at him sweetly.

At first he wanted to growl at her that he had plans for the evening and lots of them, but it wouldn't have gotten him any brownie points and there wasn't anything she could do about it. Rules were rules and duty was of paramount importance at Albrecht. Fine, they could work around it.

'I've got a table at that new French restaurant, *L'Colbert*.' I had to pull in a few favours, but they've got a space in a half-hour for us, and we'll just about be able to make it if we leave now.' Isabelle saw Kyle look towards Jenny and frown. She cleared her throat to grab his attention once more. 'What do you think of the leather?' She twirled around and displayed her petite derriere to its best advantage. If that didn't grab and hold his attention, then nothing would. She wiggled it for good measure. Kyle sighed, but it was not a sigh of displeasure. It was a heartfelt sigh of worship and adoration.

'I think that both the leather and its awesome filling are to die for, but I've got a problem. We're in the middle of something here. Any chance you could delay our reservation for another half hour?' Kyle compressed his lips in an almost pleading gesture, which showed just how much he had been enjoying himself with his new novice.

Isabelle shook her head. 'No way, hot shot. That reservation nearly involved the exchange of bodily fluids. We've gotta go. Good news is, I've got you a replacement who's reported to be the meanest thing on two legs. I've already paged him and he'll be on his way down shortly.

For a moment Kyle looked torn between indecision, but he really had no choice in the matter. Giving up a date with Isabelle would be worse than the kind of torture P was currently going through. Of course, he had no real experience with being on the receiving end of such an ordeal, but he guessed it could be likened to such a thing. He winked at her. 'OK. You need to give me two minutes, though. I need to get her ready for her flogging. That all right?'

'Yes, you do your thing, but be quick.' She waved him away and waited by the door. She had no wish to step over the dungeon threshold and she wanted no part of what was going on inside. Tapping her fingers in agitation against the metal doorframe she heard the sound of tearing, followed by a muffled squeal. She couldn't help wincing. As curiosity got the better of her she watched as he dragged Petal across the floor before lifting her up and placing her on the Objectifier. Her head was inserted into a hole at the front of the box and her backside rested proudly in the air. There was a soft 'clunk' as two semi-circular padded blocks were inserted around her neck, making sure her head would remain buried inside the large cube.

'Isabelle, come and have a look at this.' Kyle's beautiful face smiled earnestly at her.

'Umm, I really don't think we have time for this,' said Isabelle, who was beset by nerves for the afternoon ahead and could do without any further distractions.

'Come here,' he cajoled, and his finger beckoned.

As it appeared she wasn't getting out of the place until she'd had a look at his latest victim, Isabelle took a deep breath and cautiously stepped forward. It didn't take her long to discover what had been keeping Kyle so busy. The torn partitions in the latex drew her eye. She held her breath tightly. 'Lovely,' she whispered in what she hoped was a convincing, light-hearted voice. Her expression was horrified and it was just as well she had turned her back on him to view the pony. Wanting to gag, but not daring to make a sound, she simply reached back and gripped Kyle's hand in hers. 'Let's go,' she said, and tugged him forward. 'Someone else can take care of her.'

'Yes,' said Kyle, sighing, and grabbing the blanket he had laid down on the floor he threw it over her. Mainly because he knew it would send his pony into quivers of paroxysms after his earlier threat. 'He can flog her into next year. She needs to learn her place under my fist.' Kyle cocked his head to one side as he debated something. 'Do you think my replacement might take photos for me?'

Isabelle shuddered.

Ange Ou Demon?

Jenny was stupidly grateful for her reprieve, no matter how long it might be. She had passed the moment of maximum endurance and didn't think she could take any more. Like a tall wineglass made of the finest crystal, she now had a crack in her body and there was no question she was going to break. Wriggling her neck around in its tight confines, she grunted as she realised her prison was absolute. She would not get out of this mess in one piece. The wineglass would shatter and smash, and no one would know which piece was which. Becoming annoyed with herself, she tried to refocus her thoughts.

'You can do this,' she whispered to herself, keeping her eyes tightly shut and her body tensed. Stinging, throbbing pain radiated through every pore and ate away at her consciousness and limited reserves of energy. She wondered how much more she had to give. Could she survive a twenty minute flogging after what she had already suffered? She didn't think so, and that was the best case scenario, she suspected.

Seconds ticked by interminably slowly in her dark, sweaty world of fear and trepidation. She wondered if Kyle would come back for her, his earlier threats of abandonment now beginning to take hold, and she also wondered if that might actually be the better option. To be left here and discarded rather than suffer the pain of a beating. Thump. Thump. Thump. Her heart was threatening to explode, growing impossibly large as it boomed each of its beats in her ear. Add that to a dry throat, an aching jaw, tired, stretched limbs and a back that felt like Hannibal Lecter was about dine from it and things were not looking good.

Her thoughts went to Mark. Why had she not picked the one half-sane man in the room? He might have been a bastard, but he at least had a conscience. Well, a quarter of one, perhaps. Right now she would beg to be his house-slave or whatever they were called. A few years crawling around his house would be nothing when compared to a week in Albrecht with Kyle. She would make a deal with the devil himself in order to escape the current mess she was in. Kyle was going to make mincemeat out of her, quite literally, it appeared.

She lost herself then, in a dream world all of her own making. Mark's beautiful blue eyes swimming before hers, his perfect, bow-shaped lips formed in a kissable pout and his fingertips lightly streaming over her flesh.

Odd though it seemed, her dream seemed to take shape and she could have sworn she felt something lightly brush up her right leg. She cursed. She was probably hallucinating. She'd had so little food that even if she wasn't fantasising she was most certainly lightheaded. Concentrate on the daydream, she berated herself before sinking her lips and tongue into Mark's warm mouth and running her fingers through the soft black spikes of his hair. Something trailed up her left leg, imparting the gentlest of pressures, but it was distracting. Was it really coming to the point where she could not control her own thoughts? For a few seconds her mind swam around frantically in a dark void of confusion. Her brain tried to process the phantom movement, to no avail. It continued up her leg and suddenly there was a sharp *thwack* upon her backside.

This was no dream. The flogger moved over her ass in a sea of leather tentacles and whilst the soft swings didn't have a lot of power in them, it wouldn't matter when they reached up past her shoulder blades. Could she do this? It must have been the tenth time she had asked herself that question. The flogger increased in intensity and heated her ass cheeks with a warm and pleasant glow. She didn't really appreciate it, as the pain of her back had not subsided, but it was a distraction.

After it'd had its fun with her ass it moved along to the small of her back and began to wreak havoc upon her. The blanket that covered her back itched and scratched as each movement of the flogger jolted it. The pain had not subsided one iota and having a flogger rain down upon her abraded flesh was more than she could endure. It was made worse by the fact that she knew the bullwhip was waiting to begin where the flogger finished. In order to let Kyle know he'd won she screamed and dipped her head, whinnying stupidly through heartfelt sobs. Her whole body had taken on the trembling of a washing machine on maximum spin cycle. She was all over the place; sobbing, screaming, tearing at the metal cuffs and trying to wrench her limbs in half.

'For God's sake stop.'

In her dream the voice was exactly like Mark's. He placed a palm on her back, thankfully below the stinging bits, and stroked her softly, trying to soothe her. It didn't work. She knew what was coming. His hand was too close and her ordeal of being turned into something with even fewer freedoms of the average household pet was more than she could bear. Her struggling intensified.

'Stop, you'll dislocate your arms in a moment.'

There was that voice again. Exactly like his. Her subconscious was really having a whale of a time. There were hands everywhere then, freeing her neck, pulling her head out, unfastening her cuffs and tearing her ball-gag out. A series of distraught, choked hiccups followed as her blindfold was ripped off, and then her hood swiftly followed. He fished inside her ears for the plugs and pulled them both out at once, letting them drop to the floor.

'Look at me. Look at me!'

The man was holding her head between his two hands and shaking it gently to get her attention. It took her a moment to focus her eyes. They widened into the most enormous dinner plates. It *was* Mark Matthews. Oh God. What did that mean exactly? Tears poured down her face as she sobbed out her misery.

'Shhh. Talk to me. What's been going on here?'

He swept his fingers through the short strands of her hair, trying to placate her. He stroked her over and over, murmuring comforting words in her ears, and he let her rest her cheek on his chest. It was a good five minutes before she managed to stem her sobs long enough to try and get a few words out.

'Am I dead?' Jen's voice croaked on a whisper.

'Let's say you are,' said Mark, with a twitch to the corner of his lips. 'Do you consider you've gone to heaven or hell?'

A stray tear leaked out of her left eye and he fished it up with his index finger and sucked it into his mouth.

'I'm not sure,' she said. 'A few minutes ago I would have said hell, and you certainly deserve to be there, but I really shouldn't find you this attractive. Besides, if I am in hell why are you being so nice to me?'

'You're still very much in the land of the living, so quit worrying about your soul. I got rid of Kyle for the afternoon to see how you were getting along.' Mark didn't add that he'd been worried sick about her, after having heard what Kyle was capable of. He'd ditched all of his responsibilities at Zystrom and stormed down to Albrecht to keep an eye on the new boy as soon as he'd received his Intel. It was the first time in a long while that he found himself anxious about someone's wellbeing. A rather strange and unwelcome feeling, but he couldn't shake it, nonetheless.

'Let's get that blanket off you, shall we?' He couldn't understand why she was covered with one; her life would already be hotter than hell under the latex covering. Ignoring her moan of protest he pulled the thin wool covering from her back and there was a single second's silence as the blanket hit the floor, fluttering its wings earthbound.

The flogger Mark had been holding hit the floor with a thud. 'Holy fuck,' he said in horror, which was swiftly followed by, 'I'll fucking kill him.' He was staring at bright red, block capital letters which spelt the word *Kyle's*. 'When I get my hands on you, Levison!' he roared, and he felt his fingers pull into fists.

He watched as the poor wretch jumped up and gasped. He'd forgotten she'd had her ears plugged for the past hour or so. His outburst probably sounded like a bomb exploding inside her head. He examined the carnage. He could feel rage bubbling up inside him and a muscle ticked tightly in his jaw. Kyle was lucky he'd left the building. If he hadn't he'd be dead by now. He bent over her back to get a good view of exactly what had been done to her. He bit his tongue sharply.

'Why aren't you screaming?' he whispered.

'I am. You just can't hear me.' Her voice was strained.

'I'm so sorry. I had no idea the bastard had it in him.' Mark scratched his jaw and worked out what he would need to treat her. 'Hold on while I go and get some pain meds and some anaesthetic cream. Something with lidocaine should do the trick. I'll get some antibiotic ointment on you after its taken effect. Has he fed you?' She shook her head. Mark wanted to punch something, anything in fact, but he managed to keep himself in check. There were more important things to consider than his rage. 'OK, we'll sort that out too. Just keep it together for a few more secs.' She nodded but the lines of pain across her face spoke volumes. He got to work.

When he returned to apply the cream her back was curled up in agony and she was whimpering. He had no idea what was causing it for a second, but then he realised it was the suit. She was on the verge of a climax and there was little he could do to help her. At least it would be a distraction while he applied the cream, because no matter how gently he spread it over her, there was no way it would be painless.

He waited until her clit stimulator burst into a frenzy of motion, she contorted into an arch and then he liberally spread the cream all over her upper back, as fast as he could. She moaned miserably, but thankfully there were no further screams or sobs. When she stifled a bitter groan of frustration and collapsed upon the block he knew the suit had finished its cycle. He held out a couple of tablets and she took them into her mouth wordlessly. He held a paper cup to her lips and let her wash them down with water.

'Do you think you can eat something?' Jenny shook her head, which appeared to be wobbling on its hinges. He'd seen the look before. It was exhaustion. She'd been tried far too hard in the last couple of days and hadn't been able refuel anywhere near the calories needed to recuperate. Grabbing one of his staple energy gels he held it to her lips and waited until she opened her mouth. She did so obediently, no doubt incredibly thirsty after her ordeal. When she'd finished he let her have another one. The more fluids he could get into her right now the better.

'I've got a ham sandwich here. It's not haute cuisine I'm afraid, but I'm going to break it up into pieces and feed it to you. I'm not sure you're in any fit state to feed yourself.'

When she didn't argue with him he began tearing up little bits of the pre-packaged sandwich he had managed to find for her and gently popped them into her mouth. She ate slowly, but managed to devour the whole thing.

'Did you give Kyle the rather becoming hoof print around his face?' Mark's smile was wry as he looked at her.

Having finished the last bite of her sandwich she slowly licked her lips and then replied in the affirmative.

'You mustn't antagonize him. He'll rip you to shreds with only the slightest provocation.' Mark shook his head and ground his teeth together, but then he couldn't resist a smile. 'How did you do it?'

Jenny snorted in response, a little happier now the lidocaine had begun to take effect and said, 'He chained me up in one of the cells in the barn. He made sure I was standing, so it would be impossible for me to go to sleep, and he left the light on. I wanted to try and get some sleep, so I used the chain to try and scale the wall and knock the light bulb out. Unfortunately it was virtually impossible wearing hoof mitts, but I did manage to rip the anchor point from the wall. Lucky for me the floor was covered in hay. After a good search I found a pebble and had about half an hour's fun with it until I broke the bulb. Next morning I balanced on a couple of the cuff restraints, beside the door, and waited for his arrival. I'm only sorry I didn't get him on both sides.' She sighed. 'How long have I got left in this suit?'

Mark shook his head in exasperation, but he looked at his watch and said, 'About twenty minutes is my best guess.'

'Thank God,' she whispered.

'I'm going to put this antibiotic cream on you and dress the wound. I'll remove the top half of your suit and finish the rest when your belt unlocks itself. You OK with that?' He stroked her sodden hair, which hadn't fared well under the tight stricture of the latex hood. 'After that I'll give you a good sponge down. How does that sound?'

'It's about as good as it gets around here,' she whispered.

He snorted and couldn't help a smile as he severed the latex in strips and layered the antibiotic cream all over her scoured flesh. 'Haven't lost your sense of humour I see. That's a good thing I guess.' Compressing his lips together he worked on securing her dressing with surgical tape. It wasn't long before he had managed to carry her off the cube and set her down on the blanket, ready for a good rubdown. He left her for a few minutes, coiled up in a heap on the floor, while he sourced some warm water, a sponge and some soap. When he came back she was nearly asleep despite the fact that the suit had begun humming once more.

'Come on, just get to all fours for me and we'll be done and dusted in no time. Then you can go to sleep.' He began folding up the blanket beneath her. She managed to obey him, but her legs were shaking with the effort. Careful to avoid her dressing, he lathered her sticky flesh with sweet lavender soap, and using soothing strokes carefully cleaned her upper body. He then soaped her hair and massaged her scalp between his fingers. Her eyes kept flickering open and shut as he worked.

Before the suit had managed to do any real damage in its next round of torture it gave off a series of beeps before the unravelling of a locking mechanism could be heard. Using his penknife and swift fingers he peeled off the remaining latex, drawing the plugs out of her pussy and ass with the utmost care. She was red and sore. There was a reason why the suits were not designed to be worn for long periods. Applying a generous amount of lubricant to both her pussy and ass, he worked on repairing the damage the suit had wreaked upon her. Most things would heal nicely within a day, but some would stay with her for a week or more. Anger simmered brightly on the stove of retribution. He would get even for this. He might not deliver it personally, but he would make sure Kyle paid for his mess in full.

Sluicing the now tepid water down her hair and back, he gave her a thorough rinse before drying her with a couple of the softest towels he could find. The endorphins running through her body would make even the lightest of touches feel like a vicious scrape. When she groaned underneath his hands he patted her down gently and whispered soothing words in her ear. She shook her head, indicating she did not want to hear them.

'I don't suppose I can change my mind and get you back?' The fact that she laughed indicated she knew it would be impossible.

He smiled sadly and shook his head as she knew he would, while his fingers caressed her cheek in sympathy.

'I'm sorry,' she whispered.

He raised his eyes at her in puzzlement. 'Sorry for what?'

'Sorry that I didn't pick you for my trainer. I thought it was you in the training room that day, when I was on the sybian...' her voice choked and tailed off.

'How did you not know...?' Mark's teeth snapped shut. 'He had you blindfolded?'

She nodded.

'Well, doesn't that explain a few things,' he said, gritting his teeth. 'How did you find out it was him?'

She gave a low growl. 'Sound of his spurs. I recognised them from the room that day and I remembered that during the whole scene on the sybian no one had uttered a word. When I pieced it back together, what you'd said afterwards finally made sense. I thought you were nuts at the time.' She gave him a wry grin.

'I might still be, but I wasn't guilty of that. You have my word.' He rubbed her lower back in calming circles.

'I know,' she murmured. 'Kyle's a madman. You can see it in his eyes.'

'I'm inclined to agree with you,' he said, nodding.

'Can you get me out of this mess?' Her voice was stained with salty tears and mucus, but the vehemence behind it was enough for him to know she was serious.

'I don't know,' he answered truthfully. 'I could try, but there are no guarantees. The earlier terms haven't changed, either. You'd have to commit to being a personal slave and I'm not sure that would suit you at all well. It involves plenty of training, perhaps even more so than you would endure here and most of the time you would be trapped between four walls. You'd need to complete at least a term of servitude before any thought to your release would be given, and I'm talking five or ten years here. It's a long time. Besides, I'd want a willing slave. If you enter into my household you'd have to be prepared to serve of your own accord. You're of no use to me otherwise.' He drew in a deep breath and rubbed his eyes.

'Would you feed me something other than porridge?' There was no disguising the disgust in her voice at the thought of another breakfast at Albrecht.

He laughed. 'No, but you'd be fed scraps from the table and you'd always eat last. You'd get the occasional treat, but your personal exercise regime would be just as demanding as it is here. You need lots of stamina to serve as a submissive. You'd have no rights, you'd do everything I told you to, you'd still sleep on the floor and you'd have the additional duties of cleaning and cooking. I do not think the life would suit you.' He looked apologetic but firm.

'Do you think the life of a pony-girl would suit me better?' Her eyebrows raised in question.

'No,' he said, 'I don't think you're cut out for submissive duty, although your body might beg to tell you otherwise. It's a shame.'

'I want to serve you. As your house-slave, servant, whatever you want to call it. I'll do everything you tell me to, without question, although you should note I'm an awful cook. I can burn baked beans.' Jenny rambled on in an effort to put forward her plea in the best light possible. 'I can be obedient. I promise. Take me on as an apprentice and if I put a single foot wrong you can always ship me back here. That would be threat enough to behave, wouldn't it?'

'It's not as easy as that. What reassurances would I have that you wouldn't try and escape? Now you've seen our world we can't have you running to the Sunday tabloids at any given opportunity. The powers-that-be would see it as a dangerous proposition.'

'Then do something to make sure I can't. Whatever you need to do to make them accept your proposal, I'll agree to. I mean anything because *anything* is better than this. I can't stay here another day. I can't live like this.'

'That, unfortunately, is not your choice to make, but after having seen wha

Kyle's done to your back I've arranged for you to be shipped off to your little vacation slightly earlier than planned. You'll have forty-eight hours away from the beast, rather than the original twenty-four.' When Jenny trembled he ruffled her hair and said, 'It can't be any worse than spending another couple of days with Kyle, that's for certain.' She had to nod in acquiescence.

'Right, enough talking. You're dead on your feet.' Laying the blanket back down on the floor for her to settle on he said, 'Anything I can get you before you nod off?'

Jennifer Redcliff looked down at the floor, chewing her lip, and it was obvious she was debating her next question. She finally summoned up the courage she needed and her lips parted. 'May I bring myself to orgasm, Sir? Please?'

The whispered plea was almost heart-breaking. It showed just what a state the suit had left her in, for her first wish to be that of sating herself rather than sleep. He gave her a wry laugh and sat on the edge of the Objectifier. 'Lay over my lap and I'll get you where you want to go, Pet.'

No sooner had he said the words than her backside flew over his legs. Even though her upper back was now covered the word *Kyle's* in angry red lettering on an otherwise pristine bed of creamy white flesh had embedded itself in his brain. The image caused his fingers to twitch, but he swiftly diverted his attention from it. There would be time to sort Kyle out later.

Although not a finger had touched her she squirmed in heat upon his lap. She was an impatient one and exhausted or not, she was clearly in heat. He let her squirm a bit more, building up a nice level of anticipation inside her already sex-starved body before he allowed her the pleasure of feeling his hands upon her backside. He didn't need to spank her. The marks she'd acquired over the last few days were numerous and if he just pressed his fingernails lightly upon them she immediately gasped. Her skin was already super-sensitive, so he just ran his hands up and down the globes of her ass, lingering between her inner thighs, stroking and caressing the tips of her legs whilst careful to avoid her sex. He palpated her delectable ass cheeks in his hand, over and over, admiring their lovely curves. A light stroke of her lower back, a soft pinch to her inner thigh and she was panting in very short order. Rubbing a finger around the tight virginal hole of her backside he coated it with the excess lube that had spilled out from his cleansing session.

'I'm going to finger you. In your ass. It's going to be a little uncomfortable at first, but if you're a good girl and ride with it I'll reward you with an orgasm. We clear?'

She nodded. It wasn't as if she had any real choice. When his finger slowly worked its way inside her she moaned pitifully at the intrusion. It wasn't the same as a rubber plug. It was firmer and less flexible. Another finger followed and he listen to her mewl, part in pain, part in pleasure. Using his other hand to tease the lips of her sex, he caressed them back and forth with a soft touch and smiled when she ground her body into his. He upped the tempo of his fingers in her ass, while his other hand formed a two finger salute and dived inside her pussy. He didn't need to check if she was wet; he could feel the sticky welcome brigade of lust all over the tops of her legs. Curling his fingers he dived in long and deep, arching up for her G-spot. He never let the pressure in her ass subside, so she would have to work through the barrier of discomfort and pain to achieve her climax. His fingers became stiffer and more pronounced as they flew in and out of her body. He fucked her with precision and skill, and drew it out as long as he was able, watching her buck over his knees with irritable little moans. Her arms flapped this way and that, her breath came in loud pants and her heart rate roared in her chest. When she finally overcame the sensations of being finger-fucked in two holes at the same time she screamed the place down as the mother of orgasms hit her hard.

He could always tell when they'd had a good one. Their whole body would shake like a leaf, uncontrollably, and it would take a few minutes for the reaction to die down. Miss Redcliff was doing exactly that, whilst making insensible little noises in the back of her throat. It was quite entertaining. She was almost asleep on his knee when she whispered, 'May I suck you, Sir?'

Mark laughed and threaded his fingers through her hair, letting them play with a wayward strand. 'You're learning. Maybe you won't make such a bad house-pet after all. Don't worry; you can consider this a freebie today. If we do manage to get you out of here you'll have plenty of opportunities to practice your sucking skills later.'

Her soft snores could be heard before he had uttered the last word of his sentence.

Cagey

Mark let Jenny sleep for the better part of three hours. In the few days she'd spent at Albrecht she'd been taken somewhere that most people didn't get to see in a lifetime and she'd come through the other side. Well, he hoped she would. She certainly had plenty of determination.

He considered what she would be like as a house slave. Hell, he'd never taken a slave to his house, so it would be a steep learning curve for the both of them. The girls in the office generally kept him busy enough. If she was willing and he'd want proof on her part, then he'd be prepared to give it a go. Without a doubt she'd be an ogre to tame. No matter how pure her intentions, she'd had years of getting her own way in a spoilt and privileged upbringing and that would take time to work out of her. The question was: would he enjoy doing so? He pursed his lips and let his eyes raise heavenward. Probably. He hungered like a starved man to fuck her, but every time he got close to her something stood in his way. Not for much longer, though. He wanted that nubile, perfect body all to himself. Well, at least for the first few months. Then he might consider sharing her. Although he had to admit that was by no means certain.

What would Redcliff want for the sale of his daughter? That was a mind-blowing equation if there ever was one. OK, so he knew she wasn't his daughter by blood, but there must be some kind of bond between the pair.

Letting out a pent-up breath he didn't remember holding, he let his eyes focus on his beautifully naked, soon-to-be slave. She was pretty as a picture, even in her exhausted, sleep-drugged haze. If he was honest he couldn't wait to have her on his terms.

Running his fingers over her scalp, careful not to look at her back because he knew even with the dressing the anger would hit him full force in the gut, he decided he really needed to focus. Jennifer Redcliff had invaded his mind, and it appeared she was there to stay. He badly needed to fuck her. He'd held himself back because she was in no fit state to play, but it had hurt to refuse her very sweet offer of a blowjob. He consoled himself with the thought that he'd let himself have free rein when she was in his hands for good. Then he'd make her suck him ten times a day, in between the ass fucks, hand jobs, fingering and maybe, just maybe he'd consider making love to her. He shook his head in amazement. Where had that thought come from? The only thing he needed to do was screw her and return to normality with his sanity intact. He didn't have time for this rubbish.

He patted her head a little harder than necessary in order to wake her. It was time to visit the tack room ladies and get her kitted up for her next journey. He needed to put several hundred miles between them as quickly as possible. He needed to think things through. See where he wanted to go with this one. He also needed to get himself some action. Desperately.

'Mmmm,' she whispered groggily as his fingers circled her scalp gently.

'Come on sleepy head, there'll be time enough for snoozing on your journey. We've got to move and get you out of here. Kyle will back in a few hours' time and you need to be gone by then.' That captured her attention and she got to all fours, ready to crawl. 'No, you can use your feet to get to the tack room; it'll be quicker and there's still lots of work that needs to be done to get you ready for your travels.'

Offering his arm and helping to set her upright, he led the way out. It wasn't long before the steep stone steps loomed upwards and he saw Jenny's legs wobble out from under her. It was no great surprise. Mark solved the problem by scooping her up in his arms, bad backs be damned. She rested her head into the crook of his shoulder and he was amused to find he liked the sentiment. Who would have thought it? He was a man who enjoyed nuzzling. He'd do well to keep that information to himself.

When he knocked on the door of the tack room it was quickly answered by a frazzled Agnes, who didn't seem to be faring well in the hot August heat.

Pulling a sweat-slicked tendril of grey hair away from her face, she fanned herself and gave a cross-eyed grimaced to the pair in front of her. 'You'll have to excuse the hair. Hetty broke my air-conditioning.'

'Our air-conditioning,' Hetty corrected, 'and I didn't break it.'

'Hmmph,' said Agnes, narrowing her eyes at her friend, 'then what do you call your disassembling party over there?' She pointed to what once could have been an air-coolant but now appeared to be a train wreck.

'I was just seeing how it worked. I find these things fascinating,' Hetty sniffed.

'Rubbish,' said Agnes, wrinkling up her nose, 'you wanted to see if it had ammonia inside it. I know you've run out and you like to give your boys a spot on occasion before you play with them.'

Hetty's mouth hung open. 'How do you know these things?'

'I'm not as stupid as I look,' said Agnes, trying to nod sagely and failing, 'and I overheard you trying to order some of the stuff yesterday.'

Hetty grumbled, 'Well, if they'd had some in stock I wouldn't have to dismantle our cooling friend.'

'Too bad for you our "cooling friend" is filled with freon and not ammonia, though.' Agnes thumped her on the shoulder. 'I'm really not sure whether it would have been safe to use in any case...'

'Safety, schmafety. You worry too much, darling. Anyway, we've got things to do, people to see,' she sing-songed.

'You've certainly got things to do,' said Agnes, waggling her finger crossly. 'You need to put that thing back together.'

'I love putting things back together,' said Hetty, looking sideways at the vast array of parts strewn all over the room. 'I'll have it figured out in no time, you wait and see.' She gave her friend a bright smile which lacked conviction.

'See that you do, and it had better be before December,' replied Agnes, who was also looking at said parts and pondering how much a repairman would cost. If you broke things at Albrecht you were responsible for fixing them.

Turning her attention back to her guests, she directed her next comment at the trainee. 'Still no yellow collar then, dearie?' She clucked her tongue as Mark led Petal forward into the room.

'Hetty, we might have to put my retirement plans on hold. At this rate I could be eighty before I get my stable full of pony-boys.'

Hetty snorted. 'You wouldn't know what to do with them anyway,' she waved her hand expansively.

Agnes let the corner of her lips twist up. 'Oh, I have a few ideas that might keep them busy. I will have my stable.'

'Sorry, Master Mark,' said Hetty, rolling her eyes. 'She gets a bit carried away sometimes.'

Mark winked. 'I like an ambitious woman,' he said. 'From a distance, you understand, but I like them.' He grinned.

Agnes grunted. 'So, what did you do with Master Kyle?' She looked up at him with a curious expression.

Mark's expression darkened. 'I've had him kidnapped by a gorgeous woman who's going to put fifty thousand volts through him before taking him back to her lair to have her wicked way with him. While he's in lots of rather nasty restraints, of course.'

Both ladies burst into peals of laughter. 'No hard feelings then, Mark?'

Agnes grinned from ear to ear. 'So you get to babysit while Kyle goes out for his date with Isabelle? I bet Kyle didn't exactly agree to that.' She raised an eyebrow mischievously.

'Not exactly, but what Kyle doesn't know won't hurt him. Much,' added Mark for good measure.

'Hmmpf,' said Agnes, her attention already distracted with preparations for Petal's quick getaway. 'Pop her up on the table, Sir,' she said, patting the wooden bench in front of her.

Mark deposited her on the table carefully, and stretched her limbs out just enough that she would remain comfortably stable. Jenny's hands were still shaking. She'd either spied the small metal cage she would be transported in, which rested just below her, or she was suffering from hunger and lack of sleep. He guessed the ham sandwich and energy gel hadn't really managed to fill the hole that had formed in her stomach for the past few days. She had little energy to give and it would take all she had to remain on all fours for the next five minutes. If this session lasted any longer than that she'd be flat on her face. He'd see to it that the ladies moved quickly.

'What on earth happened to her back?' Hetty peered at the dressing in puzzlement.

'Kyle's doing, not mine, and better not to ask.' The look in Mark's eyes discouraged further argument and Hetty simply nodded.

'Do we know where she's going yet?' Agnes tactfully changed the direction of the conversation. She also lived for office chitchat and she'd been dying to find out where the star trainee was headed.

'To a very rich bidder,' said Mark, with a twinkle in his eye.

Agnes' eyebrows narrowed in frustration. 'We had kind of figured that out.' She gave him a pointed look.

Mark grinned at her. 'Fine. Can you keep a secret?'

'Can I ever,' said Agnes, already dribbling at the thought of telling everyone in the staff canteen the juiciest bit of gossip to hit Albrecht in quite some time.

'She can't,' said Hetty, holding two pieces of bent metal in her hands and trying, unsuccessfully, to piece both back together.

Agnes scowled at Hetty and winked at Mark. 'Tell me anyway.'

Mark tapped a finger against his cheek thoughtfully.

'Ooh, don't tease, Sir,' she said, and put half her hand in her mouth, chewing nervously at it, in anticipation of what was to come.

'Leyland Forbes won the auction and he requested an extra night, would you believe? It's supposed to run from midnight to midnight, but Forbes is apparently greedier than most,' said Mark, slanting Agnes a sideways grin.

'Isn't he the pharmaceutical giant? Have I got the right man?' Agnes looked puzzled for a moment.

'Yes, and he's the one who likes painting still-lifes of women in bizarre bondage, I do believe,' said Hetty, now tinkering with a couple of rubber tubes.

'What kind of bondage are we talking here?' It was clear that Agnes' interest had been piqued.

'He works mostly in the wacky fantastic,' said Mark, stroking Jenny's ass in an effort to calm her as Agnes got the wrist and ankle cuffs out. 'Underwater bondage, mid-air, statuesque and mirror maze are just a few of the exhibitions he's managed to accomplish. He's been known to bury them upright to the neck in glass containers filled with nothing more than sand, showcasing tits, ass and hands in a supplicating gesture. He's also famous for mounting them on plinths wearing nothing more than a pair of stilettos and a couple of rather impressive dildos. The underwater ones he creates are superb. I've seen a tank of emerald green seawater with three naked women entwined together wearing little more than the necessary scuba gear required to survive. If you frame that with an exquisite array of marine fish, coral and frayed, hessian rope, Forbes had quite a picture to paint.'

'He must paint very quickly,' said Agnes, who had attached both sets of cuffs to Petal's trembling body and was now fastening a strip of chain in the middle of both that would prohibit her from being able to stand upright.

Mark shook his head. 'He takes a good week or two over most, and sometimes it can be almost a month before he's finished with them.'

Agnes tugged on her connecting chain and was satisfied it was secure. 'Well how on the earth do they...?' she waved a hand to indicate she was looking for some words that were rather delicate in nature.

'Toilet?' Mark grinned. 'They're tubed up from head to foot and a machine takes care of all their essential needs for the duration of their bondage.'

Agnes' eyes widened. 'Oh my,' she said.

'For the most part they're paid handsomely for their services and they thoroughly enjoy it. He has ways of making them squirm.' Mark wiggled his eyebrows for effect and Agnes burst into laughter.

'If you say so.' Agnes didn't appear convinced. 'OK, we're ready to insert her plugs. Did you want to play with the wand first and loosen her up a bit, so to speak? I'll use plenty of lube, but some of her own wouldn't hurt. She looks like she's had a hard couple of days, poor filly.'

'That she certainly has. What do you think, Petal? Fancy a round with the wand? This time it's a free-for-all-come-as-you-like deal. Two for the price of one?'

Jenny hiccupped, which might have been a result of all the sobbing she had done, before managing to nod her head. After the last two days he suspected orgasms of any variety were most welcome and the more, the better. She had a lot of catching up to do.

'I'll get it,' said Hetty, who had finally decided to leave the intricate repair of the air-conditioning unit to the experts. It was electrical, after all, and she shouldn't be messing about with such things at her age. It would come out of her salary, but it would be a small price to pay compared to the constant nagging Agnes would bestow upon her every day until it was fixed.

Bustling into her closet she found what she was looking for in an instant: a white Hitachi wand with its power cord wrapped neatly around the base. Grabbing it and unwinding the flex, she zoomed back out into the tack room and found a suitable plug socket. No batteries were needed here. When that was done she passed it over to Mark and settled down to watch the show, because this time Agnes was doing all the hard work. Her misdemeanour with office appliances had consequences, more was the pity, and Hetty was most jealous of the fact.

No introduction was needed for the start of the theatrical pursuits, because the Hitachi's motor sounded like a jet airplane taking off. OK, it was more like a drill, but impressive nonetheless. There was a reason the so-called 'back massager' was the Ferrari of vibrators. It was currently on its lowest setting, but when the thing was on high it was truly incredible.

Petal, who had been almost comatose before the wand came near her, picked up her head and straightened her arms. She knew what was coming. Turning her head a fraction to the left Hetty spied Agnes generously lubricating the larger of the two shock plugs which would be inserted first.

The moment the wand touched Petal her body tensed tightly as if she was almost afraid that there might be another round of orgasm denials, but Hetty knew from experience just how intense the pressure of the wand was, even on its lowest setting. It took a few seconds before she managed to settle into its insistent rhythm and her body began pumping backwards and forwards on the bench of its own accord. Mark hadn't even gone anywhere near her clit yet; he'd focused the vibrations upon the lips of her sex and was slowly working his way towards the apex of her thighs. By the way Petal was moaning you'd almost think he was there already, thought Hetty with a wicked smile.

When the wand finally stopped teasing her inner thighs and labia, Mark upped the vibrations and moved forward. Jenny gurgled and groaned. She twisted this way and that to avoid the powerful pulsing upon her most sensitive organ, but Mark's grip was sure and firm. Within seconds she was gasping. Agnes then begun to pump the first couple of inches of the slim metal plug inside Petal's pussy, and the filly was obviously lost.

'Remember what we talked about, back in the dungeon?'

Jenny remained ominously quiet. They'd talked about a few things. Which one did he mean? Not wanting to put a foot wrong she tried to guess what he was thinking. The expression on her face said it was not the easiest task.

Mark, as usual, read her thoughts. 'I'm talking about the "O" word here and I don't mean *orgasm*. You have permission to talk as soon as you've figured it out.' He slapped her backside and the smart of his handprint was delicious in her hyper-aroused state.

'Ohhh,' whispered Jenny, rapidly charting all the words that began with 'O' in her head, and orgasm was on the top of her list, unfortunately. After discarding several more possibles, her brain finally managed to trip over the right one. 'Obedience,' she breathed.

'Congratulations,' he smiled. 'Now we'll put all that talk of yours to the test. I want you to stay as still as you can. You are not to avoid the direction of the wand.' He pressed it tightly upon her clit to demonstrate and watched to see whether she could follow instructions.

'Ahhh,' she whimpered, wanting nothing more than to wiggle and buck helplessly.

'That's it,' he encouraged her. 'Stay perfectly still and let yourself go.'

The vibrations from the wand were so powerful it was impossible for her to do anything else and she came in thirty seconds flat. Agnes timed the moment of climax with exacting precision, inserting her plug about two seconds before the poor girl exploded.

Mark did not let her have any time off for good behaviour. He dropped the vibrations down again, but made her ride out wave after wave of almost painful, orgasmic contractions under his immoveable hand. It was probably the longest orgasm the chit had ever had, and quite possibly the most painful.

Whilst Jenny was almost sobbing under the wand's irrepressible, juddering bursts, she had managed to take control of herself and she did not move a muscle from the all fours position that had been assumed. There was no sway or squirming to be seen. Mark, quietly impressed, thought it was a sign of good things to come.

Meanwhile, Agnes had herself busy with plug number two. It was shorter and fatter than its predecessor and whilst it would be a snug fit going in, when it found its anchor point it was there to stay. There was a long black horsehair tail attached to it, but unlike Petal's normal tail plug this one was designed as a removable attachment, to suit her bidder's whim.

The shiny chrome butt-plug was now getting more than its fair share of lubricant and Mark's fingers were once more working inside Jenny's ass, to prepare her for the invasion. The strain on her face began to show, her expression tightening into a hard knot as the effort of not moving became more and more difficult. He flipped the power button on the wand back up to full again and watched as her fingernails clawed the table. Agnes began to position the butt-plug at Jenny's rear. The trainee's eyes glazed over. This one would learn to love anal sex, Mark thought, although she might not think so on her first occasion. It all depended on the skill of the partner.

Agnes began to apply a little more pressure with the plug and a slow twisting motion. The tense set of Jenny's body would deny it entry for the moment. He wanted to see if she would be able to deal with that on her own, so he bent down to her ear.

'Relax for me. Let go and take it all inside you. Concentrate, push out and the experience will be a whole lot less painful and a damn site more enjoyable. Can you do that for me?' He caught her chin with a finger and watched as her eyes connected with his. A frisson of sexual tension rippled through them both and it shocked him. Although he'd seen the jolt in her eyes and had been able to mask his, his desire for Miss Redcliff had just increased to the most painful frustration he had ever felt. If Agnes and Hetty had not been in the room he would be banging the girl silly by now. So much for control. What was wrong with him? He had no time to consider the matter further.

Jenny had obviously taken his commands to heart for he heard Agnes say, 'Beautiful,' as the plug slotted firmly home. Then, he had a fiery hellcat on his hands. All her restraint was lost as her body began to writhe and jump under the weight of the wand. Her newly positioned tail jumped around everywhere for a few seconds before an ear-splitting scream could be heard. It was all he could do to keep the wand attached to her clit, the girl moved about so much, but he made her ride out every single convulsion until she collapsed on her hands in exhaustion. She was panting for breath and a few beads of sweat trickled down from her forehead.

Agnes gave the pair a few minutes of quiet time before she coughed delicately and held up a simple silver circlet. Removing Petal's thick white collar with a couple of snaps, she held up the thin metal one for Mark to examine. 'It's a shock collar, same as the plugs,' she said, with a sympathetic twist to her lips, 'so if there's anything you want to say, better do it now. You can put the collar on and lead her into the cage if you like. We're happy to give you a couple of minutes' privacy. Hetty and I will be waiting outside.'

Hetty, who had been happily enjoying a very pleasant daydream with several pony-boys, her eyes staring blindly into space, found herself yanked out of the room with rather more force than was absolutely necessary.

Mark waited until he heard the door close behind them. 'Don't worry about Leyland. He's harmless enough and it's unlikely he'll lay a hand on you. You might be in a spot of awkward bondage for a few hours, but I suspect it's nothing you can't handle. Most of his girls find his works of art rather pleasurable... in one way or another.' Mark grinned. 'Oh, and don't worry about Kyle, I'll take care of him.'

He stroked her shoulders softly for a few seconds and finally said, 'Is there anything you want to ask me before I put your collar on? You won't be able to speak after it's in place, so get it all out of your system now.' He sighed.

When she looked up at him the look in her eyes was heart-breaking. 'Promise me you'll try to get me out of here?'

He let his eyes connect with hers once again, even though the sexual tension was now almost debilitating in nature, and said, 'You have my word on it. I'll do everything I can.' Snapping the collar tightly in place he scooped her up off the bench and kissed her. He knew he would be in an evil place when they had finished, but not giving her the reassurance of his lips would be worse. The mewling little cries in her throat were reward enough, and when he finally released her lips and tongue she gasped for air.

When she made a move to speak he put a finger over her lips. 'Don't say a word. The collar will give you a shock and you've probably had enough of those lately. I'll be back for you. Now be a good girl and get in the cage. It'll only be for a few hours and you'll be asleep for most of them.'

Lowering her to the floor he watched as she eyed her barred prison warily. Her lip wobbled. The cage was fairly small and she would not be able to stand up or lie down in anything other than the foetal position. He wondered whether she would go willingly. In her position, he didn't think he would.

'It's only for a few hours and I promise no one will hurt you. You'll be back with me before you know it.' He gave her his trademark grin and a wink.

Incredibly she crawled forward and, ducking her head through the narrow entrance, sealed herself behind sturdy metal bars.

'Gotta go, darling. Be a good girl for me, won't you?' Tapping the metal cage twice with his hand he turned and got the hell out of the room before he decided to do something stupid. The ladies would have to padlock the damn thing.

It took over an hour for Mark to calm down enough to pull his cell phone out. By that time he was already en-route to London and sipping a sparkling glass of Perrier with a slice of lime. The thought of eating anything turned his stomach. When the dial tone clicked to that of an answer tone he left a short clipped message.

'Hello, Sophia. I've changed my mind. Give our friend the works and take your time about it. You'll be reimbursed in the usual way.'

When he replaced his cell in his pocket he felt marginally better about the day's shortcomings. Rome wasn't built in a day.

Under My Thumb

Mark waited until he was back in his office before he made his next call. It was one he was dreading. He'd had one of the girls cheer him up slightly, to take the edge off things, but in reality she had only made things worse. His hunger for Miss Redcliff seemed to double with each day he didn't manage to fuck her. Half of it was his own damned fault. He could have had her today, but he had too much of a conscience, unfortunately. She'd been through enough. The trick was to get her on his own terms and he could have her, if he played his cards close to his chest. He had no idea what Redcliff wanted, though, and that worried him. He guessed there was only one way to find out.

'Hello, Synstyte Petroleum. How may I help you?' The plummy voice of a receptionist answered the phone and she immediately made Mark wince.

'Can I talk to Mr Redcliff, please?' His voice was abrupt but it didn't deter the receptionist in her practised response.

'I'm sorry but Mr Redcliff is currently in a meeting. Can I take your number and I'll get him to call back at his earliest convenience, Mr...?'

'If he is in a meeting, which I doubt at this time of the afternoon, you have my permission to disturb him and haul him over to an available telephone line in which to speak to me. I have a business proposition that requires immediate attention and if he doesn't talk to me right this instant, he will most definitely lose millions and you will probably lose your job.'

'Who did you say was calling again?' The receptionist had lost her good humour and a hard edge appeared where flowers had been only a moment before.

'I didn't. The name is Matthews. Mark Matthews.'

'Give me a moment, Mr Matthews.' He was put on hold while the line played Verdi's Anvil chorus. It felt vaguely appropriate, except they were banging anvils and he was probably banging his head against a brick wall in his latest and probably futile endeavour. He suspected the secretary had got her pert little butt off her chair and was trying to attract Redcliff's attention from whatever perverted games he was currently playing out in his office. The good news was he didn't have to listen to Verdi for long because Michael Redcliff's voice barked at him less than a minute later.

'Matthews. What a pleasant surprise. Is there anything I can do for you?'

Mark did not beat around the bush. 'As a matter of fact, there is. I'd like to purchase your daughter. How much do you want for her?'

'You want to purchase her when she's achieved the black? Oh jolly good, I'll jot your name down and we can discuss figures nearer the time. Was there anything else?'

'No. I want to purchase her for use as my personal submissive. If her earning the black is important to you, we can negotiate terms. I'm willing to pay handsomely. Name your figure.'

Michael cackled with laughter that sounded oddly inhuman on the other end of the line. It was clear that the man did not laugh often. 'How much are you willing to pay? Indulge an old man's curiosity,' he said, his throat rasping from his bout of amusement.

'Several million. Sex slaves usually run up to the ten million mark. I'm willing to pay fifty. Do we have a deal?' Mark's voice was curt. He wanted this conversation over with as quickly as possible.

'That much? My oh my, she's gotten under your skin, hasn't she? Her mother had that effect on me at the start. It's a crazy type of madness she'll inflict upon you, Matthews. You should be pleased I'm refusing your request.' And just in case he'd misunderstood that last remark, Mr Redcliff added for good measure, 'She's not for sale.'

'She will be eventually, so what does it matter whether you sell her now or later? You won't get any more money for her than that which I've offered.'

'That may be true but perhaps I just enjoy watching her suffer.' Redcliff chose that moment to have a coughing fit down the phone, although it could have been laughter, Mark supposed.

'Name your price, Redcliff. Everyone has a price. What's yours?' His voice was succinct and to the point. There was no question that Redcliff would understand exactly what Mark was offering.

'Oh. It's like that is it? The madness has overtaken you already and you're helpless under its tight fist? Poor boy. Now that is a shame.' Redcliff paused and Mark knew then that there was something the old man wanted. Something he had wanted all along, but he knew without a shadow of a doubt it would not be money. A company he owned, perhaps, or an island in the Caribbean, but not cold hard cash as he had previously thought.

The wait made Mark clench his fists, but he bided his time and remained silent. Let Redcliff think he was making him squirm.

'Well, there is one thing I might enjoy, I suppose.' Another long pause, and finally Mark could wait no longer - he bit.

'And what is that, Mr Redcliff?' His tone was cold, his words succinct.

Michael made a show of clearing his throat and then a slurp could be heard. The man was drinking coffee, whilst speaking on the telephone. Charming. Get to the damn point, Mark fumed silently. There was another pause, another slurp and a sigh before he finally received an answer.

'You. Under my command for the evening. Just one night, you understand. Nothing long term. I think you'd make a delightful submissive. What do you say, young chap? I'll make sure it's a night you'll never forget...'

A note from the author

Can I just say thank you to everyone involved in the making of this book from start to finish. An especially big thank you goes to my publisher, editor and beta readers who try to erase my numerous errors and keep me on the right track. It is not an easy task!

If you would like to follow the antics of C. P. Mandara and get free previews and updates on my next release, please take a look at: http://christinamandara.wordpress.com/

Spanks, whips and smacks to all of you wonderful people who like a spot of naughty bedtime reading and plenty of erotic escapism.

Christina Mandara x

The Pony Tales conclude...

...in the sixth and final episode of Jenny's pony training. Don't miss it!

The Ties That Bind

Jenny shuddered, but the bondage she had just witnessed was by far the most innocuous. Looking just a little bit higher the artwork got considerably more interesting, or distressing, in her case, because she had no idea what would be in store for her little sojourn at the hands of the notorious Forbes.

Will Mark Matthews accept Redcliff's terms for his daughter's release, surrendering both body and mind to the enemy? Petal's sanity depends upon the fact, for in the sixth and final book of the Pony Tales she is to discover that the fate in store for her at Albrecht is not a pretty one.

Shipped off to Leyland Forbes in a steel cage, the pony-girl will have to endure all sorts of imaginative bondage and BDSM at his palatial manor, as her body is photographed intimately by several of the world's top photographers. As the day progresses she will find herself taken out to dinner in chains, before being cleverly and expertly divested of her virginity.

Trouble awaits when she returns to the stables, however. One of the trainers has taken a monstrous dislike to her and intends to prove his superiority, both in the dungeon and beyond.

Escape for Jenny is beginning to seem like an impossible dream...

Keep in touch

As mentioned in the intro pages of this book, if you're keen to write erotic fiction and would like our **Author Guidelines**, or you're a published author and have existing work, the rights of which remain with or have reverted to you, we would be delighted to hear from you at **info@chimerabooks.co.uk**.

You can also keep updated on our new releases and special offers at **www.chimerabooks.co.uk**, where you'll also find our complete list of over 300 erotic books available to download as ebooks.

Printed in Great Britain
by Amazon.co.uk, Ltd.,
Marston Gate.